A UNITED FRONT

A UNITED FRONT

CHRONICLES OF AN URBAN DRUID™ BOOK 13

AUBURN TEMPEST

MICHAEL ANDERLE

DISRUPTIVE IMAGINATION

LMBPN Publishing
PMB 196, 2540 South Maryland Pkwy
Las Vegas, NV 89109

Version 1.02, March 2023
eBook ISBN: 978-1-68500-646-4
Print ISBN: 978-1-68500-647-1

THE A UNITED FRONT TEAM

Thanks to our JIT Team:

Deb Mader
Dave Hicks
Jim Caplan
Diane L. Smith
John Ashmore
Kelly O'Donnell
Dorothy Lloyd
Larry Omans
Paul Westman

Editor
SkyHunter Editing Team

Glaine ar gcroí. Neart ár ngéag. Beart de réir ar mbriathar.

CHAPTER ONE

"**W**ho wants to go faster?"

As the question echoes over the sound system, I raise my arms and scream. The force of motion is pulling me into Sloan and trying hard to throw us from the car. Adrenaline fuels my anticipation as my heart races at double time.

Sloan is on my left, looking dubious.

Dionysus is on my right, grinning like a fool. The Greek god lifts his arms to match mine, and the two of us scream at the top of our lungs.

The backward motion pulls us with even more force, bumping in rising and sinking waves as we spin in a wild circle.

The music blares at us from all directions and shifts from loud rock and roll to a screaming siren.

Our speed increases.

There's no way to fight the centrifugal force crushing me against Sloan and Dionysus against me. We compress along the vinyl seat as far as we can go and I laugh as my hair whips all three of us in the face.

I try to wave as Kevin takes our picture from behind the platform gate, but we're going so fast, the onlookers are a blur in the distance.

"Who wants to go faster?" the ride conductor asks again.

Dionysus and I scream our approval, and the speed ratchets up another notch.

The siren wails louder, and the world spins by at an incredible rate. My cheek plasters against the sleeve of Sloan's shirt, and I'm thankful for the wide span of muscle holding my head steady.

It's amazing.

It's been ages since I've had this much fun.

Like all great things, eventually, the ride slows. The three of us can gain some distance on the bench seat, and a moment later, we bump to a stop.

My cheeks hurt from laughing and when I see the look on Sloan's face, I laugh even harder. "What? You didn't love that?"

The glare he pegs me with is hilarious. "Love being crushed by my insane girlfriend and her equally insane Greek sidekick while being spun like a lab sample in a centrifuge?"

I know all Sloan's varying degrees of grouch and grumble. His family repressed the little boy in him so long that he doesn't know how to connect with his id.

Dionysus, on the other hand, is all id all the time. "I didn't know black men could get so pale." He pokes Sloan's cheek. "You're not going to lose your corn dog, are you, Irish?"

Sloan throws the two of us a heated look, and when the mechanics of the ride release, he pushes the safety bar off his lap so he can get up and get out. "The two of ye aren't nearly as funny as ye think ye are."

Dillan and Evangeline get out of their car behind us and jog down the slope to walk out together.

"Did you like that, Eva?" I don't need to ask. The answer is as plain as the dimples in her cherubic cheeks and the bounce in her blonde curls.

Her expression has her lit up like the angel she is. How no one else in the crowd realizes she's ethereal is beyond me. "Goodness, yes. That was so much fun. Dillan and I are going to race back to the end of the line and do it again. Do you three want to come?"

I fight my instinct to join them and consider Sloan's lack of enthusiasm. "You go ahead. We'll take camera duty from Kevin so he, Calum, and Nikon can have their turn. When you finish, we'll head over to the concert center to claim our spot for the live music."

Dillan chuckles. "You're passing up a chance to go on the Polar Express? I never thought I'd see the day. When we were kids, Fi spent all her midway tickets on this one ride. The rest of us would take turns riding with her, then go off to try some of the other rides. Not Fi. She was here for the duration."

I grin. "Why mess with perfection?"

"Clear the platform, please." Yep, the ride conductor is talking to us. We shuffle toward the exit gate, and Dillan and Evangeline turn to get back in line.

"Do you want to come with us, Greek?" Dillan asks.

Dionysus grins and nods. "Absolutely. Can I be on the outside? I want to get crushed this time."

I laugh and hang back while Calum, Kevin, and Nikon get ushered in with the next round of riders.

Kev jogs over to hand me his phone and turns to follow Callum and Nikon to the car they chose.

"Have fun!" I call, searching for the best spot to take their picture.

"Are ye disappointed to be takin' a pass on the next round of fun, *a ghra*?" Sloan asks. "If ye want to join yer brothers, I'm happy to be the one takin' pictures."

I shake my head. "Of course not. Today is a celebration of life and love. I'm Team Mackenzie all the way. The fact that you didn't love the absolute best ride of the country fair, the ride that anchors all my happiest childhood memories, doesn't diminish my love for you at all. Seriously. Not even a little."

He looks at me, his brow arching. "Are ye tryin' to be funny?"

I sober. "And apparently not doing a very good job of it today. Not even the hint of a smile, eh? Nothing?"

Sloan sighs and offers me an apologetic smile. "Sorry, luv. I'm not feelin' well, and the high-speed spin didn't do much to help the situation."

"What kind of not feeling well? Is it your stomach? Do you have a headache?"

"A bit of both. I woke up feelin' grotty and things haven't improved since then."

"Woke up? That was hours ago. You should've said something."

He waves away my concern and draws a deep breath. "Ye've been lookin' forward to today fer weeks. I'll not let a wee stomach bug ruin our day."

A cold shiver races down the length of my spine and suddenly nothing seems funny anymore. "You don't actually think it's a wee stomach bug, do you? Like a wee blue bug, maybe?"

The music grows louder as the ride begins its backward spin.

Sloan studiously avoids watching the cars whiz by and presses his fingers against his lips. Turning his back to the action, he swallows. "Nothin' like that, no, but if it's all the same, I think I'll go talk to Dillan and the others in the line."

I take a few quick pics of Kev and Nikon crushing Calum and laughing their heads off, then straighten. "Lead the way, hotness. If you need to puke, give me a signal, and I'll part the sea like you read about."

I've seen him barf blue beetles once and I don't ever want a repeat performance.

"Thank you, Lady Moses. I'm sure things will settle once we join Liam and Kady and sit fer the concert."

Yeah… I'm sure they will. At least, I hope so.

"Fi, over here!" I follow the rich timbre of my bestie's voice to find Liam stretched out on one of two blankets taking up a large patch of grass. Kady, his girlfriend of the last six months, is spread out beside him, and the two of them are hogging as much space as they can while being glared at by the surrounding concertgoers.

Sloan and I pass the assigned seating, climb the concrete steps cutting into the hillside, and make our way across the manicured grass to join them.

The Markham Fair is one of Canada's oldest country fairs and has been a yearly event since 1844. There are prizes awarded for livestock, quilting and sewing, baking and preserves, harvested vegetables, and all manner of crafts. As well, there is a tractor pull, the midway, and live bands all weekend.

"Some of my favorite family memories are of Da and Mam driving us north of the city and bringing us here. They'd take us through a barn or two and lay out a couple of blankets as our home base. They'd listen to the bands while the six of us ran wild through the fair going on rides and eating midway food until we were ready to puke."

Sloan swallows and makes a face. "Let's not talk about puking if ye don't mind."

"Yeah, sorry."

The stage is set and looks ready to roll. Then there is a large floor section, an upward slope that includes the assigned seating, and general admission seats across a massive grass slope.

Sure, the people in assigned seats can see better and have a roof over their heads, but with the sound system, the video screens, and the sun shining on a beautiful October afternoon, grass seats rule.

"Hey, guys. How's your day going?" I settle on the thick Mexican blanket we Cumhaills use for picnics, concerts, and hockey games. "Great spot."

Liam is lounging on his back with his hands behind his head

and his eyes closed. With the sun warming his face, he looks as content as I've ever seen him. "Was there any doubt? This ain't my first fair."

I grin at the dirty looks the couple next to us throw my way. "I see the two of you have been making friends with the neighbors."

A sly smile curls across Liam's lips, but he doesn't open his eyes. "First come, first served is the law of the land. I can't help it if people aren't as committed as I am to having a great home base."

Sloan lowers himself to the grass beside me, and I stretch out on the blanket to look up at the sun and soak up some rays myself. "Man, what a beautiful day."

"They don't get much better in October."

"I bet this is Brenny's doing. He knew we were having a day dedicated to him and living life and he rigged us the best weather of the month."

"That wouldn't surprise me in the slightest." Liam chuckles. "Have you got sunscreen on, girlfriend? I know it's October, but I also know how you fry."

"Yes, dear." I chuckle, but he's not wrong to be cautious. With my red hair, blue eyes, and pale Celtic complexion, direct sun hasn't always been my friend.

I can't even count how many times I've come home from playing football with the boys or volleyball on the beach and have been fried redder than a boiled lobster.

Sloan, however, doesn't have that problem. His mocha brown complexion gets darker and more tanned through the summer, but he doesn't burn.

Lucky duck.

A shrill whistle pierces the air, and I sit up, searching for whichever one of my brothers is looking for us. I don't see anyone, but hundreds of people are flooding in and taking their seats.

It's funny what you get used to over a lifetime. I can pick out the whistle of any member of my clan anywhere in a large crowd even if I can't see them.

Pinching my finger and thumb together, I press it under my tongue and blow. The whistle I release in response matches the tone and volume of the first one.

Kady winces and bends her head away from me. "Shit, Fi. I think you just blew my eardrums."

"My bad. Sorry."

"Marco!" Emmet yells somewhere in the distance.

"Polo!" I yell back.

"Marco!" he yells again a minute or two later.

I see him then and raise my hand to wave. "Em! Over here."

Once he and Ciara are on their way over, I settle in next to Sloan and check on him. "How are you feeling, hotness? Any better?"

"Do ye mean is my headache any better with yer whistlin' and screechin'? No. I'm afraid not."

I wrinkle my nose and offer him a genuine look of apology. "Oops. Okay, close your eyes, and I promise, no more yelling until the concert starts. That should give you a good half-hour to rest."

"Rest?" Emmet joins us with Ciara. "Nobody rests at the live bands of the fair. This is Brenny's one-year celebration of life."

"It is." I keep my voice down so I don't disturb Sloan. "It's hard to believe it's been one year without him. It still kinda feels like he's on an undercover assignment and he's going to come home."

Liam nods. "I've felt like that more than once. I also think he was too big of a personality to truly die. He'll always be with us. I figure he's here spending the day with us at the fair, waiting for us to start raising many overpriced pints at the concert."

I chuckle. "That sounds about right."

Liam grins. "There's nothing he loved more than family and having a good time."

I point at the concession stand at the base of the hill. "Then, I guess, we better get some bevvies so we can get this party started in true Cumhaill style."

"I like the way you think, sista." Emmet straightens and checks the line at the three kiosks down on the concrete pad. "First round is on me."

I shake my head and jump to my feet. "Nope. Brendan is picking up the tab today. I'll come with you and help carry."

Liam jumps up too. "I'll come. Hotdogs, anyone? Since Brenny's buying, we might as well go all out."

The offer of hotdogs gets a yes on all fronts.

He nods. "We might as well get some for Dillan, Eva, and the Greeks too. They've been working up an appetite on the midway rides all afternoon."

"Will do."

"Do ye want me to come, luv?" Sloan opens his eyes.

I wave that away and check my watch. "No. You rest. You still have twenty minutes to feel better before things get started. This is a celebration. I want you to be able to enjoy it with us."

Emmet, Liam, and I navigate across the crowded lawn, placing our feet so we don't tromp on anyone's hands or personal belongings. By the time we make it back over to the concrete steps, Dillan, Eva, and the Greeks are funneling toward the gates at the far entrance to the stage area.

After whistling, I wave my hand over my head to get their attention.

"Are you good to line up, Fi?" Emmet asks. "I drank too many slushies and need a pitstop."

Liam and I join the tail end of the incredibly long line, and I chuckle. "Yeah, go pee. Liam and I will probably still be standing right here when you get back."

Liam grins. "True story."

The two of us spend the next couple of minutes catching up on what we've missed in each other's lives and inching forward in a go-nowhere shuffle. "So, Da's taking today on his own with your mom, and tomorrow we're headed to Ireland to set up for the big dragon first birthday party on Gran's and Granda's back lawn. Wanna come?"

"Sure. I can come for a few hours during the day if Nikon or Dionysus can snap me back to the bar before the dinner rush."

"I'm sure that can be arrang—ah, hell." The shield on my back flares to life. I straighten, scanning the crowd for the source of trouble. "Cat crap on a Ritz."

"What?" Liam telegraphs my gaze, searching the crowd. "Did you see something? What's wrong?"

"My tattoo just fired to life and is burning."

"Shit. That's never a good sign."

"Nope."

"Is it like a warm tingle or like a bonfire whooshing on your back?"

"Closer to door number two. It's strong but not a DEFCON alarm."

"I suppose that's one good thing." Liam scowls at the thousands of people coming and going. "Maybe it's a drunk and disorderly and nothing Guild-worthy."

"Maybe."

"Hey, Jane," Dionysus gushes as he, Nikon, Eva, and Dillan join us in the line. "We missed you on the spinny ride. How's Irish feeling?"

I hold up a finger to pause Dionysus's enthusiasm—as if that's even possible—and take a moment to let the rest of the group into the loop.

"Ah, Fi." Dillan frowns. "Way to bring down the party, baby girl."

I chuff. "Don't shoot the messenger."

"Fine. What's our plan?"

I consider that for a moment and sort things through. "Liam, you take the Brenny debit card and stay in line with Nikon. If the world explodes, Greek, flash him and Kady to safety. The rest of you spread out and see if we can deal with whatever is building quickly and quietly. My Spidey-senses are tingling, and I've got a bad feeling building in the pit of my belly."

"Maybe you're just gassy," Dionysus says. "Or hungry? Sometimes you get cranky if you're hungry."

"True, but this isn't that. Something's not right."

"Do you have any idea what it is?" Nikon asks.

"Nope. Sorry."

Dillan takes Eva's hand in his. "Would you care to take a stroll through ten thousand people and search for something not right?"

Eva giggles. "I'd be delighted. Have I told you how sexy you are when you're crabby?"

"No, but I'm all ears."

I groan and shoo them off, deliberately not listening to any more of their convo. If Eva finds Dillan sexy when he's a crank, both of them are incredibly lucky because D is usually grumbling about something.

Emmet arrives back a moment later. "Hey, guys. Glad you found—"

"—Liam and Nikon, if you two see Calum and Kev, fill them in. Emmet, you're with Dionysus and me."

Emmet blinks and falls in behind us. "Is anybody going to fill *me* in?"

"I would if I could, bro. All I know is my shield is flaring and something wicked this way comes."

"Oh. Is that all?"

CHAPTER TWO

As Emmet, Dionysus, and I make our way through the crowd, I text the Team Trouble WhatsApp group and make sure everyone is informed. Next, I call up Sloan's cell and phone him. It rings a few times and goes to message. "Ye know who I am, so ye know what to do."

"Hey, hotness. If you're awake, we've got a situation. If you're not, you might soon be. Hope you're feeling better."

I hang up and shrug. "Anything?"

Dionysus shakes his head. "I'm listening to all the conversations but nothing yet."

"*All* the conversations? You can hear *all* these people and what they're saying at once?"

"Of course. Why? Is that weird?"

"Not if it's a god thing, I guess."

He nods. "Then it's a god thing. Oh, and the connection is especially strong for me when people are drinking and having a good time—which most of these folks are."

Emmet grunts. "We would be too if Fi's stupid shield wasn't acting up."

I laugh. "It's not like I planned this. I'm rolling with the punches here, same as you."

"Yeah, well, we've got about ten minutes before the warmup band takes the stage and we run the risk of impacting everyone's good time."

"That might work to our advantage." Dionysus scans the people already seated.

"Ruining everyone's good time?" Emmet asks.

"No. The concert is starting in ten minutes. At least then, everyone will sit and give us a chance to see what's going on."

"Yeah, that would be good." I point toward the concrete steps leading down into the floor section. There are times when the burning of my shield acts much like the game Hot-and-Cold. Today is one of those times. It's a slow process, but we're zeroing in on the beacon of bad.

"Ticket holders only." The security guard checking tickets at the gate to the lowest seating section offers me a warm smile.

I pull out the general admission stubs stuffed into my back pocket and catch Dionysus's attention. "Of course." I tilt my head toward the gatekeeper. "I'm sure you'll find these are three tickets for the front row seating and all is in order."

Dionysus catches my drift and flicks his fingers toward me. The tingle of his magical signature washes over me and eases my tension.

The security guard scans the ticket stubs in my hand and nods. "Thank you. Enjoy the concert."

The three of us file through the gate and continue our descent toward the empty stage. Three roadies are finishing setting guitars in place and doing last-minute sound checks.

Tipping my head back to scan the scaffolding above, I search the structure of the roof and catwalks for anything that seems out of place.

"I swear when the gods get bored, they sit up on their marble dais, grab the pegs of a giant wheel of chaos, and give it all they've got. It's like a real-life version of *Wheel of Fortune* only with more bankrupt spots, and I'm sure much more laughter."

Dionysus barks a laugh and two girls with midriff t-shirts and lots of cleavage eye him up. "Honestly, it gets old after a couple of hundred years. Even gods can mature and evolve. People blame the Fates, but that's not fair either."

"No, it's not." I step down a few more stairs while I continue to search. "I've met those ladies, and they're lovely."

Dionysus grins. "They are indeed."

No. It's not the Fates we need to worry about. It's the Hecate and Eros kind of gods that cause chaos like this.

Or bad apples in the fae realm like Keldane, Prince of the Unseelie.

Or the evil souls who manage to escape their Neitherlands prison when their psychotic lover opens a rift during a sacred ritual.

Or vampires who hear the blood song of their prey because some psychotic female drugs them in an attempt to take over the empowered crime ring in the city.

Wow. It's a wonder magic is even a secret at all.

"There." I point at a white pouch the size of a sandwich bag tied to one of the cross beams of the scaffolding eighty feet above our heads. I don't know how I'm so sure, but when I focus on it, my shield tells me I've hit the jackpot. "What do you suppose that is?"

"I don't know, but there are more than one." Emmet raises his arm and points in another direction. "Look. There are a bunch of them."

I follow Emmet's gesture and yeah, now that we know what we're looking for, there's a series of small, white bags tied to the white metal frame of the roof scaffolding. If my shield hadn't drawn me to look for them, I never would've found them.

"What do you think they are?" Emmet asks.

"Hex bags, maybe?" I say.

"To hex who? And why—"

The words are still falling off Emmet's tongue when a rush of magic hits us like an EMP pulse. It knocks me, Dionysus, and Emmet staggering back but doesn't seem to affect anyone around us.

My bells thoroughly ring, and the world spins for a bit. When the ride comes to a full stop, I look at Emmet and Dionysus to make sure they're all right.

"What the fuckety-fuck was that?" Dillan snaps, jogging over to join us.

My phone rings the next moment. It's Niall Horan's *Black and White*, a.k.a. Sloan. "Hey, hotness—"

"Fi? What just happened?"

"Didn't you get my message?"

"No. I, uh… I don't know. I was sleeping until that surge hit. What's going on?"

"Not sure. My shield went off, and we tracked the hot and tinglies to—"

Dionysus snorts beside me. "Yeah, baby. You said hot and tinglies."

"I did, but not the good kind. Sorry, dude."

"Fiona, please," Sloan snaps. "Can ye focus long enough to tell me what's happenin'?"

"Sorry. All I know is that there are a bunch of weird hex bags or something tied to the metal framing of the roof. As for what they do or what that pulse was, I have no idea."

Another pulse of raw power hits and I'm knocked back for a second time. This time, Dionysus grabs my arm to steady himself, and I feel the rush of magic he holds in his cells.

"Are you all right, Tarzan?"

"He's better than that guy," Dillan says, pointing into the crowd. In the middle of a section of plastic seating, there's a guy doubled over and sprouting fur. "Shit, we've got Moon Called losing control and shifting in full view of everyone."

"Sloan, get Garnet down here." That's all I get out before I end the call and rush toward the man doubled over and splitting out of his clothes.

"Veil of Privacy."

It's already too late. People are backing away, eyes wide, and I have no idea where to take him or how to—shit, he's a grizzly… and trapped in a rage of horror. "Dionysus, get him out of here before he eats someone. I'll cover you."

As Dionysus reaches the grizzly shifter, I throw up a cloud of confusion and release Bruin. "Race up the aisle toward the stage. You're the distraction, buddy. Try not to trample anyone."

"On it."

Another scream from behind me has me spinning. "Well, shit."

Two skinheads wearing the marks of the West Village Wizards have their hands up and are throwing off blue and purple sparks like two magical arc welders.

"Stand back, puny humans," one of them shouts. "Behold the power of greatness."

Seriously? That guy's been watching too much Sci-Fi channel. "Dillan and Eva, de-escalate Mr. Greatness."

"De-escalate him?" Dillan flashes me a crazy look. "Yeah, sure, Fi. We're on it."

"I have faith in you, D." I'm already scanning the chaos of the crowd for the next disaster.

"Fi, is Bigfoot a thing because I've got a huge furry brown guy throwing people like pebbles over here."

I follow Emmet's panicked call and my mind stalls out… "Holy crapamoly."

"Right? That's Bigfoot, right?"

"All signs point to yes."

"Vampires!" someone screams to my right.

Yep, two of Xavier's seethe are standing under one of the hex bags. They're red-eyed and have dropped fang like the creatures of my nightmares.

"Sloan and Nikon, you're on Bigfoot. Emmet, you're on hex bags. Get those things down so we can transport them out of here."

Emmet scowls. "How do you suggest I do that? I left my hundred-foot ladder in my other jeans."

"I was thinking transfiguration. Be a monkey or a bird or something. You have the most experience with animal forms. Be the solution, Em."

I can't tear my gaze away from Bigfoot. He's incredible. Sure, he's dangling a woman by her ankle five feet off the ground, but he's still incredible.

While Emmet runs off to figure something out, I zone in on the vampires. If Emmet has the most experience with transfiguration, I have the most experience with vampires.

Yay me.

"Marcus and Laurent, right?" I approach with my palms up. "You don't want to do this. I *know* you don't. You two are part of Xavier's family, and that means something. Higher standards. Lots of control. This isn't you. Magic is influencing you."

I point up, where a golden lion tamarin and a squirrel monkey are racing along the metal framework above our heads, untying baggies.

Go Emmet…and other monkey person.

"You smell good, Lady Druid." Marcus takes a step forward.

"Thanks, I try, but seriously, if you two could race out toward the midway, I swear you'll be able to regain control, and all will be well."

"Or we can finally see what Xavier sees in you. Did you know we can read the imprint of another vampire who fed off you? All we need to do is sink our teeth in and quench our thirst for knowledge and sustenance."

I glance back to ensure my way up the aisle is clear. Bruin is on the stage with a faery girl with purple wings, so I decide to join him if this comes down to a chase.

"As flattering as that sounds, I'm going to pass. I gave blood last week, and you know the rules. Once a month at most."

Another scream draws my attention to where Dillan and Eva are calming the wizards. As I turn, the curved blade of Eva's scythe lops off someone's head. The detached noggin tumbles through the air, casting bloody spray over the horror-stricken concertgoers.

What. The. Hell?

"I said, *de*-escalate you two! *Deeee*-escalate!"

A woman in the splash zone doubles over, hacks, and vomits over the blue plastic chair in the next row.

I don't blame her. The way my stomach is heaving, I could go for a nice, cathartic vomit right now too.

My shield is singeing hot, and I turn to—

The vampires took my distraction as a signal to launch. As their movements blur before me, I curse and turn on my heel.

"Tough as Bark." My sneakers smack out a steady rhythm against the concrete as my body armor bursts forward. Several people notice my skin spontaneously bursting into a web of tree branches, bark, and roots.

The exposure of the empowered is knocked out of the park today. If you're gonna go down, you might as well go down in a fiery ball of flame.

"Feline Finesse." I leap up the four feet to land on the stage. *"Bestial Strength."*

I cartwheel in the air and land with my hands up and ready to defend. Where's Bruin? He was here a minute ago. Yikers. He's supposed to be my backup.

It's the work of a thought to call Birga to my hand, and I'm as prepared as I can be to defend against two vampires.

The two of them engage, their fingers tipped with claws, their eyes as blood red and creepy as any horror flick villain.

Spinning Birga, I'm able to keep them at a distance, but it won't work long.

"Bruin? A little help here?"

The roar of my bear in the distance is comforting.

The roar of two lions in the crowd is not.

Garnet tips his head back and lets loose a lung-vibrating roar. He's more pissed than homicidal but the humans around him don't realize that because they don't know him. Another wave of panic washes through the crowd and ratchets up the insanity.

In hindsight, maybe I should've assessed the danger before calling them in and adding more empowered fuel to the proverbial fire.

Oops.

People dive to the side like tipping dominoes as my bear races to my aid. We've fought in enough battles now that I'm not worried about hitting him with Birga as I dance my dance with the vampires.

If I were trying to dispatch them, that would be different. I'm not. They're Xavier's family and are under a magical thrall. I'm not going to lop off their heads as a quick fix to a bad situation.

I can't believe Eva did that.

How do I fix that?

Bruin rears up on his hind legs and towers over me. He's brutally beautiful when he's riled up, and I couldn't be prouder. He's as badass as they come.

The posturing stops our vampire attackers in their tracks. They freeze, blinking at us as if they're rethinking their decision to come at me.

"Lady Druid?" Marcus says, scanning the stage. "What's happening? Why... What have we done?"

Laurent stands down too, and his eyes return to a normal, warm brown. "I don't understand."

"Give me one second, and I'll explain." Before I do that, I pull out my phone and scroll through the Team Trouble contacts. Finding the one I desperately need, I connect the call.

Dan the Djinn picks up on the second ring. "Hello?"

"Hey, Dan, it's Fiona. We have a massive FUBAR situation at the Markham Fair in the grandstand stadium. We need your mind-washing superpowers... Come to think of it, bring everyone you can. Help me, Obi-Wan Kenobi. You're our only hope."

"Well, that was one helluva clusterfuck." Garnet storms into his office, pulling off his ruined silk shirt. He grabs a clean one from the hanger on the back of his door and stalks back out to glare at us while he does up the buttons. "Would someone like to tell me what the fuck just happened?"

Emmet holds up a glass box Dionysus devised to secure the dozen white bags he and Ciara removed from the roof of the concert center. "These were tied all over the maze of scaffolding above the assigned seating. We think they're hex bags but won't know for sure until a witch or a wizard can take a closer look at them."

"Since I have to speak to Markdale anyway about the man you beheaded, I'll have him weigh in. Speaking of which, how did one of the West Village Wizards end up in two pieces?"

"I was protecting Dillan." Eva grins. "I have been charged to act as the guardian for the Cumhaill family. We made every effort to de-escalate the wizards, as Fi suggested, but when his attack on Dillan drew him too close to death for my liking, I took steps."

"It was less about steps and more about a swing, from the reports."

Eva smiles. "I was within my purview as a guardian angel protecting my charge. Feel free to take it up with my supervisor if you wish."

"Which is who, exactly?"

"That would be Death."

Garnet growls and turns his attention back to Emmet's burden. "Whether or not they're hex bags, they'll carry a magical signature we should be able to track to a community, if not the exact perpetrator. Then we can figure out what their alignment is."

"I'm guessing dark," I say.

Garnet pegs me with a droll glare. "Someone run this down for me from the top."

When all eyes fall on me, I shrug and accept the talking stick. I explain everything I know, starting with the first pulse of energy and ending with Ciara and Emmet untying the bags and shutting down their effect.

"But the damage had already happened," Garnet says.

"Unfortunately, yes. Although, yay Emmet and Ciara. You guys did a great job."

"But we weren't able to get them down before all hell broke loose," Emmet says.

I wave that away. "You guys shifted forms and saved the day. It would've been *waaay* worse if you hadn't gotten those bags down and locked in Dionysus's magical cake keeper. Ciara, I didn't know transfiguration was one of your skills."

Ciara shrugs. "Ye forget, I've been a druid my entire life. Takin' a simple form like a wee monkey isn't such a fantastic feat."

"Well, I think it was, and I'm glad you were both there to get the job done when we needed it."

The growl of Garnet's lion is a long, low rumble that makes the hair on my arms stand on end. "The wizards won't be happy. They already hate Fi, and this isn't going to help. It would be best if you all keep to yourselves for a few days while I sort this out."

"That works for us," I say. "We're headed out of town by tomorrow noon anyway. Let me know if you need us. Otherwise, we're taking a long weekend on the Emerald Isle and will be back mid-week."

"Perfect. Hopefully, by the time you get back, the dust will have settled.

"Yeah, hopefully."

CHAPTER THREE

"I heard you played the starring role in another shit show yesterday. Garnet mentioned the djinns had to throw a two-mile memory wipe to cover the entire fairgrounds and the surrounding area."

I don't fall for the distraction.

Sparring with Merlin is very different than sparring with my brothers or even fighting against opponents.

Merlin might appear relaxed as he blocks Birga with his staff, but he's planning the offensive maneuver he'll use on me five steps from now.

I've learned this the hard way.

When I don't respond, he smiles. "Cat got your tongue, Lady Druid?"

I throw myself to the side in an aerial to avoid getting penned into a situation where my back is up against a tree. "Just keeping my eyes on the prize, old man."

"Old? Who are you calling old?"

"The guy who was around to see Mother Nature invent rocks."

That gets a laugh out of him. "Rude and inaccurate. If you're going to put anyone in that category, your finger should be pointing at Dionysus."

I jump over his staff as he attempts to sweep my feet. Checking my periphery, I make sure he's not sending any strangle vines to tangle me up and tie me down. Fool me once and all that.

When I'm sure my blind spots hold no hidden dangers, I seize the opportunity and make my offensive move. Reaching out with my connection, I fold the earth beneath his feet and rush in to keep him from bounding out of my trap.

Except when I move in, a gale-force wind hits me from behind, and he vaults over my head. With my forward momentum, there's nothing to do but navigate my landing so I can get out of the pit I created before he closes me in.

Spotting my landing, I've already envisioned my next move. The moment my boots meet the earth, I command the soil to raise me up and out of the hole.

A fireball hits me square in the back and knocks me face-first into the grass. I lose Birga in my attempt to save my face and curse as my staff is sucked across the forest floor and into my opponent's hand.

"Dammit." I push myself up to my knees and brush the dirt from my palms. "You make it look so easy. I honestly thought I was a decent fighter until we started sparring with you."

Merlin offers me a sympathetic smile. "Don't be disheartened, Fi. I have more than a millennium of battle, magic, and strategic experience over you. Your skills are developing very quickly for a new fighter. These things take time."

I glance at where Dillan and Emmet are squaring off against Sloan. It still takes the two of them to best the skills he's amassed over a lifetime of growing up a druid...and he's even stronger now that we're training in the Don Valley River System.

"Time is something we don't have. Once the Culling starts, we'll face gods and demons and a dozen other dark fae opponents who are stronger than us. If the balance of good and evil rests in our hands, we must be better than skilled. We have to be powerful fighters."

"Then honestly, there is work to do." Merlin steps over to where I'm still sitting on my knees and extends his hand to help me up. "If it makes you feel any better, you and your brothers have a years' worth of experience and a decade's worth of proficiency. Druids work at building their connections and their craft over entire lifetimes. It's all very new to you."

I regain my footing and try to calm my frustrations. "I know. We get our asses kicked more often than not. If it weren't for you, Sloan, and Wallace patching us up all the time, we wouldn't have survived this long."

"Again, give yourself a break. You and your brothers came into this a year ago…less than that. Your brothers didn't even start until you got home last fall."

"I understand that. But if we're supposed to be heroes in our own lives, we need to be able to hold our own against powerful forces. The idea that my brothers are unprepared for the coming fight makes me sick. I can't lose anyone else."

"Then the answer is simple, cookie." He tosses me Birga and steps back, striking a ready pose. "We'll practice hard and leave everything on the forest floor. I'll even ask a few of my empowered friends to step in and play the part of our enemy opponents. In two months, destiny will be what it will be. All we can do is meet it with as much strength and skill as we can muster."

What can I say to that?

He's right. No matter how much I wish it were different, we're a year into our training as druids, and there's no way to be any further along than we are.

"I wish we knew for sure who we'd be coming up against."

Merlin tilts his head to the side, his long, dark waves brushing his shoulders as he lifts his staff. "We know a handful. We'll study the strengths and weaknesses of the opponents we know and anticipate the rest."

Birga sings on the breeze as I spin her in my hands, ready to begin again.

Yeah, we know a handful of our opponents.

Melanippe is an immortal Amazon. Mingin is a banished Hunter-god dark soul that merged with Riordan McNiff, an experienced druid. The Barghest aren't particularly dangerous, but Droghun will be pissed about Dionysus sending him to Antarctica, and they're loyal to Riordan. Then we have dark wizards, and I'm sure some demons, and likely a trickster or two...

"We need a bigger force," I say.

"As your messenger said, *Ní neart go cur le chéile.*"

There is strength in unity.

Yeah, no shit, weird rocking chair lady...no shit.

Merlin and I engage in another round of muscle-tearing, back-aching melee training and I take the beating until I think I'm going to drop. "Okay, I surrender. My arms are going to fall off."

I send Birga back to her resting place in my forearm tattoo and stagger over to grab my water bottle. My muscles feel like rubber, and it's surprisingly difficult to walk when your legs are Jell-O.

Flopping onto the grass, I sip my water and try not to look as wiped as I feel.

Merlin scoops a towel off the pile and dabs his face. Ha! What a faker. He's obviously doing that for my benefit because he's neither sweating nor winded.

"You, Cazzie, and the others are coming to the birthday party, aren't you?"

"Wouldn't miss it. Cazzie and Saxa plan to teach the young ones some of the ancient fireside songs as their gift."

"I've been thinking about that. I think the party is my gift to them but is that enough? What do dragons really want?"

"Shiny things. They love all things that glitter and shine. That's why the Queen of Wyrms and Cazzie both have a treasure horde they protect. They love all the baubles, coins, amulets, and trinkets. Anything like that."

"All the glittery things. Got it."

My phone rings and I log roll a few times to reach my jacket instead of trying to get up. Normally I'd let it go to message, but by the ring tone, I know that it's Samuel or one of the other Hunter-gods, Ahren or Quon Shen. "Hold that thought, master Merlin. This could be important."

I rummage through my jacket pocket to find my phone, accepting the call right before it goes to message. Sweat drips down the crack of my butt, and I wriggle in my yoga pants as I sit up.

"Samuel? Is that you?"

The line stays muffled at first, then the background noise clears, and a deep, Sam Elliot-esque baritone answers. "Fi, it's Ahren. Listen, Samuel wants me to let you know we're closing in on Melanippe and Mingin. We nearly caught them outside a small village in Budapest. They gave us the slip, but it's easier to track them now because the taint of their evil is growing."

"I guess that's a good news and bad news situation. The more powerful and evil they become, the easier it is for us to locate them."

"Yeah, but the harder it is to take them down."

"Do you need help? Do you want me and my posse to meet you and join the fight?"

"That time is fast approaching. Right now, be ready. Things are escalating, and we think new players are taking the field."

"Any idea who that might be?"

"Nothing solid yet. Have you had any brushes with ancient sorcerers lately? Quon Shen got hit hard when we tried to intercept a meeting between Mingin and a new guy on the scene. He said the magic signature that washed over him felt like old sorcery."

"How old are we talking?" I hold the phone out while I press the button to put it on speaker. "I'm no expert on ancient sorcerers, but I have a friend here who might be."

"I can't say how old he was or from where the source of his power stems. Quon Shen would know better than me. He spent time sharing the plains with ancestors back to the Ming Dynasty. He simply said ancient sorcery."

"Did he happen to mention what this person looked like?" Merlin asks.

"Oh, that I can help you with. I got face-to-face with the asshole. He has long dark hair, a scar across his cheek, and two different colored eyes."

Merlin stiffens. "One green and one brown?"

"That's right. Do you know him?"

My throat tightens, and I swallow against the constriction. "Is it an ugly red scar that goes from his cheek up to his ear?"

"You got it on one, Fi. Do you know that jerk?"

I meet Merlin's scowl and exhale. "Unfortunately, we do. That's Morgana's son, Yvain. Long story short, we had a run-in with him back in the ninth century when he was trying to free his mommy dearest from her magical imprisonment. I thought maybe we had left them in the past...well, I hoped we had."

"Afraid not, Lady Druid. He's here, and he's a nasty son of a gun."

"Yeah, I can't imagine time has improved his disposition much. Where are you now? I'll round up the team and will meet you. We were coming your way tomorrow anyway, so we've already cleared our schedule. If things are escalating, you do need help to take them down."

"You're right, but I think you're jumping the gun. Let us track them down and give you a call back. If you and yours are ready to roll at a moment's notice, that'll be soon enough."

I hate the idea of not being there if they need me, but maybe Ahren's right. Merlin is stepping up our training schedules. Perhaps it's better to work on becoming stronger fighters for when they call us in to help.

"All right. Thanks for letting us know. I'll make sure we're all ready for your signal. Keep us in the loop and stay safe."

"Will do. Watch your back, Fi. You seem to have made a negative impression with all the evil superpowers. Watch yourself."

I meet Merlin's worried gaze and nod. "Always."

After ending the call, I turn to address Sloan, Nikon, and my brothers. I hadn't realized they closed in while I talked to Ahren, but it's good they're here because this affects all of us. "How much of that did you hear?"

"Yvain is here, and he's joining forces with Mingin and Melanippe," Sloan says.

"Seems like it."

"He'll be after his mother's grimoire." Merlin pegs me with a hard stare. "You've never told me what you've done with that dark tome. Are you sure it's secure?"

"I honestly don't know. I was confident it was safe and secure against everyday power-hungry magical assholes, but Yvain, Mingin, and Melanippe are *uber* assholes."

"It's secure." Sloan's confidence goes a long way in making me feel better. "It's sealed in the iron tomb you crafted to contain it and placed somewhere that no one will ever find it or stumble upon it. It's as secure as it can be."

Merlin nods. "All right. I'll accept that for now but understand that if Yvain starts closing in on its location, we might have to put more security protocols in place."

"Understood."

Sloan doesn't seem to like that idea any more than I do. It

seems to me, the more attention we pay to where we buried the book, the more likely someone is to be able to find it.

"What about removing it from our minds and memories altogether?" I ask. "Because honestly, the only way they're going to find it is to pry the information out of our minds."

"Either that or torture you or someone you care about until you tell them where it is," Merlin adds.

I don't like the sound of that, but he's not wrong. I'd like to think I'd never succumb to torture, but to save someone I love from being killed, I might break down. "Agreed. Sloan and I are the only two people who know where it is, and we should strike it from our memories."

"What if we need to know where it is to keep it safe?" Dillan asks. "There is power in knowledge. That's a saying for a reason."

"I get that, but I don't think they'll find it."

"I'd like to be able to agree with you, Fi," Merlin says, "but Yvain is sensitive to his mother's power signature. If he gets close enough to feel it, he'll find it."

Sloan frowns. "All right. We'll put additional safeguards on the area and a warning spell to alert us to anyone potentially finding it and remove its location from our minds. There's not much more that we can do."

That seems to satisfy everyone's concerns.

"Okay, that's settled. Let's get back to training. We have two months to become the best we can be if we plan on saving the world's alignment from tipping heavily toward the dark side."

Merlin nods. "Everyone. Back at it."

CHAPTER FOUR

Gran's and Granda's back lawn is one of my favorite places on Earth. From the view of their little gnome house with thatched hat roofs and cobblestone walkways to the family grove on one side, the treehouse Dionysus built us on the other, and the sunken practice rings way off in the distance at the far end.

It's everything that makes me happy as a druid, a woman, and a kid…because the firepit in the middle of it is where we have our family bonfires at night.

Perfection.

As we materialize upon the vast green carpet of manicured lawn, everyone releases hands, and we separate. Dillan sets Jackson down. I let Meggie go off to run to Gran, and Aiden and Kinu head straight inside to get the twins settled in the spare room.

"Welcome home, kids." Granda sets the stick in his hand onto one of the large rocks by the bonfire. "We've got almost every-thin' ready."

I hug my grandparents and look around. "Where's Da and Shannon? They're here, right?"

"They are, though I think yesterday was too much fer yer father. He may have bent the elbow a few too many times and is payin' the price today."

That doesn't surprise me.

When we talked to Da about spending the day at the Markham Fair celebrating Brenny, he said he didn't have it in him. I have no doubt in a few years, things might be different, but for now, he's still lost in grief.

To some extent, we all feel that way, but it's different for him. Brendon was his child. I know part of him feels responsible for his death because, like all my brothers, he became a cop to follow in Da's footsteps.

While it's true Brenny was shot while he was undercover, the actual incident was outside a store when he stepped in front of the bullets meant for a woman and her daughter.

That could've happened if he was on the job or not. Brenny would've stepped in as their shield whether he was a cop or not.

"Maybe one of Ciara's remedy pills will help." Emmet extends his open palm back to his betrothed.

Ciara digs in her purse and comes out with her hand-painted pill holder. "Happy to donate to the cause."

Emmet closes his fingers around the little container and jogs over to the ladder leading up to the treehouse.

The flutter in my chest signals Bruin shifting position, and I leave Emmet to take care of things with Da.

Are you ready to hang with the family, buddy?

I was born ready, Red.

I release Bruin, and he appears on the lawn next to Manx, Doc, and Daisy. The four of them race off into the grove and are gone.

"Welcome home, luv." Gran pulls me into her embrace, and I accept the affection and breathe her in. Gran always smells like summer blossoms and home-cooked meals. She's the living representation of love and comfort in our family, and I've missed her.

Gran eases back and studies my expression. "What's the craic, luv?"

"Not much craic these days, Gran."

Her smile fades, and she washes me with a knowing look. "Ye put too much on yer plate, sweet girl. Ye need to take better care of yerself."

"I've told her that for years." Liam bumps my shoulder. "She's as stubborn as rocks."

"Am not." I scrunch my nose at him.

"Ye absolutely are." Sloan steps in to hug Gran next. "It drove me batty in the beginnin', but I've come to realize there's nothin' to be done about it. Ye'll do what ye do, and all anyone else can do is mitigate the fallout."

I bark a laugh. "That doesn't flatter me at all. Are you sure you want to go with that, Mackenzie?"

Liam chuckles. "Whether it flatters you or not, the man's not wrong."

I stick my tongue out at my bestie and focus on Sloan and Gran hugging. My heart melts a little to see the two of them together. Yes, Gran and Granda were his pseudo grandparents as he grew up, but when we first met, and he interacted with them, he was stiff. He's much warmer and cuddlier now.

If nothing else, being a Cumhaill has taught him the healing power of hugs, laughter, and of a family being a source of steadfast strength instead of a point of pain and disappointment.

Gran eases back and lifts her hand to cup his jaw. "Lovin' my wee girl suits ye, lad. Lugh and I couldn't be happier."

Sloan ducks his head and kisses her cheek. "I'm blessed in more ways than I can count."

"That's true," Dionysus says, joining us with Nikon. "But if you *were* to count, having two handsome, ancient Greeks in your life would be at the top of the list, right?"

I giggle. "Hells yeah it would."

Sloan goes with it and nods. "Aye, that's true enough. If not on the top, very near to it."

Dionysus leans in, kisses Gran's cheek, and gets his hug. Nikon follows right behind him and does the same. By the time we're milling around catching up, Emmet comes out onto the treehouse deck with Da and Shannon.

The beauty of Ciara's drinking cure is the immediate results. The first time I took it, I was in a shot-for-shot pissing match with Riordan McNiff. I won the challenge but would've paid a heavy price for it had she not come to my rescue.

Since then, it's saved us more than once.

So, when I gaze up and study my father, I know the dark patches under his eyes and the slump in his shoulders has nothing to do with the morning after the night before and everything to do with the reason he was drinking in the first place.

"Hey, Da. How's retirement in a treehouse going?"

He forces a smile and nods. "I can't complain. Although, the retirement part of it hasn't really started. Between finishing my rotation at the station and getting called in by Maxwell fer the task force, we've only had a couple of days to relax. It's been more like a vacation. We haven't even started to unpack."

Shannon is smiling in the background, but I get the sense that she's putting on a happy front.

That's concerning.

Jackson comes running, waving his arms at my dad. "Granda! Daddy says I can be a dragon rider like Auntie Fi when I grows up."

"Ye don't say." Da makes his way over to the ladder to climb down. "Aren't ye afraid ye might fall off and splat on the ground?"

Jackson busts up laughing. "No, Granda. Dragons have handles. You gotsta hold on."

"Oh, right." Da finishes his descent of the last couple of rungs. "I forgot about the holdin' on part."

He swings Jackson up into his arms and hugs him before looking up toward Shannon. "Come along, *a ghra*. If ye fall, I'll be sure to catch ye this time."

"This time?" Liam scowls up at his mom. "You fell off the ladder? How high were you?"

Shannon flicks her hand at her son and frowns. "Let's not talk about that. Ye'll jinx me."

I meet Sloan's gaze and point up at the deck. "Hotness, do you mind?"

"Of course not." Sloan *poofs* away and appears a split second later on the deck next to Shannon. "May I help ye down?"

"I appreciate the offer, dear, but I won't get any better at things if I avoid them. I'm certain the problem was my shoes. I was wearin' my slip-ons and slipped right out of them, and away I went."

Dionysus frowns. "I don't like it that Shannon fell out of our treehouse. She could've hurt herself."

"Och, I think she *did* hurt herself, sweet boy," Gran whispers. "She's spent most of yesterday sittin' on a heating pad on the couch and limpin' to and fro."

I meet Dionysus's gaze. "You have been so incredibly generous, and I heart you huge, you know that, but do you think you could maybe make Da and Shannon a little love nest on the ground so we don't have to worry about them breaking their necks getting up and down from our treehouse?"

"Or their hips," Dillan adds. "Old people tend to break their hips."

"Who are ye callin' old, ye mouthy git?" Da points at him. "I'll take ye on any day of the week and twice on Sunday."

Dionysus isn't paying any attention to them. He's solely looking at me. "But *you* like the treehouse, don't you, Fi? We're Tarzan and Jane...Swiss Family Robinson...all the good things, right?"

"Absolutely." I grin, showing him how serious I am. "It's perfect, and I wouldn't change a thing for us, but it's not a good fit for Da and Shannon. We want them to be safe and happy."

"If they have their own wee house, ye'll have yer place back to yerselves," Gran adds.

Dionysus grins. "I do like that idea. Niall has such strict rules about clothing."

Da laughs. "Only that ye wear some."

"Exactly." He nods, looking annoyed. "It's strange how important it is to you."

I slide an arm around his back and hug him against my side. "Some people don't embrace your nakedness, Tarzan. Their loss. Now, what do you think about a second little forest home?"

"Do you want it out here beside the treehouse?"

Gran waves Da and Shannon over. "If ye had yer pick of things, where would ye like yer love nest situated? It seems our boy here is in the mood to grant us a wish, and we thought we might be able to save Shannon's backside."

Da shrugs. "As long as it has a bed and a kitchen, I'm happy. I leave it up to Shannon."

Shannon looks shocked. "Are ye serious? I name a few things, and it'll happen?"

Dionysus checks with me. "Why? Is that weird?"

"No. It's so incredibly generous that it seems unreal to us. Your godliness is still new to us."

"Oh, then if that's all it is, sure. Name it, and I'll make it happen. Then we get the treehouse back, right? And I can be myself?"

Da chuckles. "Aye, ye will and ye can."

Dionysus steps behind Da and Shannon and stretches his arms over their shoulders. "Let's walk. Tell me what your dream house looks like, and I'll see what I can do."

As they stroll off, a gust of wind picks up my hair, and the ground rumbles with the weight of dragons landing in our midst. A moment later, Dart drops the glamor he cast to fly across the Irish sky, and we're looking at him, Saxa, Bryvanay, and Utiss.

Their presence stops all the casual conversation. Then Merlin and Empress Cazzienth land as well.

"The big chocolate dragon is Merlin, and the champagne one is his bonded companion, Empress Cazzienth."

"My word." Gran gasps beside me, her hand fumbling at the base of her throat. "They are beautiful together, aren't they?"

"They are."

We wait for them to settle, then Merlin shifts into his human form, and they come to say hello.

Gran bows her head and slides her foot back in an old-fashioned curtsy. "Welcome to our home, Empress. It is such an honor to have ye here."

Granda doubles over at the waist and bows. "Welcome. Fiona speaks highly of ye. It's our pleasure to have ye as our guests."

Merlin bows to my grandfather in return. "A warm and hospitable welcome indeed, Lugh. Thank you." He steps into our circle and takes Gran's hand, bringing her knuckles to his lips. "It's lovely to see you again, Lara."

"Dragons!" Jackson yells, running from the house with a cookie in each hand. Aiden is chasing him but has Meg in his arms and is losing the race. "Is it time to be a dragon rider? I'm ready!"

Merlin jogs forward to snatch him up before he charges Utiss and takes him over to meet Cazzie. "Jackson, this is my dragon companion, Empress Cazzienth. Cazzie, this is Jackson Cumhaill, Fiona's nephew."

Cazzie lowers her head and flutters her long, golden eyelashes. "It is a great pleasure to meet you, young Jackson. Merlin tells me you want to grow up to be a great dragon rider like your auntie."

Jackson's chocolate-smeared smile is too cute. He shifts both cookies to one hand and reaches out to touch one of the ridges on Cazzie's snout. "Yous *soooo* pretty. You sparkle like yous on fire."

He's not wrong.

My first impression of Empress Cazzienth was that she reminded me of a dazzling opal glistening in the firelight. She has two glorious gold and burned orange wings, a strong tail that ends in a treacherous-looking ball-spike, and the most beautiful champagne scales that shimmer and catch the light like magic.

"Why, thank you, young rider. That is sweet of you."

"Will you be my dragon?"

I chuckle, but Cazzie and Merlin take his question very seriously. "I am already paired with a rider, sweet boy. You see, for every dragon, there can be only one companion to bond with. My human is Merlin."

Jackson twists in Merlin's arms and grins. "You picked a pretty one."

Merlin grins. "She is very pretty, but the truth is, she picked me. It's the dragon who chooses a rider, Jackson. Not the other way around. They are wise and magical creatures, and they will feel the pull of bonding long before a human will. If you truly want to be a dragon rider, you need to honor your place as a druid and grow up to be a good and honest man."

Jackson looks a little lost, so I help him out. "You've gotta be a good boy and earn a dragon's love by being kind and brave and honest."

"I can do that." He grins. "I takes care of my sisters and help Mommy when she can't find her slippers. That's a good boy thing."

Merlin nods and sets him down. "It definitely is. Now, let's introduce you to the others. Who knows, maybe at the birthday party tomorrow, you'll meet the dragon destined to be your companion."

Aiden groans. "But it won't be time to ride a dragon, buddy. You gotta be sixteen, remember?"

"I remember," Jackson says. "We can still make friends, right?"

I grin. "Yep. You can for sure make friends."

CHAPTER FIVE

The next morning, I stretch under the covers and look up at the upholstered panel above our heads. King Henry is very masculine and has a carved depiction of woodland animals and stags with large racks of antlers. Anne Boleyn is much more feminine in design and décor but equally comfy.

Taking stock, I roll onto my side and find Sloan lying next to me. Normally, he's up and dressed and all spiffy by the time I get up, so finding him lounging in his boxers still beneath our mass of blankets is a treat.

"Hey, you."

"Hey, back."

"Is everything okay?"

"Why wouldn't it be?"

I inchworm closer and drape my arm over the sculpted ridges of his abs. "Because you're here lazing about with me instead of attacking the day like you usually do?"

"Maybe I want to laze about in bed with you. Maybe, instead of attackin' my day, I plan to attack you. Did ye ever think of that?"

I waggle my brows. "I'm game, of course."

"Of course."

"Or at least I would be if you were serious."

He pegs me with a sultry smile. "What makes ye think I'm not serious?"

"Because I know you and can tell when you're mind-spinning and avoiding something."

He smiles wryly. "Maybe yer not as smart as ye think. I've been watchin' ye sleep for some time now and was about to wake ye."

I chuckle. "That might be true, but I'm still right about you avoiding something."

He draws a deep breath and exhales. "It's this place. It winds me up, I suppose."

I draw a deep breath too and get a lungful of damp castle. He loves the smell. It makes me think of wood rot and mold. We agree to disagree.

"Did you talk to your parents yet? Do they know we're here?"

He tilts his head and lifts his shoulders. "I texted Da this mornin' and said we got in late and were in bed. He said he had a late-night house call and didn't get back. He'll catch up with us after nine."

"Uh-huh, it's becoming clear now. Your dad's not here to act as the buffer, so you're hiding in bed, so you don't have to face your mom alone."

He rolls his eyes. "I don't hide from my mother. There's no shame in enjoyin' a private moment with the woman I love. I thought maybe ye'd like to join me in the shower and start our day off right."

I burst out laughing. "You want me to be the bad example and corrupt your morning, so you don't have to face your mom."

"Yer ridiculous. I was bein' romantic."

I chuckle. "You were being a chicken and seducing me to back you up."

"Does that mean yer turnin' me down?" He throws the sheets back to pivot and puts his feet through the curtains.

I rock on my back, follow him through the fluttering draperies, and into the chill of the room beyond.

The moment my feet hit the stone floor, I run behind him and jump onto his back. Clinging to him like a koala, I reach around his shoulder and nip his jaw. "I never said that. Seducing me is a totally valid mode of avoidance. I was just calling you on it."

He twists his mouth to meet mine and laughs, course-correcting toward his bathroom. "Yer crazy, Cumhaill. Ye know that, right?"

"Crazy in love, maybe. So really, that's your fault."

He chuckles, only stopping once we're in the bathroom and he locks the door. "Och, well, if I'm the cause, I guess it's my responsibility to take care of ye."

I drop my feet to the floor and make quick work of the t-shirt I slept in. "It's important to embrace your responsibilities."

He runs an appraising gaze over me and nods. "It is at that, *a ghra*. Very important, indeed."

Sloan and I eventually make it out of his childhood room and down to the clinic to say good morning to his dad. Wallace has made great strides over the past months to bridge the gaps in the relationship between him and his son. It's been a rocky road at times with his parents, but I've enjoyed watching Sloan and his dad starting over.

Family matters.

Having a fam jam support system is such a part of me and who I am. I couldn't imagine not having it.

"Kids! There ye are. I was about to come to look fer ye." Wallace is chatting with one of the other healers in his clinic and ends the convo to come over to us. "What a wonderful surprise."

Sloan hugs his dad, and I'm next in line. "We mentioned we'd be coming for the dragons' first birthday celebration. Did you forget?"

Wallace winks at me and forces a smile. "I suppose I did. It's been a crazy time, and I couldn't be happier to have ye here. Will ye be stayin' at the castle or Lugh's and Lara's?"

Sloan casts a subtle glance around the clinic and answers his father's question. "All of Fi's family and friends are at Lugh's for the next few days, so I thought we'd stay here while the rooms are full...as long as things remain civil."

Wallace's smile falls, and now he's the one looking around to ensure privacy. "Let's have some breakfast, shall we? There are some things I need to tell ye."

That doesn't sound ominous at all.

Sloan meets my curious gaze and shrugs. Okay, so he doesn't know any more than I do.

We follow Wallace through the long, stone passageways of Stonecrest Castle and end our journey in the formal dining room.

The space has always painted the picture of exactly what I imagined a formal dining room in an ancient Irish castle would be. There was a long, uber-polished table with enough chairs to seat a football team, a tall hutch with expensive china plates, and heavy, expensive drapes that matched a century-old hand-woven rug.

Not anymore.

I blink as we come fully into the room. It's empty. No drapes. No hutch. No carpet. No mile-long table with forty chairs.

"Wow. Are you remodeling?"

Wallace gestures at the only furniture in the space—a round, wooden table with four chairs and a simple vase of cut flowers on it. "In a manner of speaking, yes."

Before he joins us, he touches the intercom button and leans close to speak. "Dalton? Sloan and Fiona are joining me in the dining room for breakfast. Would you mind fixing us up something?"

"My pleasure."

Wallace leaves it at that and joins us at the table. Looking around the room, he swallows and looks a little embarrassed. "I suppose I'll need more furniture in here to help balance out the room, won't I? It seems a little silly with only a wee table, doesn't it?"

Sloan shrugs. "The room is for eatin', Da. Any table is fine. Now, what's going on?"

"She left." Wallace draws a deep breath and nods as if simply saying it out loud solidifies things. "It seems yer granda was right all along."

"Left?" Sloan repeats, glancing around the room. "Left how? Left on a trip? Left fer the day? Left—"

"Left me," he says matter-of-factly.

Sloan pauses with his mouth open for a moment. "She up and left the life ye built over the last thirty-five years?"

"It seems so."

I reach across the table and rest my hand on Wallace's. "I'm so sorry. We didn't know."

"No, ye couldn't have. I didn't tell ye."

"When?" Sloan's voice is clipped. "How long ago did this happen?"

Wallace shrugs. "A month…maybe a bit longer."

"We've texted since then. Ye could have told me."

"I wasn't in much of a condition to talk about it at the time. I lost more than a few days in the confusion, but I'm back on track now. I'm glad yer here so I can tell ye in person. I'm sorry, son."

Sloan frowns. "Ye don't need to apologize. I'm only sorry ye didn't lean on me when ye were hurtin'."

Dalton comes into the room with a tea tray, scones, and jelly. He unloads the tray onto the table and straightens. "Shall I wait to pour?"

Wallace shakes his head. "It's fine, Dalton. I'll pour in a moment, thank you."

"I'll be back with yer breakfast shortly."

"You rock, Dalton," I say.

He offers me a smile. "It's nice to have ye back, Miss Fiona, and of course, yer a welcome addition to the household as always, young sir."

Sloan nods and waits until we're once again alone in the dining room. "What happened, Da? Is it done? Might she be havin' a tantrum and come back?"

"Och, I don't think her new man would think too highly of that. No. It's well and truly over."

Sloan recoils. "Her new man? What the hell? Are ye sure she's involved with someone else? Did she maybe just say so to hurt ye?"

"No, no. She and Arthur have always gotten on well at socials and fundraisers. Apparently, they're getting on quite well now."

The dismay in Wallace's voice is there in his eyes too. Thirty-five years. That's heartbreaking. I've never been a fan of Janet Mackenzie, but at least I respected her place as Sloan's mother and Wallace's wife.

Sloan reaches forward and pours a splash of milk in each cup before topping it with tea. "What happened? How did things go so wrong so fast?"

Wallace accepts the tea, stirs, and takes a slow sip. "I've spent the past weeks runnin' it over in my mind and, in hindsight, maybe it shouldn't have been such a surprise."

"No? Were ye havin' difficulties?"

"Not that I realized at the time. When ye started to strengthen yer own mind, she wanted me to bring ye back in line. We argued a bit then. When ye willed the fortune into Fi's care, she demanded I fight yer wishes. The arguments grew. Then, when I came back after spendin' the weekend with ye in the summer, I made it clear I supported yer choice and was happy to remain here and run my clinic regardless of whether or not I control the Mackenzie money."

"And she left?"

"Aye, she packed a bag and walked out the door."

"I'm so sorry, Wallace." I blink at the moisture stinging my eyes, guilt heavy in my heart. "I never wanted anything Sloan and I shared to come between you and your wife."

"Och, no, Fi. None of this falls on yer heads. It's simply how things evolved, and here we are."

"Aye, here we are. Yer right about that." Sloan sets his teacup down on its saucer and stands. The chair legs scrape the floor as he rises and rounds the table to open his arms to his father. "Fi's right. We never wanted to cause a rift in yer marriage."

Wallace rises to accept his son's support. The two are both well over six feet tall and resemble one another a great deal. "That's just it, son. Our marriage didn't even factor in. When it came down to it, it was all about the money."

"That's disgusting."

"It's good to have ye home, son."

Sloan steps back from the hug, his eyes too glassy. "Ye'll not face this alone. Yer far too good a man to stay tied to a woman who doesn't see the treasure she had. There are better things on the horizon. I promise ye that."

"Hells, yes, there are." I swipe at the tears now brimming and warming my cheeks. "You might not be totally familiar with the power of Cumhaill loyalty, but now that we know what you're going through, you've got the full force of our family behind you. If you need anything, consider it done."

Wallace hugs me next, and my breath shudders. When he steps back, he chucks my chin like Sloan always does and looks down at me. "Ye needn't let it bother ye so, Fi. It'll be fine."

I nod. "I know. It hurts my heart that she threw away two such amazing men. You both deserved better."

Dalton pushes through the dining room door with a tray of

bacon-scented wonder. When he sees the three of us in our state of tears, he freezes in his tracks. "Apologies. I can come back."

Wallace steps back and gestures to the table. "Not at all, Dalton. Ignore the display of emotion. There's nothing like a hearty breakfast to set things right."

I take a moment to hug Sloan while Wallace and Dalton get us set up. "I'm so sorry, hotness."

He presses his cheek to the top of my head and holds me tight. "Don't be, luv. Ye always say things happen as they're supposed to, and I've grown to believe it. I'll not mourn a woman who thought so little of my father or me that she'd walk straight into another man's life."

"Exactly right, son." Wallace reclaims his seat and flaps his napkin loose before settling it over his lap. "We'll be fine on our own."

Sloan holds my chair out for me, and we join Wallace at the table as Dalton takes his leave. Sloan picks up his juice glass and raises it toward the center of the table. "To new beginnings and the wonder of what the universe has in store."

I raise my glass and *chink* the other two. "*Slainte Mhath.*"

By mid-morning, Gran and I are arranging a dragon buffet line at the far end of the lawn for our happy birthday lunch party. Sloan, Nikon, and Tad are portaling in and out every few minutes to make pickups, and I take our quiet moments to fill her in on Janet Mackenzie walking out on Wallace.

"I admit, Wallace and I haven't always seen eye-to-eye on things where Sloan is concerned," Gran says, "but I've always respected the man and gave him credit fer puttin' up with the likes of Janet. That woman is as hard and cold as a glacial icicle."

"I feel bad for Sloan too. I know they weren't getting along, but I think he was still hoping she'd come around like Wallace did."

"Likely not, luv. Janet is most concerned with how things affect Janet. Getting her to recognize that the love ye share with Sloan is genuine and healthy fer the both of ye doesn't benefit her one bit. She simply wasn't interested in whether or not it could work, solely that ye stood in the way of her claimin' her financial reward."

"That's really crappy."

"It is at that. The good news is Wallace has seen her true colors and is still young and vibrant enough to find happiness."

I cast a sidelong glance at my grandmother and grin. "You say that like you might have some ideas about where happiness might lay for him."

Gran winks at me. "Wallace Mackenzie is a successful, well-respected member of our community. I have no doubt that when word gets out to the right sort of people, he'll find more than a few ladies who'd like to help him mend a broken heart."

I chuckle. "I take it you know 'the right sort of people?'"

Her smile is radiant, and I see quite clearly where I get my matchmaking talents from. "Leave it with me, luv. Wallace is now in very good hands."

"The absolute best. Thanks, Gran."

Tad *poofs* in with a deer, and I point at the end of the line. "I think you're finished. Feel free to wash up and join the boys. The libations are flowing at the fire."

Tad straightens, rubs his palms together, and strikes off across the lawn. "Och, well, if ye insist. I suppose you could talk me into a pint or two."

Gran and I finish with the birthday feast preparations and talk about the fun we have planned for the next few hours. Since we wanted to ensure all twenty-three dragons plus their mother, plus Cazzienth and the Icelandic dragons got their own meal, we had to widen our supply chain to include Scotland and more of the UK.

Thankfully, the family members of the Druid Order, living both here and abroad, are well-informed about the importance of keeping dragons happy and well-fed.

They came through for us big time.

"Och, that's a lot of dead animals." Ciara's disgust is plain in her expression.

She and Emmet are on their way back from a walk down by the training rings. By the look on her face, she wishes they didn't have to pass this on their way to the house.

I raise my finger and count down the line. "Roadkill, poaching, die off, butchering… Thankfully, we have quite an underground food chain built up."

"Well, you ladies killed it." Emmet screws up his face. "No pun intended."

Gran looks over the long line of dead and nods. "I'm sure the local farmers would thank us if they knew the lengths we've gone to keep their livestock out of the mouths of babes."

I chuckle. "I'm sure they would. Waste not, want not, right? One man's roadkill is another dragon's smorgasbord delight."

Ciara gags and groans.

Emmet grins. "Don't harsh on the buffet line, babe. I bet it'll be as popular with the dragons as chocolate chip pancakes are for us."

"Mmm, with extra syrup," I say, licking my lips.

"Noice, Fi. We should slather maple syrup on their brunch and make it authentically Canadian. It would be super birthday special."

"Sounds delish."

"Sounds disgustin'," Ciara snaps.

Emmet laughs and ignores her. "Gran? Do you still have any of those gallon jugs of syrup I brought you last winter?"

Gran grunts in amusement. "Ye brought me ten of them,

sweet boy. Aye, there are still eight in the back pantry. I'm set fer life, luv."

"Excellent. Then you won't miss a couple if I spruce up the dragon death row."

"Not a bit."

"Yer disgustin'." Ciara strikes off to go back to the house.

Emmet laughs and waves over his shoulder. "Don't worry. I'll take care of it. The syrup topping and the fact that we grossed out my betrothed."

Merlin is striding down the lawn to join us and knuckle bumps Emmet as they pass. "Trouble in paradise? Ciara looks off."

"She's a little green in the gills about the culinary offerings for the dragons," Gran says.

I shrug. "I don't know why it grossed her out. Dragons gotta eat."

"Yes, they do." Merlin holds up his phone. "On that note, Patty is texting me. He doesn't want to send the birthday beasts too early for that reason. He's afraid there will be a stampede for the food, and you won't be ready."

Nikon snaps in at the end of the row with two bighorn sheep. "Are we done? Please say we are. I smell like a slaughterhouse."

I nod. "Other than Emmet topping off the carcasses with maple syrup, yes. Awesome, Greek. Thank you."

He nods. "Anything for the next-gen of dragons. I've been thinking about it. Maybe I'll mix and mingle and see if any of them wants a rider. I'm immortal anyway. I might as well be a badass crimefighter and have adventures with you two."

I love that idea.

"You already are a badass crimefighter, Greek, but yeah, I'd love to share the sky with you."

"I would too," Merlin adds. "You'd be a welcome addition to the twenty-first-century dragon riders club."

I blink and give him my full attention. "We have a dragon riders club? Who's in it other than us two?"

Merlin grins. "No one. It's very exclusive."

"Apparently." I give the buffet line one last look and give Gran a thumb's up. "To answer your question, Merlin. Yes, you're clear to tell Patty we're ready."

"Release the hounds!" Nikon shouts. "And get the women and children out of the splash zone."

I laugh. "The children will be confined to the upper deck of the treehouse for the day. I'm not taking any chances with Jackson and Meg ending up as Scooby Snacks for juvenile dragons."

Merlin shakes his head. "That won't be a problem, Fi. They consider you their human mother. Jackson and Meg are yours. They won't harm them."

I chuckle. "Says the man who rushed to scoop up Jackson and safeguarded the kidlet as he charged the Iceland dragons last night."

"Charging them is the key point. Utiss and Bryvanay aren't accustomed to children and certainly not being rushed by humans who aren't afraid of them. Me scooping up Jackson was simply showing the two of them that Jackson is mine and therefore they won't harm him."

"Great to know, and thanks for caring. Much appreciated."

"My pleasure. This is the first dragon birthday celebration for a new generation of mythical creatures. I don't want anything to mar it."

Me either.

Nikon looks down at himself and grimaces. "I really need a shower and change before the party."

"Tad went to the treehouse to wash up."

"No worries. I'll pop home and be back in twenty."

The absurdity of that never ceases to amaze me. Nikon can be anywhere on the planet in the blink of an eye. It's amazing.

He's amazing. I think about Gran's plan to smooth out the hurt and loneliness of Wallace's life and smile at Nikon. There's more than one great man in our life who could use a love match.

"You do you, Greek. We'll be here when you get back although you might want to bring another keg. This party is well underway."

Nikon glances up at where the humans gathered by the fire. "Not a problem. Back in a flash."

After Nikon snaps out, Gran, Merlin, and I walk up the lawn. I glance over at my blue boy playing with Manx, Bruin, Doc, and Daisy. What a difference a year can make.

Dart senses my attention and glances over. *Is everything all right?* he asks over our private mental channel.

It's perfect, buddy. Happy birthday.

Thank you. And thank you for my party.

My pleasure. Your siblings are on their way, so let's get this party started, shall we?

Looking forward to it.

CHAPTER SIX

Maple syrup on roadkill goes over incredibly well. At least that's how it seems from the sidelines. Once the dragons arrive, there is no holding them back beyond the brief moment when Patty explains that even though there are almost thirty dead animals to choose from, it's still one per customer. Cue the start of the day's chaos.

Kids these days, amirite?

In addition to the food, children's birthday parties imply birthday games...but when you're celebrating the first birthday of twenty-three dragons, pin the tail on the donkey, hide-and-seek, and three-legged races get modified for the intended audience.

"How did dragon polo in the pond go?" Evangeline asks as Sloan and I trudge back up to the bonfire area.

The two of us are drowned rats, drenched from head to toe after getting body-checked into the pond in an adolescent effort to get us to play with them.

"That depends on who ye ask, I suppose," Sloan grumbles. "The kids had one hell of a good time. I can't say Fiona and I felt the same."

I wave away his mood and laugh. "Gokin and Mizuchi thought it would be more fun for us if we were in the water too. It was an honest mistake. Really, the fact that they were so enthusiastic about us joining in was sweet."

Gran chuckles and points at the treehouse. "Go change yer clothes and hang yer wets out on the rail, so they dry before dark."

I hold my hand out for Sloan. "Would you mind doing the honors? Straight into our bathroom, please, so we don't traipse water."

While I expect him to *poof* us up into the treehouse, the moment we materialize, I realize we're in the ensuite of his bedroom at Stonecrest Castle. "Right. I forgot our stuff is here and not in the treehouse."

"Only for a night or two." Sloan tugs at his wet clothes. "Although, after hearing about my mother, I might prefer to stay close to home fer a few days more, if ye don't mind. Ye know, to show Da a little extra attention and support."

I'm stuck in my wet jeans with the denim suctioned to my thighs. Sitting on the floor, I thrust my legs into the air and wave my feet. "A little help."

Sloan tosses his clothes onto the shower floor and returns to act the part of my white knight. Grabbing the waistband of my jeans at my hips, he peels them off my legs and tosses them inside out on top of the heap with a heavy *plop* and another gruff grumble.

"Why are ye layin' there laughin' at me?"

I roll onto my feet, grab one of Sloan's super-sized velvety towels, and wrap myself in cozy bliss. "No reason. I find you funny when life takes an unexpected detour. You get all cranky pants and dour."

"If that were true, I would be cranky pants and dour almost all the time. When I'm with ye, life is always takin' an unexpected detour."

"Point to you, Mackenzie." I tap his bare shoulder as I shuffle past him and go to my dresser. One of the last times we stayed here, he had the foresight to add new furniture to the room and stock it with a full wardrobe.

One thing you can always count on with Sloan is that he'll anticipate your needs long before you realize what you'll need or when you'll need it.

"So? What do ye think about that?"

"What do I think about what?"

"About sleepin' here and spendin' some extra time with Da."

I pull out a fresh pair of yoga pants, some dry undies and socks, and a knit top. "Yeah, I think we should. I don't suppose it matters where we lay our heads to sleep as long as we can get back quickly if anything happens."

"What are ye expectin' will happen?"

"Ahren told us to be ready for anything. Yes, they're chasing down Mingin and Melanippe, but Yvain is now in the mix, and there's always the occurrences of life taking an unexpected detour."

"Aye, there's that."

I finish changing, pull on a dry pair of socks, and go to the closet to see if I have any sneakers—yep—that's my guy. Ready for all contingencies.

"I heart you hard, hotness."

Sloan finishes tucking his polo shirt into his ripped designer jeans and blinks up at me, looking confused. "Right back at ye, *a ghra,* but what makes ye say so?"

I shrug. "I just think it needed to be said."

He lowers his chin and slides a dry belt through the loops around his waist. "Well, that's thoughtful and appreciated. Now, should we get straight back to the party or would ye like to play hooky for a bit?"

I laugh and hold my hand out for him. "I like where your mind's going, but it's my party, so I think we need to be there."

"As ye wish, but don't say I can't be wild and spontaneous."

I love that he thinks delaying our return to the party is wild and spontaneous. "I wouldn't dream of it. You, Mr. Mackenzie, are the warrior of wild, the earl of excitement, the veritable imp of impromptu."

Sloan rolls his eyes and takes my hand. "Now yer just takin' the piss."

The familiar signature of Sloan's wayfarer energy washes over us, and we *poof* back to the back lawn.

The scene has changed in the ten minutes since we left. I can't quite put my finger on it, but the party's energy has shifted. I scan the dragon activity at the bottom of the lawn. They're racing and rolling around in the sun, having fun.

I smile at Dart, playing with Scarlet and Saxa and the rest of his siblings carousing around.

"They seem to be having a fun time."

Gran, Patty, and Merlin have gathered halfway down the lawn and are watching the show.

"That's an understatement, luv," Gran says.

"Excellent. That's what today is all about."

Merlin rubs his hand over the dark stubble of his jaw. "Maybe, but we were saying that it's like they're hyped up and under the influence. I think maple syrup might be the catnip of the dragon world."

I laugh and take another look.

They seem extremely wound up, and some of them are rolling and rubbing themselves on the grass where the buffet line was.

"Seriously? Is that a thing?"

Merlin shrugs. "It's hard to say. Maybe they're really excited about their birthday party."

"I have a feelin' it's more than that." Patty points at where the

Queen of Wyrms is swaying high in the air and blowing spurts of fire. "Her Utter Sophisticatedness isn't one for such spectacles. I think it's fair to say she's hopped up on Canadian tree sugar."

"Note to self. Syrup might've been a bad idea."

Merlin shrugs. "So far, it's fine."

"Well, let's hope it's only a recreational high and no one steps too far out of their lane. No cause for alarm."

Gran grunts. "Twenty-eight out-of-control dragons would be cause for alarm."

"True story. I really don't want to explain to Garnet and Maxwell how I single-handedly exposed the existence of dragons and leveled the magic and mystery of the Emerald Isle all in one day."

Merlin chuckles. "It wouldn't be single-handedly, Fi. We'd fall on the sword with you."

"Thanks. That makes me feel loads better. Okay, keep an eye on the situation and let me know if I need to be worried."

I leave the three of them and stroll over to chat with Da, Shannon, and Ciara. They're sitting on the large stone seats at the fire pit, watching the boys in action.

Dillan, Aiden, Nikon, Emmet, Calum, and Kevin are each contained in a clear inflatable sphere and running around the lawn bumping into one another and laughing like fools.

They look like iridescent soap bubbles rolling and bouncing over the rich, green grass. "What's the craic?"

"It's savage craic fer sure." Da laughs.

"The day drinking has taken hold, I see."

Ciara nods. "They're makin' the most out of the party. No fault. No foul."

"They're called human hamster balls." Dionysus jogs over to us, grinning. "I thought they looked fun. Do you want to try one? I have enough for everyone. Irish, how about you?"

Sloan's eyebrows climb so high on his forehead it's ridiculous. "Maybe after a few pints, Greek."

Dionysus deflates a little but turns his attention to me. "How about you, Fi? Are you game?"

"Hells yeah, I'm in. How does it work?"

Dionysus grabs my hand and the two of us race over to the ground at the base of the treehouse.

"You need to take your shoes off."

I do as he suggests, and he helps me get into the ball and zip me up. From the outside, he hooks up the air pump and inflates the ball around me. The outside wall is double-layered with about a foot of air in between. That leaves me with a couple of feet all around me to maneuver.

"This is so cool." I raise my hands, testing the strength of the bubble around me. I'm literally inside a massive, clear beach ball. "Are there any warnings or things we're supposed to watch out for?"

"I have to be careful not to overinflate," he says, watching the gauge. "The instructions say not to overinflate, or the ball will explode and cause damage to the product."

"What about damage to the person inside it when it explodes?"

He shrugs. "The warning didn't mention that. Apparently, that's less important."

"Not to *me*, it isn't."

Dionysus waves at me and frowns. "Hush. I need to pay attention."

I silence my objections because, yeah, I'd rather him pay attention and the plastic bubble surrounding me not explode. After another minute, he detaches the air pump and *clicks* the little nozzle flap closed.

"You're set. Now me." He steps into one of the empty balls still lying on the grass, zips it up, and it's instantly inflated around him.

"Hey, if you were going to cheat, why didn't you magically inflate mine?"

He waves that away. "You deserve the full experience. Now, let's join the party."

It takes a few minutes to get the hang of navigating. I soon realize I need to keep running and pushing against the plastic in front of me to get my groove on.

Dionysus and I play hamster ball games while we get used to things. I wish I had my sunglasses on. October sunlight is bouncing off the iridescent plastic and making everything sparkle and glitter like opals in the sun.

I bounce off Dionysus a couple more times, and I get knocked on my butt. It's crazy. I should've taken my socks off as well as my shoes so I could get traction.

Deciding to go ahead and do that, I make quick work of pulling them off. Then, as I run around, my socks are flipping and flying next to me, and I can honestly say I now know what it would feel like to be inside a running dryer.

"Oh, ho ho." Dillan eyes us up as fresh targets. "Look who's coming to play with the big boys."

I laugh at his posturing and course correct to join the main game of ball bouncing. That is...until Dillan calls to the others to attack me.

"Game on!" Emmet shouts, turning toward me.

"You better run, Fi." Calum laughs, gunning for me.

I scream, get back to my feet, and start running to gain some momentum.

"I'm coming to save you, Red," Nikon shouts, laughing as Calum slams into him and knocks him flying. "I'm *not* coming, Red. Save yourself."

I squeal and angle my bubble toward Aiden. "You'll be nice to your baby sister, won't you, Aiden?"

He snorts and barrels into Dillan, knocking him rolling backward. "It's every man for himself, Fi. There are no favorites in human hamster balling."

"Noice." I pause for a second to catch my breath and target

Emmet, who is racing straight at me. He's got a ton more speed behind him than I do, so when he hits, his momentum bowls me over.

I flip ass over end, and the world spins.

That's not good enough for my brothers.

Dillan starts ramming me and flipping me down the lawn. The craziest part of these balls is that you can't get your footing as easily as if you weren't in an eight-foot bouncy ball.

I'm half-laughing, half-screaming as I'm tossed on my back and bounced onto all fours—the whole time, getting smacked in the face with my socks. "So rude. Give a girl a chance to get the hang of things."

Dillan laughs. "Ha! We've been drinking all afternoon. You're sober. You already have the advantage."

I can't argue with that, but sober or not, I'm getting a little seasick. I'm still screeching when the rumble of the ground beneath my bubble registers.

Twisting to see what's happening, I gasp.

Oh, shit. "The dragons are coming!"

I push up to my feet and run.

It's not the same halfhearted run to escape playing human bumper-ball with my brothers. It's a full-tilt, give it everything, kinda run. I push against the plastic wall in front of me and race toward the shaded space under the treehouse.

"The dragons are high on dragon-nip. Save yourselves. Seriously, find shelter. They're off their meds." As I'm running, my mind is racing, wondering what inspired the attack.

The fractured light is blinding me now that I'm facing the house. Merlin's words hit me... *Shiny things. They love all things that glitter and shine.*

Awesomesauce.

We've become life-sized baubles for them to play with.

I make it under the shelter of the treehouse with little problem. That is, until the plastic rolls over the forest floor and punctures my ball. The integrity of my bubble doesn't so much burst as it deflates in a whiny hiss.

Doesn't matter. I haven't got the time to worry about that.

Grabbing the zipper, I yank it over my head and split the seam of my plastic prison. Pushing out into the fresh air of the forest, I run barefoot to try to help.

Dionysus and Nikon have flashed out of their balls and are running to help my brothers. They grab the two closest to them, and Aiden's and Kevin's balls disappear and are out of the game.

Merlin and Da are racing toward Emmet. Scarlet has caught up to him and is bouncing him on the end of her snout like a seal in a circus act.

While they try to help him, I focus on Dillan. The dragons surrounded him, and Cadmus is bearing down on him at full speed with his three-horned snout pointed directly at the bubble.

"Dillan!" I shout, running hard. My thighs are burning, but there's no way I'm going to get there in time. "Cast *Resilient Sphere!*"

If he doesn't get that spell cast in time, those horns are not only going to pierce the plastic of the ball, but they're also going to pierce him.

"*Resilient Sphere,*" I repeat.

My heart is thundering in my chest and with everything in me, I will him to listen.

Merlin has finished securing Emmet and must have heard the panic in my voice because now he runs toward Dillan too. "Fi's right. Cast *Resilient Sphere!*"

"Cadmus, stop," Patty shouts, racing as fast as his short stature allows.

There's no stopping an adolescent dragon who's closing in on the shiniest, most exciting thing he's seen in his one year of life.

The breath in my lungs freezes solid at the moment of impact. I watch in horror, each millisecond of time and eternity, waiting to see if Dillan managed to secure the ball from destruction.

The moment he's thrown into the air, I let out a gasp of relief. The hamster ball is intact, and though Dillan is getting tossed in the air, he's alive and whole.

I slow down, patting my chest to catch my breath, but my elation is short-lived. Tossing the ball into the air has given the dragons an idea for a new game, and Dillan has become the opal snitch for a game of Dragon Quidditch.

CHAPTER SEVEN

"**D**art, we need to fly." I race across the grass toward my blue boy, hoping he's sober enough that he's in his right mind. He turns his head, and I feel his eagerness to help and his need to quell my panic.

He supersizes in an instant, and I race straight toward the dewclaw on his elbow. *"Feline Finesse."*

As my spell takes hold, I lunge, grab the hook of the claw, and vault onto his back with an aerial grace I could never manage without magic.

"I'm with you, Fi." Merlin darts off the other way toward Cazzie.

Dart waits until I arrive at his first spike and grab the center handle of the leather saddle. "We're good, buddy. Let's go."

"I'm here too, Red." Nikon appears behind me at the saddle on Dart's second spike.

I barely get a chance to acknowledge Nikon's arrival before Dart's claws dig into the earth, and we launch into the air. The force that he exerts to get us airborne is incredible. I widen my stance and secure my footing, holding on tight while the g-force of his strength pulls hard on my muscles.

Searching the sky above, I look for my brother.

The moment my mind catches up with my intention, I realize it's much easier to find seven dragons cartwheeling and tumbling through the afternoon sky than it is one human in a see-through bubble.

"There, do you see him?"

I see him, Dart says into my mind. *Kaida evaded Torrim and passed him to Abeloth. It was a great pass.*

I appreciate Dart's commentary, but now is not the time to admire a great play. "Greek, do you think if we get close enough, you can grab the ball and snap him back to the ground?"

"That was my idea. Midflight portaling is tricky. If I get it wrong, or if the dragons bump the ball in a different direction, you'll be diving to rescue me instead of Dillan."

Yeah, well, that won't work either.

"I have faith in you, Greek. Let me know what you need. If you get any other great ideas, I'm open to those too."

"I'll be sure to let you know."

I know we're getting closer to Dillan when I hear him swearing. My middle brother is salty at the best of times, hostile most of the time, and downright cranky when the world throws him for a loop.

He also has one of the most colorful vocabularies for choice words of anyone I know. I don't think Da has heard half of the gems he can come up with when truly inspired.

By the sounds of it, he *is* truly inspired.

The wind rushes past my face in a shrill whistle, throwing my hair in every direction including into my eyes. I reach up with my free hand, shielding my vision and searching for a way into the chaotic jumble of dragons playing.

"Any of those great ideas coming to you yet?"

Nikon chuffs behind me. "Nothing yet. Looks like it might be a Hail Mary dive."

"Hold that thought, Greek," Merlin says, flying up fast on my left. "If Cazzie and Dart can run block, we might be able to push the other dragons out of the path and get a clear shot at Dillan. If we can avoid them launching him all over the place, you'll have a better chance at grabbing him for a portal."

"Works for me," Nikon says. "Tell me when you're ready for me to make a go of it."

Merlin meets my gaze, and I know he's checking to ensure I'm steady.

I am.

Yes, my brother might be in mortal danger, but I'll fall apart later. Right now, I'm solely focused on saving his testy tuchus. "What do you need me to do?"

Merlin whistles, and Saxa, Bryvanay, and Utiss rise from below and behind me to join the rescue effort. Seeing them all here in the air is not only humbling but also breathtaking.

"Thanks for helping, guys."

Merlin takes charge of coordinating the efforts, and the dragons get their instructions. The dragons we brought from the ninth century are mature, experienced, and don't seem to have fallen so deeply under the spell of the maple syrup sugar rush.

"Fi...Cazzie and Utiss will escort you above the play while Bryvanay and Saxa divert the other dragons. Get as close as you can to Dillan so Nikon has the best chance of success."

"Got it. Are you good, Dart?"

One daring rescue coming up.

"How about one *successful* daring rescue?"

Our success goes without saying. We're Team Trouble, after all. Success is what we do.

"I love that confidence, buddy."

Cazzie and Utiss pull up on either side of Dart and escort us in like two MIG fighter jets over private airspace. Then Bryvanay and Saxa force the young dragons back and away from their shiny new toy.

Merlin's instinct on their dominance parting the way is on

point. The Irish dragons fall back without hesitation, allowing the senior dragons to isolate Abeloth, who is currently balancing Dillan on his wing.

"Are you ready, Greek?" I ask.

"Ready as I'll ever be."

I hear the nerves in Nikon's voice and can't blame him. We're thousands of feet above the earth, and even though he can snap out and relocate safely on the ground if this goes sideways, that won't help Dillan.

"You can do this, Nikon. I have faith in you."

"That makes one of us."

"Then I have enough for both of us."

"Are you coming on to me, Red? Now is not the time. I need to focus."

I smile at him over my shoulder. "Sorry, I guess I couldn't help myself."

Nikon winks, focuses on the hamster ball a hundred feet down and to our right, and snaps away.

There's a split second when my stomach lurches and I almost close my eyes. I don't want to see what happens next, yet I don't want to miss a single moment.

Life can be trippy at times.

Between the span of two racing heartbeats, Nikon disappears from holding the saddle handle on the second spike and reappears starfished on the top of the glittering ball of delight.

He's there for only a split second, then he, the ball, and Dillan are gone and hopefully safely on the ground.

"Did they make it?" I search the ground below.

My eyesight isn't nearly as sharp as a dragon, but we might be too high for even them to see.

How about we land and find out? Dart asks.

"Yes, please." I hold the saddle with both hands and close my eyes, the stress of the moment closing in on me. "Landing would be good."

Are you all right, Fi?

"Fine, just a little overwhelmed. I'm looking forward to having my feet on the ground." That's the understatement of the century. As much iron will and bravery as I have in the face of danger, my family's mortality is my Achilles' heel.

I close my eyes, grip hard on the handle of the spike saddle, and wait until I feel the gentle jolt of us stopping. My eyes lift, my neck turns on a swivel, and I search the surroundings until I find him.

I don't remember the brief moments between releasing the saddle and racing into his arms. The only thing my brain focuses on is Dillan standing on the lawn of my grandparents' home, surrounded by family and friends, and as pale and pissed off as I've ever seen him.

"Are you all right?" There's nothing left in my legs to stop me from running, and I crash straight into him.

I hug him as tight as I can to be sure he's real. Then Sloan's arms come around us...and Da's...then Calum's...and Aiden's... and Emmet's...

The Clan Cumhaill love-in crushes the breath from my lungs, but I don't care. I'd rather be gasping for breath and deflated than crying over the loss of another one of my brothers.

"Can't breathe..." I grunt.

There's a throaty choir of laughter, then the pressure eases, and oxygen returns to my lungs.

I ease back to meet his gaze. "Are you alive?"

"I feel like a floppy leaf of lettuce after a turn in the salad spinner, but yeah I'm alive."

"Well, good. You dying would've ruined the party for me in a big way."

He chuffs. "Yeah, for me too. And Eva would've been so sad. If one of us died when she wasn't here to guardian us, she would've been devastated."

"No more maple syrup for dragons," Granda says.

Patty lets out a long exhale. "I think that's a wise decision, Lugh."

I nod. "Yeah, good call, Granda."

Emmett smacks Dillan on the shoulder and grins. "While you were up there, Kevin and Calum were reminiscing about how Kev's hamster always peed in his ball when he was scared. Naturally, *I* said you're far too much of a manly man to pee your pants *buuuut* some thought it was a real possibility."

He points at the front of Dillan's jeans. "Congrats, dude. You really are a manly man."

Cue a round of snickering and Dillan raising both middle fingers to the crowd. "You all suck...except you, Fi. You're my favorite sibling ever. At least you came to save me."

I flash Emmet, Calum, and Aiden a wide grin. "I always knew I was the favorite."

As the moment devolves into a rush of sibling sparring, I step away and hug Nikon. "Thank you for the save, Greek. I heart you hard."

The fact that he turned out to be the hero of this crisis is no surprise. The fact that with my arms around him, I feel how badly he's shaking. "Are you okay?"

"Better now. Do you mind if I hold onto you for a little longer?"

I snuggle in tighter, ready to stay there. "I'm yours for as long as you need. Hug away, my friend."

Nikon asks for little and gives so much.

He's forever taxiing us around the world and getting drawn into whatever danger and chaos are circling my life. If he needs a little TLC, he's come to the right place.

When he finally eases back and meets my gaze, he seems steady and pulled back together. "Sorry about that. It really mattered, you know?"

"I know exactly how you feel. I could go up against demons, vampires, and sorcerers all day long and come out exhausted but steady. Once the conflict involves someone I love, my nerves go to mush, and the panic sets in."

He draws a deep breath and exhales. "Your family has become my family. You know that, right?"

"I know that…and that's a good thing because we love you as one of our own."

"Yeah, we do." Emmet joins us. "That was a great save, Greek. You did good."

"Yeah, you did." Calum comes in for a hug.

Kevin is next. "That list of 'we owe you one' just keeps getting longer."

Nikon steps back, the warm tan of his Mediterranean skin blushing pink. "Glad I could help. Now, if we could spend the rest of the party without the death-defying theatrics, that would be great."

"We can try." I slide my arm around his hip and turn him back toward the party. "But who are we kidding? It probably won't help."

Nikon leans into me and kisses the top of my head. "Well, at least we can try."

The rest of the party goes off without a hitch. The dragons eventually settle down, Cazzie and Saxa teach them fireside songs of their ancestry, and Utiss and Bryvanay spend time teaching them wing and tail maneuvers, glamor tips, and how to make the most of fire breath.

"Quite a party ye put on today, Red."

I lower my pint to *clink* glasses with Patty. "It's been a great day, hasn't it?"

"Aye, it has."

"They seem to be having a lot of fun."

"Yer right about that. I'll likely not hear the end of it fer months to come."

"Well, at least you have something to talk about in the lair."

"There is that."

The two of us had originally set up the birthday cakes on the edge of the patio before Merlin nixed the idea and said that having twenty-three adolescent dragons blow fire toward Gran's and Granda's house would be a gross error in judgment.

We took his wisdom under advisement and immediately moved into the clearing down the lawn.

"How is the Queen of Wyrms dealing with her children growing up and getting more independent with each day that passes?"

Patty makes a face at me and grunts. "Och, I think she plans to pretend it isn't happening and ignore their evolutions as long as she possibly can."

"The old head in the sand approach. As much as I respect that, it won't change the fact that they're growing up and are going to need to branch out and find their own places in life."

"I understand that, and if *you* want to bring it up with her, you go right ahead. I prefer not to have my eyebrows singed off."

"I look better with eyebrows than without. Good point."

Emmet jogs over to chat with us and smiles at the five massive cakes baked into children's kiddy pools. "Wow, these are fun. I hope there was magic involved in making these cakes because if not, that's cray-cray."

"The cakes were my doing, lad," Patty says. "As the only father these wee miscreants have ever known, I have to do my part in celebrating their milestones."

The wee miscreants part strikes me as funny, but I don't say anything. Patty can think of them however he wants to. He's been a father to them since the moment they hatched. He has every right to be proud.

"Are we ready to sing?" Gran hikes Meg higher on her hip.

"All set." I give Gram a thumbs-up and step to the side to get out of the way of the inevitable stampede. Pressing my finger and thumb together, I give a shrill whistle to get everyone's attention. "It's time to light the candles. Everyone gather 'round."

Dionysus appears at my side and looks at me with a curious gaze. "Light the candles? I thought the custom was to blow them out."

"For humans, it is, but Patty and I thought the dragons would have more fun lighting the candles than trying to put them out."

Patty nods. "Ye see, not all of them have the gift of fire breath yet. We thought lighting the candles might be an incentive to try harder."

Dionysus frowns. "Are you sure you want to hurry them into that ability? If these were my children, I'd rather they couldn't shoot flames out of their mouth at any given moment."

"When lookin' at the fire safety of things, yer right, but these dragons have grown up as hatchling mates, and what one can do, the others envy. In the end, it's safer if there are no hard feelings among siblings."

"Jealousy among siblings is something I can relate to all too well," Dionysus says. "I see your point."

Yes, I'm sure he does.

Being an illegitimate demi-god heir of Zeus and having more power than many of his full-blooded god siblings left Dionysus in the crosshairs of jealousy for his entire life.

It did serious damage to the way he relates to others.

Which is why I'm so proud of him and the progress he's made over the past few months.

The rumble of the ground signals the incoming horde of dragons. I scan the seething sea of emerald green, scarlet red, and royal blue, searching for my blue boy. I know a mother shouldn't have favorites, but Dart and I connected when he first hatched and laid eyes on me.

I am here, Fi, he says into my mind.

I follow the echo of his voice and find him among the crowd now positioning in front of the five cake stations. I blow him a kiss and stay well out of the way while Patty explains what's up next.

"No need to push, kids. Ye'll all get yer chance to light yer candles. Now, this is a teambuilding exercise. I've rigged the sparklers not to go off until everybody has a chance to light them with their fire breath.

"If ye don't make fire, don't get down on yerself. Every bit of magic is bein' added up fer the grand finale. The more you give it, the greater the fireworks show at the end. Yer all part of the success."

Smart man.

One by one, the dragons step up behind one of the five cakes and give a long throaty blow. More of them than I realized command the flame of fire breath.

I knew Dart could, but over the next five minutes, at least half of them send a stream of flame at the glittering number ones perched on the top of each cake.

The ones who blow fire get congratulated and file off to the side while their siblings have a turn or two to try and when the last of them have finished, the number ones atop the glittering gold mountains explode into a hissing spray of fireworks.

Jackson and Meggie stare wide-eyed at the dancing unicorns, shooting rainbows, and pyrotechnic animals hopping, fluttering, and swimming through the night sky.

The young dragons seem equally entertained by Patty's light show. Who am I kidding? We all are. What's not to love about magic unicorns prancing through the air?

"So cool." Jackson's eyes are as big as dinner plates as he takes it all in. "I loves magic. It's amazeballs."

I stare up in wonder. "Yeah, buddy, it sure is."

CHAPTER EIGHT

It's only eight-thirty by the time we say good night to the dragons. It takes us an hour to clean up from the party. Then we call it a night. My brothers are, no doubt, going to spend the next many hours drinking and carrying on, but I'm truly gassed.

Nothing sounds as good to me as a hot bath and climbing into bed with my guy.

Even Bruin seems okay with leaving early, which is unusual, but things have been busy lately. Maybe we all need to take some time for self-care.

The moment we arrive at Stonecrest Castle, I release Bruin, and he and Manx trot off to get into whatever trouble they can find in the hours before bed.

Have at it, boys.

Really, how much trouble can they get into at a private estate in the middle of Irish countryside nowhere?

"Ye look tired, *a ghra*."

"You know me so well. I'm exhausted. What do you think about a private soak in the hot tub, then falling into bed and snoring for the next ten hours?"

"I'm good fer the hot tub, I'll leave the snorin' to the professional, and I'll gladly take six hours, not ten."

"To each their own."

The two of us undress and grab our towels. "Bathing suits or birthday suits?"

Sloan chuckles. "Yer not in Canada anymore, Toto. On this side of the pond, far fewer people get twisted up about bein' naked."

"What about naked in front of your father?"

Sloan chuckles. "With all yer near-death brushes with mortality, Da has seen ye naked almost as much as I have."

My cheeks flush hot, and I punch him in the pec. "That's mean."

He's laughing at me. "Don't act like it's not true."

"I'm not that bad…and most times, he's patching up my leg or my side. Nothing risqué about that."

He chuckles. "He's a medical professional. There's nothing risqué about him healin' ye in any way. Besides all that, he's not one fer the hot tub. In all my life I don't know that he was in it a dozen times."

"Oh, so that left it open for you to use to entertain your female conquests."

Sloan shoots me a droll stare. "Do ye want to go soak or do ye want to talk yerself into a tizzy? Because once ye start talkin' about my past indiscretions, ye tend to ruin yer mood and get somber."

He's not wrong.

I draw a deep breath and exhale. "Right. I'm the one with you now—"

"Now and always if I have anythin' to say about it."

"Thank you, that's sweet."

"It's true. Now, hot tub or no?"

"Yes, definitely." I check the tuck of my towel and grab my phone while Sloan wraps his hips. When we're ready, I hold my hand out to him. "Will you provide the transportation for the evening?"

"As ye wish, milady." He takes my hand, and the two of us *poof* to the private courtyard off the back of the castle.

We materialize, and I'm about to say something when the throaty cries of a woman fill the air. I freeze in my tracks and study what's happening in the hot tub.

Holy crapamoly.

Reaching out, I reclaim Sloan's hand and...

We're not *poofing*...

Why aren't we *poofing*?

Wallace is chest-to-chest with a brunette and getting ridden like a prized stallion, and we're standing here watching, and I *soooo* don't want to be watching.

Wallace's eyes are closed, and he's got one helluva satisfied look on his face...

Dammit, we're still here.

Digging my nails into Sloan's hand seems to snap him out of his state of shock, and he blinks at me. I widen my eyes at him, and finally, we *poof*.

Thank you, baby Yoda.

"What the hell, Mackenzie? Why did it take you so long to get us out of there?"

Sloan is standing in the middle of his bedroom with his mouth hanging open. "I don't know what to... What the hell was that?"

"That was your dad cleaning off the cobwebs and getting his rocks polished. He obviously didn't expect us home so early."

"Obviously."

"And he's working on healing his scars of rejection."

"Obviously."

Now that we're back in our room and we got away without interrupting them, the horror of embarrassment dies down.

"Hey, hotness? Do you think we should mention to your dad

that sex in a hot tub isn't a good idea? It can increase the chances of getting a UTI."

Sloan scowls at me. "No. Ye won't mention that to him. In fact, ye won't mention anything to him because we weren't there, we saw nothin', and we will agree to bury those images so deeply in our minds that they will never surface again."

"I don't know. When we walked in and interrupted Da and Shannon that time in the upstairs hall, I seem to remember you teasing me about it more than once."

Sloan's complexion pales. "Please don't."

I laugh. "Oh, I think I definitely will. Besides, this is a good thing. Not only is your dad moving on, by what we saw, he's breaking out his moves."

"Feckin' hell, Fi, don't. I'm beggin' ye…"

"You know what they say…the best way to get over a woman is to get under another."

Sloan groans and heads into the bathroom. "Ye've got two choices here. Either ye stop goin' on about my father shaggin' Siobhan, or I leave ye here on yer own. If ye choose to spare me yer witty commentary, I'll draw ye a lovely bath, give ye a rub down, and make it very much worth yer while."

I pinch my lips together and consider the offer. "So, you think you can buy my silence with a happy ending massage?"

"I'm hopin' so." He steps close and takes my hands in his. "Seriously, Fi, findin' out my mother left fer a wealthy family friend was bad enough. To walk in on my father makin' a woman I've known my entire adult life cry out like that…I can't deal with it. Not yet."

I sober. "Fine. I'll be good."

"Thank the goddess."

"In six months or a year or maybe two, I'm digging up this moment and teasing the hell out of you. Who knows, maybe by then, good ole Siobhan might be your new mommy. Won't that make dinner table talk interesting? Remember the time you were orgasming in the hot tub…"

Sloan frowns. "Ye just can't help yerself, can ye?"

I laugh and close the door before he can escape. "Fine, I'll be good. I promise." I point at the tub and smile. "I accept your terms. I saw nothing. I heard nothing. We were never there."

Sloan lets out a long-suffering sigh and heads over to start drawing our bathwater. "Thanks. I owe ye one."

The next two days are blissfully uneventful. We spend our days split between the Cumhaill Shire and Stonecrest Castle. We have bonfires at night. Kinu and Aiden get to have a bit of a break while Da and Shannon and Gran and Granda take turns taking care of the twins.

They're five months old now, so in some ways easier to manage and other ways more difficult.

Still, having this much family around means we can properly celebrate Brendan and spend time with Da while he's hurting. We're all hurting, there's no getting around that, but it hurts a little less while we're spending time together.

"Is Nikon pickin' up Liam this mornin'?" Sloan asks as the two of us *poof* into the living room of the treehouse on the fourth day.

"No. Not today." Calum glances up from the nude men puzzle that he, Kevin, and Dionysus are working on at the table. "Kady is back from her weekend taking care of her sister's baby shower and wanted to spend the day catching up with him."

"Nice. I'm glad that's working out for them."

Dillan comes out from the back rooms fresh from the shower. "Yeah, me too. Kady deserves someone amazing. Liam fits the bill."

"Is that the waitress at the family pub you used to date?" Evangeline follows him out to the kitchen with equally damp hair.

"That's her. She's a great girl but doesn't handle the stress of calamity and chaos well. Even from those first few weeks of being a druid and watching Fi get sucked into the vortex of mayhem she's always spinning around in, I knew we weren't a good fit in the long-term."

"You did a good thing by letting her find happiness with Liam, bro," Emmet says. "Seriously."

Dillan takes the compliment with a nod.

"Is Ciara here?" I ask.

Emmet shakes his head. "She's spending the day with her mom in Dublin, and they're meeting her dad for lunch. She asked if I wanted to come, but she wanted a day with them to herself."

"Being an only child, she probably misses it being only the three of them sometimes."

Emmet nods. "She does. I think we still overwhelm her at times."

"Things are good though, right?" I ask.

"Oh, yeah, but she misses her life here."

I don't want to look at that too closely. If she misses her life here, what does that mean for Emmet? I suppose time will tell.

I shuffle over to scope out the progress on the puzzle. "Wow, you guys have made some real progress."

Kevin grins up at me. "We're a dedicated group."

Dionysus chuckles. "In the spirit of life imitating art, Suede and I are hosting a party this weekend. There will be nudity, drinking, and merriment. You're all invited."

I poke through a couple of pieces looking for any that might fit. "Awesome. When this weekend?"

"*All* weekend," Dionysus says. "All the days and nights. You're welcome to drop in at any time."

"I take it things are going well with Suede?"

"Very well. I find that I enjoy having a girlfriend much more than I expected."

"That's all that matters. I'm happy for you both." I place my piece and return to chat with Evangeline.

"Hey, welcome back. It's good to see you." I hug Dillan's girl-friend and join them at the breakfast bar. "How was your trip to the Choir? How are things going with your change of designation?"

The angel sends Dillan a dimpled smile and shrugs. "We're making it up as we go along. All I know is that I'm supposed to keep you all safe in the months leading up to the Winter Solstice. Since you're all healthy, I figure things are going well so far."

Sound logic. "You can't be the first angel to want to try something new."

"I don't know. If there have been others, I don't know who and no one is talking about it."

"Are there rules against it?"

She shakes her head, and her blonde curls bounce around her face. "No, it simply doesn't happen. Angels don't step out of line. Maybe I'm defective."

Dillan chuffs. "There's not one thing about you that's defective, angel. You're perfect however you are and if they don't realize it, fuck 'em."

I pour myself a glass of juice. "You might not want to voice that opinion until after you've finished the transfer. No need to piss off Death before he reassigns you."

"Exactly." Eva wrinkles her nose at D. "When I spoke to Death about being a guardian, he assured me protecting your family was the way to change my stars."

"Well, we're happy to have you on the team. I spoke to Merlin about that last week, and we're going to start tightening our plans for our offensive and defensive objectives coming up to the Culling. We're happy to have you fighting on the side of the good guys."

"I'm happy to be on the team. Although…"

Dillan frowns and straightens on his stool. "Although what, babe?"

"I don't know for sure, but I think Death might want me to fail so I remain a reaper."

"What makes you think that?"

Sloan and Emmet get up from the couches and come over to join the conversation.

"It's just a feeling. A family like yours, with the dangers you face and the level of violence rising against you... Well, if the Choir remains invested in good triumphing evil, you should have several guardians watching over you, not one. They should be experienced warriors who can keep you all safe. Not a novice trainee."

I don't like the sound of that, and by the look of the faces around the breakfast bar, neither does anyone else.

"Do ye think he's set you up to fail?" Sloan asks.

"It seems ungrateful to say so, but I do."

I down the last sip of my juice and set the glass on the polished counter. "Maybe she was set up to fail, or maybe *we* were."

The crease in Sloan's brow deepens. "If that's true, the question then becomes, why?"

"And, who?" Dillan says. "Who in the Choir of Angels would be invested enough in the Culling's outcome to want us to fail?"

Emmet sighs. "Well, shitters. There's no way the answer to that is good, is there."

I shake my head. "Nope. I don't think so."

The long, eerie howl of a wolf breaks the silence, and I hustle over to rummage in my coat pocket. "That's Samuel's ringtone."

After digging out my phone, I swipe the green icon and answer the call, hitting speaker as I set it on the end table by the couch. "Hey, Samuel, what's up?"

"Ahren says you're on standby and ready to move."

I grab my coat and pull it on as the line crackles, and there's the pounding of footfalls and the huffing of breath. "Samuel? Where are you?"

"We're in the Bavarian Alps," he says, his voice odd. "Quon Shen is sending you the coordinates now. We've been hunting them for days in the snow, but we need backup. I'm afraid if we don't get them soon, we're going to lose them again. There's something strange going on in these mountains, Fi."

"We're on our way. Give us five." I hang up the call and check my incoming texts to ensure Quon Shen sent us the coordinates. "Okay, I've got the location. Who's coming?"

It's Calum, Emmet, Dillan, Eva, Sloan, Dionysus, and me.

"Da will kill us if we leave without telling him," Calum says. "Besides, it'll be good for the old man to face some danger to get his mind off Brenny."

"I'll tell him." Sloan turns to point at me. "Don't ye dare leave without me."

"Who, me? Never in a million."

Sloan *poofs* out, and my brothers laugh at me. Okay, so I might've left Sloan behind once or twice. In my defense, it's never on purpose.

I open the door and shout for Bruin and Manx to saddle up and then make a quick trip to pee before we leave. By the time I return, Da and Sloan are there, Bruin and Manx are present, and Tad and Nikon have joined the entourage.

Awesomesauce.

"Tarzan, can you snap us home to grab our winter gear? We'll freeze our asses off in sneakers and autumn coats."

"No need, Jane." Dionysus flicks his hand toward the room, and immediately, we're all decked out in alpine hiking gear from the bottom of our spiked boots to the pompoms on the tips of our tuques.

"Awesome, dude," Emmet says. "You rock, Greek."

"Thank you. Consider me your private Bass Pro Shop only I'm a Badass Pro."

I chuckle as I zip my phone in my fur-lined pocket. "Of course, you are."

CHAPTER NINE

After all the times the fam jam has been called to action at the drop of a hat, I don't get excited as much as start mind-spinning about what we might be walking into and what it means to us strategically, physically, and in the sake of our safety.

I hate to say the adventure has lost its shine, but you can only get stabbed, punched, poisoned, beaten, possessed, or kidnapped so many times before it's less of an adventure and more of an impending possibility of the world blowing up in your face.

Not so for our Manxy man.

I've never seen Sloan's lynx companion so jazzed about a mission before. Then again, this mission isn't just *in* his wheelhouse.

It *is* his wheelhouse.

Lynx are amazing hunters and trackers in mountainous and snowy landscapes. The long tufts on his ears act as hearing boosters, his wide, furry paws act as snowshoes while traveling over the crust of snow, and his eyesight is so strong in this habitat that he can spot a wee mouse from two hundred and fifty feet away.

Go Manx.

"Where are Samuel and the others?" Calum asks.

The ten of us pivot to search the coordinates Quon Shen texted me. We're standing in the center of a rocky plain with a mostly green valley down the slope of the mountain we're on and a smattering of snowy rock above. It's not as cold as I expected, but with the chill of fog in the air and the breeze, it's cool enough.

I frown at the picturesque landscape. "I don't see them. Does anybody have any idea where they've gone?"

Cue a round of blank faces and shrugged shoulders.

"Well, it's been less than five minutes since I talked to Samuel, so they can't have gotten far."

"Over here, Red." Bruin draws my attention toward an area where bits of dried vegetation are poking through a light snowy ground cover. "Manx is onto something."

"On to what?" I ask.

The group goes quiet as Sloan and I stride over the crunchy ground and check in with Manx. "What are ye thinkin', sham?"

Manx has his nose to the ground and is sniffing around the area. "There are some grotty smells here, not all of which are human. I think Fi's friends might've come up against some local creatures and gotten into a scuffle."

"Like what kind of creature? A bear? A wolf?"

"We have beavers living close by," Emmet adds, pointing at a group of gnarled trees by a frosted creek.

I cast my brother a look. "What kind of danger do you think a beaver would pose to Samuel, Ahren, and Quon Shen?"

"I don't know. You were rhyming off local animals, and I was helping."

Dillan barks a laugh. "You could be right, bro. I'm thinking maybe the local beaver population united against the interlopers. They likely smacked their tails against the ground so vigorously that an avalanche swiped the Hunter-gods downslope."

Emmet rolls his eyes and flips D the bird.

"I could fly around and get an aerial view," Eva says.

Da likes that idea. "Even if GPS coordinates take things down to the minute and seconds, the location can still be over a hundred square foot area or more. Maybe we simply haven't come across them yet."

"It can't hurt, angel," Dillan says. "Be careful."

Eva looks skyward and bursts into a golden mist as a white dove flaps her wings and takes flight.

Amazeballs.

I think about the theory of the Hunter-gods being somewhere close by and do a gut check.

Da might be right about the area of GPS coordinates, but I don't feel like that's what's happening here. I filter through the distractions and go back to what Manx was saying. "What kind of creatures were you talking about, buddy? Have you got any ideas?"

He shakes his head, his beige and gray fur catching the breeze. "The scent isn't somethin' I've ever smelled before. It's definitely animal, and it's part of this forest. Beyond that, all I can tell ye is that there was a group of them and they can walk on four feet or two."

Okay, now my mind is spinning.

"What makes you say that?"

"Just the way the tracks are falling. To me, it looks like half a dozen four-legged creatures came down the slope, there was a skirmish here, and when they cleared out, almost all of them were walking on two feet...other than the one they carried and the other they dragged."

Dillan comes over to see where Manx is indicating and pulls up the hood of his cloak. My brother might be a giant pain in the ass, but for our druid party, he's one helluva ranger-slash-rogue.

The two of them track the damage in the crust of the snow, back and forth in the little clearing where we're standing, and eventually expanding up the slope.

When they get back, Dillan pulls his hood back, and we all

close in to hear what he has to say. "Manx is right. Whatever these animals are, they came down the slope in a stalking prowl. They hunt like wolves and are intelligent. They spread out, circling to come in at your friends from all sides."

"You said 'like' wolves, but you don't think that's what they are?"

Dillan shakes his head. "Manx is right about their mobility. They came in on four feet and left on two. Wolves don't do that."

"Shifter wolves might," Nikon suggests. "There could be local Moon Called who live higher in the Alps. They would smell wild, be intelligent, and also be able to stalk in on four feet and leave on two if they captured trespassers in their territory."

"That makes as much sense as anything," I say. "Especially when you consider that three men with shaman abilities and the fae gifts they possess were set upon and taken to a secondary location."

"Maybe they went willingly and weren't prisoners."

I consider that and shake my head. "No. Samuel knew we were coming. He would've left Ahren or Quon Shen to wait for us and tell us what happened."

"Why would Bavarian shifters kidnap three Hunter-gods who were here on a mission that had nothing to do with them?" Calum asks.

"I suppose we can ask them when we find them." Da turns his attention back to Dillan and Manx. "Is there anything else ye can tell us about them, boys?"

"They're very big," Manx says. "Their feet are longer than and twice as wide as any man I've ever come across."

Dillan nods. "Agreed. If we compare the depth of the footprints of Samuel, Ahren, and Quon Shen with the creatures, I'd guess they're a solid two to three hundred pounds heavier."

"Garnet's lion has tackled me to the ground. I can honestly say he weighs more than four hundred pounds."

That comment goes over like a lead balloon.

What? Is it the prospect of a half a dozen five-hundred-pound foes that are making them glare at me or the idea of me being taken to the ground by possessed Garnet's lion? I'm going to guess it's the latter.

Eva's dove drops into the group, her shift in form both graceful and beautiful. "There's no one around, but I sense the coming of death farther up the mountain."

"So, your reaper radar is still online?" Emmet asks.

Evangeline nods. "I don't think being a guardian trainee negates my reaper abilities, no."

"Then we should get moving." I point the way Eva gestured up the mountain. "Manx and Dillan, you two are on point, and Bruin, we need you to ghost out and do the long-range intel gathering."

"Always a pleasure, Red."

Bruin vanishes and does one breezy lap around me before he's gone. I smile and pull my hair away from my face with my glove. "Everyone else, keep a watchful eye. Whether we're dealing with territorial shifters or not, the Hunter-gods tracked Mingin and Melanippe here, so there is evil afoot."

We spend the next half-hour hiking up the rocky slope. The boots Dionysus equipped us with are amazing. As the terrain gets more inhospitable, our footing on the jagged stone, snow, and ice patches stays manageable. It might even be enjoyable if we weren't hiking after the people who kidnapped my friends.

A gust of wind sweeps through the group, and I brace against its bite. Even within the shelter of the pine forest, it's becoming lung-chillingly cold.

Flakes of snow are melting in my hair and making my curls take hold in a 90s Mariah Carey hair kinda way. The precipitation is dripping off the pines and ice-encrusted firs looming above us.

"Is it my imagination, or is it getting noticeably colder with every minute we climb?" I ask.

"It's not your imagination, Jane." Dionysus is trudging on, his boots *crunching* along the snowy path. Exhaling, he reaches through the wispy cloud of condensed breath and frowns. "That's just not right."

"Missing the tropical climate of ancient Greece?"

"At this moment, I am. Maybe it's important for me to suffer through moments like this to truly appreciate the beauty, warmth, and fertility of my home."

"Absence makes the heart grow fonder."

"That's what they say."

"My heart would fondly like to know we're still on course. It seems unlikely that Samuel and the others were simply stumbled upon by a group of shifters who lived this far up the mountain. What were they doing so far down the slope? Why would they care if the Hunter-gods were there and drag them back?"

"All good questions." Da lifts his wide-beamed flashlight to pan across the path in front of us. "What do ye say, boys? Are we still on track?"

Dillan and Manx both turn their heads and nod.

"What about you, Fi?" Da asks. "Is yer shield weighin' in at all?"

I straighten and pay closer attention. "Nope. S'all good here. So far, at least."

Sloan stops ahead of me, raises his palms, and accesses his powers. My skin tingles as his energy permeates the area.

"Whatcha doin', hotness?" I ask.

"Scannin' the trees and the forest beyond to sense if there are any disturbances."

"And? What's the word?"

"The pervasive evil they sense has unsettled the forest and her creatures, but at the moment, they find us the most curious. Apparently, they don't get a lot of visitors up here."

I scan the forest and see nothing beyond shadows and the tall eerie silhouettes of trees caught in the fading light of day.

"Bruin? Are you back, buddy?" Nothing comes back to me. "I guess not."

Evangeline is hiking up the slope with a spring in her step and smiling like a little girl on a sunny sidewalk. It baffles me that a walking thundercloud like Dillan ended up with a sunshine and rainbows girl for first love. Then I take a moment to study Sloan.

It proves that opposites attract.

"Hey, Eva? Are your acute angel senses picking up anything?"

She smiles out at the forest around us, and I swear a faint, golden glow illuminates her. "Nothing beyond the sweet scent of pine, the quiet strength of an ancient forest, and the joy of spending the day with family and friends."

Not helpful.

I might be getting cranky, but I can't smell the pines anymore because my nostrils are freezing shut, my cheeks sting from the bite of the wind, and I'm starting to worry that Emmet's right, and we've veered off course at some point and failed my friends in their hour of need.

Dionysus blows into his palms and cups them over his face. His distaste for the cold is growing.

"Yeah, I know how you feel, Tarzan—"

A blast of wind drives stinging snow into our faces, and I spin away from its force. Dionysus ducks his head and braces himself until the assault ends.

When the air stills, he tilts his head to the side, a deep furrow creasing his brow. I wait, watching as he reaches into his snow pants and adjusts himself.

"Everything okay there, Greek?"

His ears are bright pink, but that might be the cold. "I don't know. I've never been a snow bunny before—how shall I describe it delicately?"

"Your frozen balls just crawled up inside to get in out of the cold?" Calum asks.

The bewilderment on Dionysus's face turns to sheer amusement. "I'm not the only one it's happening to?"

The guys all laugh.

"It's normal." Da waves away his concern. "Ye'll find it happens in extreme cold. Now that ye live in Toronto, I suppose it'll happen to ye again."

"Fascinating." He holds out the waistband of his snow pants and glances down at himself.

I giggle. "Yep, there are all kinds of learning experiences to take in when you step outside your box."

"Apparently." He reaches down the front of his snow pants again and adjusts things. "When will things go back to normal?"

"As soon as you warm up," Dillan says. "Don't worry. You'll thaw out in plenty of time for your house party this weekend."

Da nods. "Dillan's right. It's nothing to worry about, son. Ye'll be good as new as soon as ye warm up."

Dionysus seems content with that answer, and we continue our hike.

"Hey, lads?" Tad says a few minutes later. "I hate to bring down the party, but I think we've got a serious problem." He holds his gloved hand out and uncurls his fingers to show us a stone glowing in the palm of his hand.

"Shit. Is that what I think it is?" Calum asks.

"If ye think it's one of the stones Samuel enchanted to track the tainted souls that escaped the Neitherlands, then it is."

"Isn't that how you first figured out your dad migrated to the dark side?" Emmet asks.

"Aye, it is."

"So, he's here." I scan the trees with a heightened level of urgency. "Ahren said it was getting easier to track him and Melanippe because their taint was growing. Be careful, everyone. They were tough to battle the last time and have leveled up since then."

"Yeah, well, so have we." Calum closes ranks, pulls off his gloves, and stuffs them into his pockets. A moment later, he calls his bow to his palm. "Come out, come out, wherever you are."

Dionysus and Nikon suddenly arm themselves with double-ended javelins and shields. Da calls his staff, and Dillan's jogging back from his place leading the group.

D takes one look at us and calls his daggers forward. "Like that, is it?"

Tough as Bark. My armor activates as a protective shell over my skin, and I call Birga to my palm. "Yep. Just like that."

"Then, I guess I should mention that we're here." Dillan hikes his thumb over his shoulder. "Whoever we were tracking, they led us to a walled compound ahead. You know how you thought it might be shifters we're dealing with?"

"Yeah."

"It's not."

I frown at my brother and wave in front of my chest. "So, spill it. What are we dealing with?"

His sadistic grin makes my bowels knot. "Your friends are being held captive in a compound full of eight-foot-tall, five-hundred-pound yeti."

"Yeti? Bullshit. You're making that up."

"Oh, that I was, little sister, but even I couldn't have come up with this one."

Yeti. I let that sink in and sigh. "Well, crap."

"Yeah. That pretty much covers it."

CHAPTER TEN

The compound is a large, gated village with a twenty-foot wall surrounding its perimeter. Inside, there are sentry towers at the four corners and another four along the lengths of the long walls. There are two main buildings, three outbuildings, and a courtyard at the base of a stone cave. It seems the yeti community lives within the mountain.

Sloan frowns. "This isn't ideal."

Dillan nods. "No shit."

"Be nice, D," I scowl at him. "It's not Sloan's fault we're the underdogs here."

"Underdogs? If the Hunter-gods are inside that mountain, we're fucked. We don't know the layout inside or what their skills or powers are or how closely entwined they are to the darkness of Mingin and Melanippe. We're completely fucked."

I don't like the sound of that, but I can't argue.

Glancing at my father, I hope to see a brighter outlook coming from him. Da is deep in thought, but I can't tell if he's actually any more optimistic than Dillan or not. "Da? What are you thinking?"

"We'd need to hit at least four of the sentries in a coordinated strike. The way they positioned the towers, we might get away with not taking them all out once the dark of night has fully fallen."

"Unless yeti have night vision," Dillan says.

Da frowns. "Agreed, that wouldn't be ideal."

"Considering the distance between them, I can take out two relatively quickly."

"If your arrows pierce a yeti's hide," Dillan says. "If not, they flick your arrow to the side, and we're fucked."

I huff. "Seriously, D. Stop saying that. You're not helping."

"Actually, he is." Da frowns. "Yer brother's right to poke holes in the plan. We don't have enough information to know what kind of attack will be effective."

"So, maybe we bypass the sentries completely and portal into one of those buildings," Nikon says. "Four of us can portal, so maybe we go in with stealth instead of steel."

Da tilts his head from side to side as he considers that. "That might work better. Although, we don't know if yeti can smell the scent of a human or not."

"The animals might know about what the yeti can do," Manx says. "I can ask around in the forest here and see what I can find out."

I check in with Sloan, and he nods. "Aye, that's a decent idea. Be careful. We're in uncharted territory. The animals of this forest might not have the same temperament as the animals ye call yer friends in the Don."

"Don't worry, sham," Manx says. "I'll be fine."

The familiar breeze of Bruin's bear swirls around me. *Hey, buddy. Did you find out anything interesting?*

I haven't gone into the compound yet. I checked the perimeter and didn't find any patrols or other hunting parties in the forest. Fer now, I think yer biggest worries are within that wall. I'm going to check the compound now.

Can I give you a different task first?

If ye like. What are ye thinkin'?

Manx wants to ask around in the forest and is on his own. Will you keep an eye on him and keep him safe?

Of course.

Thanks. At least then, if things go south, he'll have you to step in. He can't ghost out of danger. If you need to go full Killer Clawbearer to keep him safe, you have my permission.

Don't worry. Nothin' will happen to him on my watch. I promise ye that.

"Report back as soon as ye can." Sloan scrubs the fur of Manx's cheeks. "And stay sharp."

"Have faith, sham," Manx says.

"I have no doubts in yer strengths. I simply worry."

"No need. I'll be back in two flicks of a lynx's tail."

Sloan chuckles. "Ye haven't got a tail. Ye've got a wee stub."

"Rude. That *is* my tail." Manx flashes us a smile, turns from the group, and bounds away.

I watch him go and wonder if we made the right call. Man, I hate having loved ones in the line of fire. "Just FYI, Bruin got back, and I asked him to escort Manx. He'll keep an eye on him."

Sloan looks markedly relieved. "That's good to know. Thanks."

"All right," Da says. "Tad and Calum, portal around the compound one more time. I want to know what kind of weaponry they carry, if any, what they use those buildings for, and if there are women and children in the courtyard or only males. If this breaks into a battle, I don't want families involved if we can avoid it."

"Yes, Da." Calum shifts to take Tad's hand.

"Dionysus, I know ye can't involve yerself as a god in mortal matters, but if ye could pop off somewhere to find out about yeti, that would be a big help. We didn't know they exist, but someone must, and information might be the most important factor in this battle."

"Yes, Da," Dionysus says. "I'll be back in a blink."

"I will too," Nikon says. "Politimi might know something that can help us. She fixated on secret societies and little-known races for centuries, and she's a tenacious bitch when she wants to be."

Politimi scares me. There's no denying it.

"Thanks, Greek. Good luck."

When he snaps out, Da looks at the rest of us. "The way I see it, we've got three separate issues here, and we have to decide our priorities. In my mind, the first and most important objective is findin' the Hunter-gods and settin' them free."

I nod. "Agreed."

"The second thing to consider is are we avoidin' Mingin and Melanippe or do we still intend on takin' them down here and now?"

"We take them down," Dillan says.

"But that splits our focus from rescuing Samuel and the others," I say.

"All right, first the rescue and then—"

"Oh dear." Eva straightens. "I'm being called for a death within the encampment."

I stare at her, and my hearing rushes in my ears. "Who's dead?"

"I won't know unless I answer the call."

"Then go," I say, maybe with a little too much authority. "Sorry. Please go. If it's one of my friends, I need to know. There's no one I would rather have escort them to their ever after."

"I'm supposed to be your guardian."

"We'll guardian ourselves until you get back."

She doesn't look convinced, but Dillan backs me up. "We'll be fine, angel. Take the opportunity to grab us some intel. If you're there in an official capacity, no one will see you or know you're there."

Eva nods. "It will be my pleasure to help the cause. Please stay safe while I'm gone."

"We promise." I cross my fingers over my heart. "Good luck."

Eva disappears, and my mind is now stuck on wondering who died within the yeti compound.

"You mentioned three things to consider," Emmet says. "Rescue the Hunter-gods, whether or not we're still actively going to try for Mingin and Melanippe… What's the third issue?"

Da glances toward the yeti compound's gate and frowns. "How and why a yeti population that keeps to themselves is involved with Mingin and his dark plans in the first place."

"Evil is as evil does," Emmet says.

"Maybe, but we can't lump them into the dark and dangerous camp simply because our enemies are here."

"Guilty by association," Dillan says.

"Last time I checked, innocent until proven guilty was the foundation of our oath." Da casts a fatherly glance over all of us, and yep, we've been told.

Dillan does another perimeter sweep with his hood up and returns to our little hideout in the trees as Dionysus and Nikon snap back. Each of them is smiling, so I'm encouraged, but before they can fill us in, Calum and Tad *poof* back too.

"All righty then." Emmet holds up his palms. "Let's hear it. Who's first? What do we know?"

Nikon raises a finger and starts us off. "Politimi said the Bavarian yeti are a sweet and private colony. She spent time here in the early 1800s. She said one of the basic tenets of their society is noninvolvement. She couldn't believe that a scouting party of yeti has taken the Hunter-gods hostage."

"Well, they have," I say.

"Or that's how it looks," Da corrects.

Dillan shakes his head. "We're not wrong on that, Da. I can't tell you why, but Manx and I went over every inch of that site where we first materialized. That's exactly what happened."

"Well, in my experience, societies don't radically change their stance on guiding principles they've lived by fer centuries without a drastic reason. Maybe the question we need to ask ourselves is why did they take the Hunter-gods?"

I honestly wish I knew. It's not much of a stretch of the imagination to guess the presence of Mingin and Melanippe had something to do with it. "Did Politimi say anything else?"

"Just that they might be big and hairy, but they're kind souls, and if we do anything to harm them, she'll kick our asses."

"Well, it's not like we came here to pick a fight."

Nikon shrugs. "You asked if she said anything else. Take that for what it's worth."

I look at Dionysus next. "How about you? Were you able to find out anything?"

Dionysus smiles. "I visited the Fates and asked Atropos and Clotho if they would look into what's been happening, both past and present, within the compound."

"What did they say?"

"I can't tell you." He flashes me an apologetic smile and shrugs. "You know, it's the whole sanctity of godly insight and us not influencing the course of human nature. They made me promise."

I throw my hands up. "How does that help us?"

"We have yet to see, but I'm sure being kind and goodhearted people, you're struggling with how to navigate a bad situation and keep your family safe."

I don't know what to say about the expectant look on his face. "Yeah, I'm sure that's true. Thanks, Tarzan."

I move on to Tad and Calum. "What did you find out about the compound and how it's run?"

"Well, I didn't see my father, but the evil sensing stone has gone molten in my pocket. So, he's here somewhere."

"Try not to think of him as yer father, son," Da says. "The moment he merged with the tainted soul of Mingin, he ceased being Riordan McNiff. He's just the evil who now possesses his body."

I reach over and squeeze Tad's shoulder. *Poor guy.*

"Wow. It's so sad when evil moves in and takes over." Dionysus flashes a crazy grin at all of us, scanning the group. "Families, right? What wouldn't you do to stop evil from harming those you love?"

"Just about anything," I say. "It's fair to say we all would go to great lengths to keep those we love safe."

"Exactly right." He lunges forward and points at me. "Even something you wouldn't ordinarily do."

"Dude? Why are you acting like such a wackadoodle? Is the alpine air freezing your gray matter?" I'm accustomed to Dionysus being a little off-center, but this is weird even for him.

Da shakes his head. "It's nothing like that, is it, son? I hear what yer sayin', and at the same time, I assure ye that ye said nothing at all."

I blink at my father. "Is cray-cray contagious? If it is, I think we have a raging case going through this group. Can we try to stay on topic?"

Sloan squeezes my shoulder and gives me a patient smile. "We *are* on topic. The thought just occurred to me—and in no way came from any other source here—if Mingin and Melanippe infiltrated a peaceful colony of yeti and somehow leveraged the safety of their families, it might force the community members to act out of character to safeguard those they love."

"Yes!" Dionysus snaps across the group, grabs both sides of Sloan's head, and lays one helluva kiss on him. When he pulls back, our god of good times is all smiles. "I agree with that possible reasoning for why the yeti are involved. Good thinking Sloan."

Hilarious.

Dionysus is as subtle as an earthquake, but I suppose he did keep his promise and didn't tell us what the Fates revealed to him.

I chuckle as Sloan wipes his mouth, looking annoyed. "All right, moving forward under the assumption that the yeti are acting under duress, we can assume that if we remove that pinch point of leverage, they will release Samuel, Ahren, and Quon Shen."

"How do we do that?" Emmet asks.

Tad grins. "I have an idea."

CHAPTER ELEVEN

"When Calum and I went on our scouting mission to assess the workings of the yeti compound, we noticed one of the guards in the far left sentry point check on several children hiding in his watchtower," Tad says.

Calum nods. "From what we could tell, they can't get them out of the compound because Mingin minions are guarding the exit."

"How does this help us?" Sloan asks.

Tad rubs his hands together and exhales a puff of warm breath. "I bet, if Nikon introduces himself as Politimi's older brother and assures them we can take the kids somewhere safe, we could garner some favor."

"Where will I take them?" Nikon asks.

"They might have an idea about that," Da says.

"And if not?"

Tad shrugs. "Somewhere safe and remote."

"Gran's and Granda's." My instincts kick in to tell me I'm exactly right. "Gran's and Granda's is heavily warded against intruders. They can feed them, and their place is remote enough so that no one will drop in and expose the existence of yeti."

I check in with Da to see what he thinks about the idea. He tugs the elastic of his knit cap down on his forehead. "Aye. It's a good plan. Nikon, go talk to the guard, and if he agrees, we'll evacuate as many of the innocents as we can before we try for a rescue of Fi's friends."

"I want to come too." I hold my hand out to Nikon so I don't get left behind. "Maybe having a woman with you might help."

Nikon checks with the group. "Any objections? Is this our plan?"

Sloan steps in and squeezes my hand. "I agree we can't all snap in there at once, or we'll spook the guard. Still, I think it's important that ye let them know there are ten of us here, and if they direct us to where the innocents are, we have others who are here to help."

I reach up and kiss Sloan's cheek. "I'll tell them."

"If it looks like they're too hostile to work with, get out of there before ye overplay our hand. There's no use tellin' the enemy how many are in our party or where we are."

"Understood."

"Should I go too?" Dionysus asks. "If the guard doesn't know who Nikon's sister is, he might know who I am."

"I'm not so sure," I say. "No offense, Tarzan, because you're incredibly memorable, but this community has isolated themselves in the Bavarian Alps for centuries and likely a lot longer than that. They might not know Greek mythology."

"I'm not a myth," Dionysus says.

"No. You're a legend."

He grins at me. "Thank you for noticing."

"Keeping the group small for first contact is best," Da says. "We don't want to overwhelm."

I smile. That's my father's polite way of saying Dionysus might be too much fabulous for the situation.

"Do either of you speak yeti?" Dionysus asks.

I frown at Nikon, and he tosses the same look of confusion back at me. "Do you speak yeti, Tarzan?"

Dionysus stretches, looking smug. "Sweet, sweet, Jane. Of course, I do. I am a chip off the old Olympus block. I speak every language."

"You mean you knew there were yeti and let us flail all afternoon?"

He sobers. "No. I didn't know there were yeti, but I speak *all* languages. I don't have to learn them. They're simply available to me when I communicate with strangers from strange lands."

"Like a built-in universal translator," Emmet says.

Cool. "Fine, Nikon, Dionysus, and I will take the first run at things and loop you all in right away."

Da nods. "Aye, do that."

Nikon takes my hand and checks with Tad before we snap out. "Far left sentry tower, you said?"

Tad nods. "The young are crouching below the line of the railing, but they're there."

Good enough.

Dionysus hooks his arm through mine as the warmth of Nikon's energy snap takes us from up the slope at one end of the compound to standing in the watchtower at the opposite end.

The moment we materialize, the guard turns. He's a mountain of a male with shaggy off-white fur, massive hands and feet, and a leather sash chock full with an enviable collection of knives. In a graceful blur of motion, he draws a wicked-looking blade and steps between the children and us.

The three of us raise our hands, and Dionysus takes over. "We come in peace," he says, his voice calm. "We know someone invaded your compound and we offer you our help."

"Who are you? How did you get here?"

I take that one. "Nikon Tsambikos is an immortal Greek with the ability to portal. You might have heard of his sister, Politimi Tsambikos. She spent some time here a few centuries ago."

"Very good, Jane," Dionysus says. "I didn't know you speak yeti."

I roll my eyes. "I don't. He's speaking English, you dope."

"He is? Oh, that's disappointing. I thought we were sharing a moment."

"Who are you?" The yeti guard repeats, taking a striding step closer to block us from the three smaller versions of yeti.

I gesture across our group. "Nikon Tsambikos, Fiona Cumhaill, and Dionysus, Greek God of Wine and Fertility."

The sentry considers that. "What do you want?"

"We want to help." I make eye contact with the kids. "We're part of the crew tracking the evil people who invaded you. We came to help the three men you captured at the base of the slope. We wondered if the invaders forced your people into servitude and if so, we want to help."

"There's nothing you can do."

"Don't be so sure. As I said, Nikon is an immortal Greek with the ability to portal and Dionysus is a god of Olympus. We can do a lot. If you tell us what's been happening here, I swear to you we can help."

The young whimper, and it hurts my heart. "Don't be afraid, kids."

"They're not afraid," the guard snaps. "They have been trapped up here for two days. They are hungry and uncomfortable and miss our queen."

"How many members are in your community?" I ask. "Of those, how many are women and children?"

His gaze narrows on me and a strange rumble releases from his throat. "Is that what this is about? The dark ones couldn't force our men to talk, so you're trying? I'll never put our young in danger."

"No, of course, you wouldn't. That's not why I asked." I check in with Nikon and Dionysus. "How do we prove we're not trying to hurt the kids?"

"Let them play with our kids?" Dionysus suggests. "If they've been stuck up here for two days, maybe having cookies with your young would make them feel better."

"You have young?" the guard asks, looking skeptical. "I never would have thought it."

"They aren't technically mine. My brother has young, and I care for them."

He studies me for a moment and nods. "That makes more sense."

"Why? Why couldn't I have young?"

He shakes his head. "It's not for me to say."

"Well, now we're invested because I'd really like to know."

"Is it because she's ugly, Kimne?" one of the kids asks.

"Hush now," the guard says. "The poor thing can't help that she wasn't blessed with hair and curves."

I look down at myself with that lens and chuckle. "Okay, enough about me. Back to the problem at hand. Who all is at this party of yours? I'm guessing a man with black spider webs veining across his skin and an alarmingly tall woman who looks like a character out of a Marvel movie."

He nods. "I don't know what a Marvel movie is but yes, that's them."

"By the look of things down there, they brought friends."

"Half a dozen men."

"What about a man with long, dark hair with a scar from cheek to ear who has two different colored eyes? Is he here too?"

He shakes his head. "No. Not him. Or at least not that I have seen."

"Okay, well, that's good."

"Kimne?" one of the young says. "They are standing up. Can we stand?"

"It's fine," I say. "I cast a privacy spell to hide us from being seen or heard. You can stand and those intruders down there won't see."

The guard stares at me for a moment. He's hella-intimidating, but he has the prettiest ice-blue eyes. "Do you swear you speak the truth? If you harm these young, I will rip your hips from your belly and throw the pieces of you to the wolves."

"That's quite an effective visual. No need to lay out the plastic sheeting. I would never hurt kids or innocents. We're here to save them from our common enemies."

Kimne takes a moment to consider that and nods at the kids. "You may get up and stretch."

The three of them unfold from the heap of white fur on the floor of the sentry tower and stand.

"How old are you guys?"

"Sixteen winter seasons," one of them says.

"Twenty," the next one says.

"Twenty-three," the third one says.

"Huh, I'm twenty-three, too." I glance down at the girl I would've guessed was about eight. "I think our species must age differently." I glance at the guard. "Not to be rude, but out of curiosity, how old are you?"

"Six hundred and twelve," he says. "And I highly doubt a female of twenty-three will be able to help us out of the situation we find ourselves in."

"You'd be wrong," Nikon says. "I'm twelve hundred, and Fiona saves me all the time."

"Same," Dionysus says. "I'm from the time before time when gods and giants ruled the world."

"Is that old, Kimne?" the twenty-three-year-old one asks.

"Yes, Laisly. That is old."

Silence settles around us for a brief moment. Then I get back to the problem at hand. "How many women and children do we need to evacuate to get the innocents out of this compound and away from danger?"

"There are nine young in our community, but our women would never abide getting evacuated. They will stand and fight once the children are safe and our queen can unleash her wrath."

"Could we be lucky enough that the children are all in these towers hiding?"

"No."

"Poop. Well, it couldn't hurt to hope."

Dionysus agrees. "Where are the others?"

"Before I tell you that," Kimne says. "You will take me to where you believe these young will be safe."

"That I can do." I step closer to the kids. "So, for the magic of the portal to work, we're going to all hold hands. Don't let go until we're at my grandparents' place. You can eat and play with the young of my family while we work on saving the others."

"You swear they will be safe?" Kimne asks.

"I swear it. You'll see."

The seven of us flash from the Bavarian Alps to the back lawn of Gran's and Granda's house. There's no one out there, so I run and stick my head in the back door. "Hey guys, can everyone come outside for a sec? We need to make a good impression."

"A good impression?" Aiden comes around the side of the house. "That lets these two out."

I laugh and hold my hand out for Jackson. "I want you kids to meet some new friends. They're going to be staying for a bit while we sort out some trouble at their house."

"Trouble?" Granda says, coming outside. "Why doesn't that surprise me?"

Gran comes out the door behind him, and I step out of the

way, so their view is unhindered. "Sweet Mother of Nature's grace," Gran says. "What have we here?"

"Kimne and his yeti people are being held prisoner by Mingin and Melanippe. They're using the kids as leverage, so my best idea was to take the children somewhere safe while we sort things out. They're hungry and tired and have had a really bad couple of days."

"Och, the poor dears," Gran says. "Well, don't worry about a thing. I'll have yer bellies filled and yer spirits lifted in two shakes. Now, tell me. What do yeti eat? Are ye carnivores, omnivores, or herbivores? I'm gonna make a wild guess and say ye need to eat a fair bit of meat to fuel muscular bodies this large."

She's not wrong. "So, everyone, this is my family. We have Lugh and Lara, that's my brother Aiden, and these monkeys are Jackson and Meg. Inside the house is Kinu, their mom, and the two newest members of our family."

Jackson, ever the social one, walks right up to the kids and smiles. "Yous got fur. That's cool. Do you want to see the bear fort under the treehouse?"

"How about we get them something to eat first, buddy? Their tummies are really empty."

"Then do you want to see the fort?"

"We make forts in our trees too," the smallest yeti says. "We can climb really high."

Kimne frowns. "I don't want you three climbing while you're here. Eat, and play with Fiona's young, but mind yourselves. There are a great many dangers in the world, and our kind must be ever vigilant."

"I'm sure that's true, sir," Granda says, "but not here. Yer kids are safe to be kids here. We'll protect them as we would our own."

"Your kindness is well received."

"And unending," I add. "We have six more yeti young to bring to safety, so we'll be back."

"Then I best be off to the kitchen. How about a beef stew? Will that suit ye?"

Kimne nods. "Anything from your hearth will meet with appreciation."

"Wonderful. I'll get started right now."

As Gran strikes off to the house, I meet the gaze of the children. "The moment we have everything fixed at your compound, we'll take you home. In the meantime, have fun, eat lots, and we'll be back with the others."

I check with Granda, and he nods. "We'll be fine, *mo chroi*. Focus on bringin' their troubles to a happy end. We'll do our part here and keep the young safe and well-tended to."

I glance up at Kimne. "That's the plan. Are you good? Do you trust me now?"

"More than I did, but not completely."

I shrug and take that as a win. "Fair enough. Your people haven't had much luck with strangers the past few days. You can hold your decision until the end. Have fun, kids. We'll be back."

I hold out my hand for Kimne and Nikon and address the Greeks. "We better check in with Da and the others. Then Kimne can tell us where the other children are so we can bring them here to safety. Does that work for everyone?"

That seems to be a yes...although, as Kimne said, he's holding out on his final decision until he sees how things progress.

Fingers crossed they go well. I'd like to add yeti to my list of strange and cool friends.

CHAPTER TWELVE

"There ye are." Da frowns at me as Nikon, Dionysus, Kimne, and I arrive back at our little hiding spot on the slope above the yeti compound. "Ye took yer sweet time, didn't ye? Here we all sit, worryin' about ye."

I gesture at the eight-foot yeti standing beside me. Somehow, my father seems to have missed him and solely focuses on giving me a dressing down for making him worry.

"I didn't miss curfew because I was at a party, Da. We were dealing with things. Kimne, this is my father, Niall Cumhaill. Like you, he is also very protective of his young."

Da realizes then that we have a guest, and despite me being gone for the past fifteen minutes, I had a job to do. Which I successfully achieved, I might add. "I'm sorry, *mo chroi*. Ye know this week has been difficult."

I step over and hug my dad. "It's fine, Da. The good news is, we have three children safely tucked away at Gran's and Granda's, and Kimne agreed to help us find and secure the other six so his people will be free to fight back and defend their queen."

"So, it's the young and yer leader both they're using as leverage?"

"Thorra is a brave and fierce warrior. Still, she would never endanger the young over a matter of the world outside. The ones who came here seek not only shelter but strength in numbers to their cause."

I snort. "Yeah, I bet they do."

Kimne looks at me to explain.

"In two months, there will be a head-to-head battle between good and evil. In the magical world, there is an upheaval of powers. Race leaders and individuals are rallying strength so their interests might gain a foothold during this event. Melanippe and Mingin want evil to win. My family and friends stand on the other side and fight for justice and peace."

"My people have no interest in fighting the battles of men but have yet to free ourselves from the dangers of not complying."

"We'll help ye with that," Da says. "Tell us where ye believe the other children are and we'll level the playing field so yer people can take their stand."

"I don't suppose the other kids are in the other sentry towers so we can evacuate them easy-peasy, eh?" Emmet asks.

I grin. "I asked the same question. Sadly no."

"No," Kimne repeats. "From what I heard, two are in the attic of the alehouse, one is hiding in the well house, and three are in the audience room with Queen Thorra and the interlopers."

I hold up a finger. "Just for clarity...when you say interlopers, does that mean Mingin and Melanippe or the three men you captured this afternoon?"

"No, I meant the evil ones. The other men were bound and taken within the caves. I assume they're prisoners."

I don't like the sound of that. "Bruin, I'm glad you and Manx are back safe. Can you ghost into the mountain and scope out the intel of what we're dealing with?"

"Way ahead of ye, Red. I've already given my report in yer absence."

"Awesome. How about I get the abbreviated version then to catch me up?"

"It's a twisty maze of rocky tunnels with little or no order to the layout or design. I recommend that we don't go into the mountain if we don't have to. There's no way to navigate the tunnels without being seen and discovered by the yeti who live there."

I check in with Kimne, and he stares at me looking blank. Right. He isn't druid and can't hear Bruin speak. Either that or he's stunned that I'm talking to a massive grizzly bear.

It's tough to tell.

Regardless, there's nothing I can do to help Samuel until we secure the children. That was the deal, and I intend to live up to my end. "Kimne, you're with us for the rescues or members of your community might mistake us for bad guys."

Sloan nods. "A good point. I'll come with ye this time, and maybe we can recruit a few more yeti citizens to the cause."

Kimne straightens. "We are a private people, not weak. This has been a violation of our home and lives. Once we are certain our young are safe; we will do what needs doing to rid ourselves of this evil."

"We'll help you," I say. "But first, the kids. Would the two in the attic of the alehouse be next? Can we get to them without tipping off our enemy that your people now have allies?"

Kimne looks at Nikon and Dionysus. "The alehouse is the long building with the sloped roof. I saw two intruders go inside before you appeared in my station. I assume they are drinking their fill."

"Da? Should we take out a couple of Mingin's men at the same time?"

"Aye, we could, but we don't know if Mingin empowered them in any way. We can't endanger the rescue of the children. The cooperation of the yeti to release Samuel and the others is secondary to safeguarding the young."

"Agreed."

"What if we don't try to defeat the enemy but simply take them out of the equation?" Dillan asks.

Da frowns. "We don't kill fer the sake of killin', son. No matter how vile the opponent."

Dillan waves that away. "I wasn't suggesting we kill them, but literally take them out of the battle. We have four people here who portal. Nikon and Dionysus can do long-distance without penalty."

"Because we're fan-Greek-tastic," Dionysus says.

"Undisputed," I add.

Dillan rolls his eyes and continues. "If we go in as a force, Sloan or Tad can go with Fi and Kimne to rescue the kids and take them to Granda's. At the same time, the Greeks can portal Mingin's men into the Bat Cave holding area, and Garnet can take care of them on that end."

I like it. "Then they are truly out of the fight."

Da considers it for a moment and nods. "All right. I think that will work. Fi, make sure Garnet or Anyx will be there to receive them. There won't be time to lose waiting around for an exchange of custody."

I pull out my phone and frown. "No service."

"Oh, baby, consider me your hot spot." Dionysus shifts to stand beside me and a rush of magical energy tingles in my cells. "Did that sound dirty? It was supposed to sound dirty."

I chuckle and send the text to the Team Trouble group. Once the message is gone, it only takes a moment before the high-pitched *ping* of his reply. "Anyx is at the office with Zuzanna. Garnet is heading there now. They'll be ready."

Da nods. "Then it looks like we have a plan. Everyone, saddle up."

When everyone is ready, Da gives us the signal, and we flash into the yeti alehouse. Unsurprisingly, even though the yeti are an isolated society, the tavern resembles any other pub I've ever been to...except the tables and chairs are for eight-foot-tall customers.

Are they customers?

Do yeti have currency and commerce or is the alehouse simply a watering hole where they gather outside the mountain to share a few pints?

"Fi? Are ye with us, luv?" Sloan grips my arm and tugs me along behind him.

Nikon and Dionysus zone in on the two humans sitting at the corner table. They snap over to them and are gone in a blink. The four yeti in the bar stand and raise their hands, ready to defend themselves.

Kimne speaks to them in a language I don't understand, but by the way the gazes in the room turn to study me and mine, I assume he's explaining what's going on.

"Yeah, hi, I'm Fiona, and this is my family. Are there any bad guys upstairs or are we good to escort the children to safety?"

The yeti turn on Kimne and another rush of indistinguishable chatter flares up.

I wait for a bit, but when the argument doesn't seem to be coming to a close, I interrupt. "Are we still doing this or not?"

"We are." Kimne holds up his massive hand to stop the argument. "If I might alter the plan slightly, Deene and Sira will come with us and stay with the young. They aren't as welcoming as I am and don't feel comfortable entrusting our children with you."

"That's fine but understand I'm entrusting them with my family and will be equally upset if they do anything to harm those *I* love."

"Then we understand each other," a female says. "No harm comes to our young, and no harm will come to your family either."

"Since we never had any intention of harming your young, that works. Now, if we've finished with the posturing, can we get the kids to safety and move out before the enemy discovers us?"

Kimne sweeps a massive arm through the space and leads the way up a wide set of stairs. The wood of the open staircase creaks with the weight of his frame, but I assume he's not the first man of his size to climb them and try not to worry.

At the top of the stairs, I straighten in the attic and scan the stacked furniture and large, hand-hewn crates. The place is a bit lost in clutter, but still, I don't see any sign of where the children are hiding.

"Here." Kimne moves a large wooden crate from its resting place against the back wall and then reaches to the roofline to trip a switch.

Once he runs his fingers along the seam of the wall and ceiling, something *clicks*, and he swings back a section of construction to reveal a panic room behind.

"Come out, young ones. Fiona and her family have become new friends. They're going to take you to safety where you can stay with Deene and Sira and the other children until this is over."

Two yeti children as young or younger than the others timidly step out of the shadows of the hidden room. They blink at the brightness of the day's light, and I give them a moment to adjust to the strange humans standing before them.

"Hey, kids. Like Kimne said, I'm Fiona, and this is Sloan and Tad. They have the magic ability to take you somewhere safe. I don't want you to be afraid. Everything will be all right. My gran is already cooking a big stew feast for the other children. You'll be safe there."

After a moment, the children gather their courage, and Kimne and I lead them back downstairs to where Deene, Sira, and my crew await.

"All set?" Sloan smiles at the children. "Did Fiona tell ye there are two human children to play with where yer going?"

"We are not allowed to play with human children," the younger boy says.

I shrug and hold my hand out for Sloan. "Today is a special day. Jackson and Meg aren't only human children. They're young druids. They can know about you without there being any danger."

"We shall see," Deene says, her voice thick with mistrust.

"Yes, you will. Everyone hold hands, and we'll go."

No one does as I ask.

Kimne steps in. "For their magical transport to work, the males make contact with us. There is nothing to fear. I went with them already, and it was fun."

Deene and Sira pull the children closer, each of them lifting one into their arms while glaring at me.

I fight not to roll my eyes; thankful Kimne was the yeti who got us started down this path instead of these two. Once we're all on the same page and everyone is in contact with one another, I check in with Sloan and Tad.

"We dropped the others on the back lawn, so I think that would be a good spot."

Sloan nods and *poofs* us out.

We materialize in Gran's and Granda's back yard to the squeals of children and the laughter of Aiden and Kinu. "That's it, Laisly," Kinu calls. "You've got him, honey. Run fast before he gets away."

The kids are in the hamster balls and are running willy-nilly across the back lawn bumping into one another and laughing their heads off. Even if their psychological ages are similar to what I'd gauge as six to ten-year-olds, they *are* yeti, so they're quite tall.

I grin and take in the horror of Deene and Sira. "They're fine. It's a game. There aren't any dragons here today, so we're all good."

That doesn't seem to reassure them at all.

"Can we play?" the older of the two asks.

"Of course, you can," I say. "But aren't you hungry? Do you want something to eat? The other kids were hungry and started with my Gran's beef stew."

They shake their heads.

"I was able to sneak them food often enough," Sira says, thawing a little. "They were fed, but thank you for your concern."

I nod, waving at my niece and nephew. "Perfect, then let's get you set up for fun. Come, I'll introduce you to Meg and Jackson."

"No need." Aiden jogs over. "Kinu and I can handle the introductions. Didn't you say there were nine kids to rescue? I'm sure the sooner, the better. We're good here."

I have no doubt. Aiden and Kinu are the perfect couple to handle this. They're parents, and they both work with the vulnerable sector. Aiden is a cop and a druid so he can handle himself, and with Kinu's experience with child welfare, these kids couldn't be in better hands.

Deene and Sira might not want to acknowledge it yet, but they'll soon see.

"Perfect, we'll regroup with Da and work on liberating the child in the well house."

"Good luck." Aiden glances up at the full height of the protective escorts. "I'm Aiden, and that is my wife, Kinu. Welcome. Come, kids. I bet your friends will be happy to see you and explain how the game works."

I leave him to get things sorted out on this end and close my hand around two of Kimne's fingers. There's no holding his wrist or his hand. His palms are the size of snow shovels. "Ready to liberate the next little one?"

Kimne nods. "Ready."

The well house rescue goes off without any trouble, and soon we've finished escorting the six "easier" recoveries to Gran's and Granda's. When that's complete, we reconvene in the attic of the alehouse to consider our next moves. We still have the three kids held inside the mountain cave, and those are in full view of Mingin, Melanippe, and the remaining minions.

Kimne said six men were working with them.

We took out two.

"So, what's our plan?" I ask my father.

Our group, the remaining two yeti from downstairs, and Kimne are in the long, chilly attic. I don't know if Kimne spoke to them about us or if they're simply more accepting than Deene and Sira, but they seem keen on helping us help them.

"The way I see it," Da says, addressing the group. "Nikon will snap to the front gate to capture the watchman at the same time Dionysus detains the one patrolling the compound. The two of you will portal them directly to the detainment cells at the Acropolis, and Mingin's force will be down from six to two."

"Not that they are the problem anyway," I say.

"No. They're simply cogs to keep the yeti in line. Bein' a peaceful species, Mingin likely didn't expect to meet with any resistance."

"Let alone the ten of us." Dillan waggles his ebony brows.

"I certainly didn't expect it," Kimne says.

I grin. "We *do* enjoy making life interesting."

"Ye do it well, *a ghra*. I never know what to expect from one day to another."

I chuckle. "Okay, so once four of the six are taken care of, we head into the mountain, is that it?"

"Aye, that's the idea." Da scans the group and seems to be wondering about something. "Kimne, could ye draw us up a sketch of what the queen's audience chamber looks like so we can get our bearings?"

He glances at the female standing inside the door, and she heads down the stairs. "Caith is our artist. She'll do better."

Da nods and gets back to our planning session. "So, the way I see it, we no longer face the difficulty of getting lost or discovered in the caverns. If Kimne and his people escort us in, we'll get to the audience room of the queen without getting lost."

"What if we run into one of the other two minions?" Dillan asks. "They might give us away."

Da shakes his head. "We'll put Nikon and Dionysus at the front and the back of our party. If we get discovered from either direction, they can pounce and do their disappearing act before the men can sound the alarm."

"The other two men have been guarding the door to the audience room," one of the yeti from downstairs says. "There is always at least one there."

"What about Mingin and Melanippe?"

"They have our queen confined to her seat of power and are tormenting our brethren."

"Where are the last three children?" I ask.

"They are there, as well. That is the only reason our brethren are allowing the torment. It was made very clear that to challenge them meant the young would suffer the same torture."

I hope there's a special kind of hell for people who torture and victimize kids. How soulless and twisted do you have to be to think that's okay?

"Where are the three captured men being detained?"

"I don't know for certain, but I assume they will be deeper in the tunnels. We don't have a place for prisoners, but over the centuries, if we've had to take in a stranger, we've kept them in a section of the underground we can lock off and secure."

"They're not." Caith returns. "The others said the woman

wanted the three chained in the audience room so she could toy with them."

"It's a party," Emmet says.

"Except they missed the part about the feasting and frivolity," Dionysus says.

"I'm sure Melanippe is enjoying herself just fine. She lied to Samuel, Ahren, and Quon Shen for months and played her part as their friend."

Knowing her, she's enjoying tormenting them.

Caith hands my dad the map of the audience room, and he lays it on the crate in front of him so we can all close in and see. "There are two entrances to the room?"

Kimne nods. "One from the surface corridor and one from the internal corridor that leads deeper into the mountain and toward our private residences."

"Is there a way to get to the internal entrance from here without going through the audience room?"

Kimne nods. "Several ways, yes."

"All right, then we'll make our entrance from both sides in a simultaneous strike. Nikon and Dionysus are on minion duty. Tad and Sloan, yer going straight for the wee ones. Once that's settled, we free the Hunter-gods, and it's on."

Our heads bob in a round of anticipation.

"Oh yeah, baby. It's on."

CHAPTER THIRTEEN

The interior of yeti mountain—my pet name for it—is everything I imagined and at the same time, not. The stone tunnels make perfect sense because we're inside a mountain. The torchlit corridors and the chill in the air are also no surprise. The smooth floors give me pause, but then I realize that for an unknown number of centuries, yeti have shuffled their tennis racket-sized feet over the same paths.

That's bound to wear things smooth.

I also hadn't considered the spacious corridors and high ceilings, but then again—yeti—amirite?

We arrive at a split in the tunnel and Da signals for Sloan and me to take Calum and Dionysus with Caith around to the far side of the queen's audience room. We're going to come in from the entrance from the residential side of the tunnels while Kimne leads Da, Dillan, Emmet, Tad, and Nikon in from the direct corridor from the outside.

We all know the plan.

Our watches are synchronized.

We have our priorities well laid out. Rescue the three young yeti. Release the three Hunter-gods. Kick the shit out of Mingin and Melanippe. Not that we have the ability to do that at the moment.

It took all of us at top fighting form plus a rocket launcher to stop them last time, and last I checked, Dionysus wasn't packing any Javelin missiles this time around. Sad face.

Caith takes us around the corner and stops dead. I nearly run right into the back of her, but stop myself before I put my hand up and use her butt as a bracing point.

Awkward.

"What are you doing here?" a man with a thick accent snaps. "You walking rugs are supposed to be confined to your quarters—"

I can't see around her, but Dionysus must because he snaps out from beside me. The moment he's gone, Caith turns back toward us, wide-eyed. "It was one of the intruders."

I got that. "Dionysus grabbed him okay?"

"He barely made contact with him, and they disappeared."

I nod back at the others. "That's perfect. That's exactly what we wanted to happen."

"What do we do now?"

"Just wait. He'll be right back."

"Where did he take him?"

"To our detainment cell in Toronto."

"Is that past London?"

"Quite a long way past, yeah. He'll be right ba—" The air snaps, and Dionysus is with us once again. "Did everything go according to plan?"

Dionysus winks. "Was there any doubt?"

"Not really, no." Turning back to Caith, I gesture for her to carry on the way we were heading.

The fact that our enemies sequestered the yeti in their quarters means the corridors are empty. We make quick work of navigating through the warren of tunnels, and when we're in position, I thank Caith for the assist.

"Now, you're free to join the fight or hang back and see how things go."

Her long, shaggy white coat sways as she shakes her head. "Once the young are safe, I will rally my people. This is not your fight."

I shrug. "Melanippe and Mingin are two very bad people we've been after for months. If we'd captured them sooner and stopped them, you and your people wouldn't be their prisoners now. So, yeah, it sorta is our fight too."

"Then together we stand."

When we arrive at the entranceway to the queen's audience chamber, I throw up a veil of invisibility and cast a spell to avoid detection. Melanippe might be a traitorous bitch, but she's also a very strong ancient power.

We spent time on the astral plane together so she knows the signature of my energy. I don't want to tip her off to my presence before we safely evacuate the last of the yeti kids.

"Can you guys see the kids?" I whisper to Dionysus and Sloan across the entryway.

From their vantage point opposite me, they can see more of the room than I. Hopefully, between the two, they've got a solid visual on the three yeti kids so we can get them out of here and throw down.

Sloan nods at me, and Dionysus winks. "We've got this, Jane. How much time do we have?"

I check my phone and look at the timer counting down. Turning the screen toward him, I feel the anticipation building in my cells.

Less than a minute.

Leaning into the doorway a little, I try to get a better look and take in the scene.

Samuel, Ahren, and Quon Shen are pinned against the far wall, suspended by an unseen force. Whatever magic is at work, it isn't pleasant. In fact, by the agonized looks on their faces, it's downright painful.

I tighten up and continue to take a lay of the land.

I've got a straight view of the troublemakers, and their smug smiles make me want to throat-punch them.

Melanippe is seated to the right of the yeti queen, and Mingin is on the queen's left. The three of them are gazing out on the room, straight-backed and eerily still.

The only sound in the room is the quiet whimpering of the three bundles of fur curled up on the floor in plain view of a very creepy-looking Evil Riordan.

I know Da said we can't consider him Riordan McNiff anymore, but it's eerie to see someone you know sitting right in front of you and disassociate that person from who they used to be.

Although, it's becoming easier.

I never liked Tad's father but admitted he was a heart-throbby, posh, fit man who made his fifties look good.

Now...not so much.

Now he has black spider webs veining his skin and looks like the evil within him is leaching across his body in ugly ebony fault lines. The smoky black smog seeping from his pores further punctuates that aesthetic.

That isn't Riordan at all—that's all Mingin.

When Mingin's tainted soul breached the rift in the Newgrange tomb and escaped the Neitherlands, he was nothing but a giant hack of tailpipe pollution.

He's come so far.

The man glares out at the room, his eyes alight with a freaky glow. Staring at him, I hear Vincent Price's evil laughter in my head. You know...that long, evil cackle from the end of Michael Jackson's *Thriller*.

I try not to judge, but in my opinion, possession hasn't agreed with him.

Poor Tad. It must suck balls to know his father chose to star in this freakshow rather than be the figurehead of his family.

"Where are Mingin and Melanippe?" Sloan whispers. "Can ye see them?"

I nod. "They're sitting on either side of the queen."

"Keeping her in line."

I check the countdown again and hold it up for Dionysus to see.

Four...three...two...one...

Dionysus and Sloan both disappear, and Calum and I wait with Caith. The moment they're gone, I flip to the other side of the entrance to watch what happens with the yeti kids.

Unlike the other three rescues where we moved in slow and explained who we are and what we're doing, there's no discussion.

Sloan, Dionysus, Nikon, and Tad appear as planned, and Sloan, Tad, and Nikon vanish equally quickly. We agreed earlier they'd each take one child and Dionysus would stand guard and power them up if there were any wards or blocks to overcome.

Four guys to portal three little—okay, well, not so little—yeti kids might be overkill but everything to do with our plan hinges on this part.

It goes well.

Mingin is incredibly powerful, but apparently, the advantage of a surprise attack goes to the druids and the Greeks. Now to free the Hunter-gods.

Calum and I rush the room from the residential hallway while Da, Dillan, Emmet, and Kimne breach the room from the exterior corridor. I call forward my armor, draw my weapons, and release Bruin, ready to throw down.

The pounding rush of footsteps brings Da, Dillan, Emmet, and Kimne into the mix. We're in the throes of engagement when my shield flares hot.

It's weird...I used to think the flares of warning were random, but I'm beginning to understand what's a physical threat versus a warning versus an urging to take notice.

I break stride and reevaluate. "Wait! Hold!"

A sickening dread grips my intestines as my ears flood with the buzzing of a swarm of angry bees. The sudden onslaught of stimulus makes it hard to think. "Wait. Something is wrong."

"What is it, *mo chroi?*" Da puts on the brakes, scans the room, and settles his gaze on me. I'm not sure what he reads in my expression, but it doesn't look good.

"This is a mistake," I assure him. "Everyone take a step back."

"Have you lost your conviction?" Kimne asks, annoyance thick in his tone. He's fashioned himself a club and is gripping it, ready to bash in some heads. "You said you would fight and we would have our justice."

"And you will...it's not that. I have a magical warning system telling me to take a moment to rethink. It's never failed me yet, so I tend to listen to it."

"Can we at least set Samuel and the others free?" Dionysus asks.

I hold up a finger, trying to figure out what's wrong. Everything I see makes me think we need to act, but my instincts are screaming otherwise...

"Focus, Fi," Da says. "Yer right. Yer instincts have never failed us. What is it?"

I take another look at the three of them sitting behind the queen's table. Melanippe, Queen Thorra, and Mingin are in a row. I cast a scattered glance around the chamber, my anxiety rising. "Does that look normal to you?"

Da studies the three of them and frowns. "Now that we've stopped to examine things, no."

"Exactly. Everything we knew was prompting us to strike but what I *feel* doesn't agree. Where's the taint of Mingin's evil?"

I wait while everyone does their gut check and catches up with me. "The last time we faced him, his dark power was like a hand closing around my throat. The taint of his dark juju coated my mouth with a nasty acrid tang that made me want to scrub my tongue with a wire brush. Where is that?"

"You jest," the lead male in a flock of yeti snaps. "If you're afraid to fight, stand aside, little girl. We are not."

I extend my arm, placing Birga's green marble tip in the path of anyone planning to rush me on this. "Give me thirty seconds to figure this out."

I glance around the room, but Sloan, Nikon, and Tad haven't returned yet. Okay, without Sloan's ring, I'll have to do this manually. Raising my palms, I focus on the three people frozen in place before me.

"Dispel Magic." I release my spell and feel its intention bump up against an opposing force. There's a momentary shimmer in the energy, and I'm more certain than ever something is very wrong.

"Emmet? Can you give me a boost, please?"

Emmet jogs over, and so does Dillan. With the hood of his cloak up, Dillan has a keen ability to see the unseen and find what's hidden. He stands beside me while Emmet moves in behind us to grip each of us by the shoulder.

"On three, D. One, two, three…*Dispel Magic.*"

The illusion wavers and the yeti in the room growl. The images of Melanippe, Thorra, and Mingin fight my command for a bit and dissolve, leaving us with only the truth before us—three terrified young yeti children are bound to their seats, gagged and immobilized.

"What evil is this?" Caith hisses, rushing forward.

"It's a misdirect," Da says, joining her.

"Fi? What about the Hunters?" Dionysus asks.

I tear my attention away from the confusion in front of me and search my instincts. "Yeah, go ahead. You guys break whatever spell is going on there, and I'll help with the kids."

By the time I'm shoulder-to-shoulder with my father, his hands are weaving their magic, and he's casting. It might only be my opinion, but druid casting spoken in Irish seems more authentic.

Maybe even more magical.

Even with Emmet there to act as his amplifier, it takes another five minutes for us to untangle the spells woven over the kids and release them from confinement.

When we finally break through, Dionysus calls me to the far wall where Samuel, Ahren, and Quon Shen are on the ground. The three of them are barely holding onto consciousness but are agitated and giving Dionysus and Calum a hard time.

I kneel next to them and move into their line of sight. "Hey, it's all right. We've got you now. Just give yourselves a minute to recover from your ordeal."

"Portal." Samuel winces, and his eyes flash gold.

I glance at Calum, and he shrugs.

"Them," he says, his body twisting as he fights the ascension of his wolf. "Not them."

"Give him space." I step back as Calum grabs Quon Shen and Dionysus grabs Ahren, and we give Samuel the space he needs to shift. "It's no wonder he can't hold back his animal. His wolf is probably howling mad and ready to sink his canines into Melanippe's jugular."

"Shit, Fi, he's seizing." Calum brings my attention back to Ahren, who is starting to convulse. "We need to get them to Wallace."

I straighten and glance around for Sloan... "Why isn't he back yet?"

"Do you want me to take them?" Dionysus asks.

"That would be great. Can you take all three?"

Dionysus rolls his eyes and laughs. "Can satyrs lick their own cocks?"

I have no idea. "Yes?"

"You bet your butt they can and do. Why do you think they're always late and get nothing done?"

"I honestly hadn't thought about it."

"Well, think about that until I get back."

He flashes out, and I blink at Calum. "Do I have to?"

He laughs. "It's hard not to now that he said that."

"Fi. Over here, *mo chroi*. We need a moment."

I offer Calum a hand up, and the two of us stride back to where Da and Kimne are having an emotional conversation. I can tell before he opens his mouth that I'm not going to like this. "What's up?"

"We've got a problem."

Oh, goody. "Lay it on me."

"If the three we thought were Melanippe, Mingin, and the yeti queen were the three yeti young, who were the three children we portaled out of here?"

I glance at where the three children were huddled and play it back in my mind. "You think it was Melanippe, Mingin, and the yeti queen with a glamor?"

"I do," Da says. "Now they're at our home with our family."

A rush of nausea hits me, and I scan the room. "Sloan, Tad, and Nikon never returned. Maybe they figured it out and are holding them back."

"Where's Dionysus?" he asks.

I pull out my phone and text him. When he doesn't respond immediately, I pull out the pendant he gave me in the citrus orchard when we first met. Gripping the etched depiction of him, I focus with everything I've got.

"I need you, Tarzan. Drop everything and come."

The air snaps in the same moment and I meet his panicked gaze with mine. "What's wrong?"

"Everyone who's going grab hold," Da says as our crew tightens ranks and some of the yeti join also.

I take Da's hand and grip Dionysus's wrist. "To Granda's. Mingin escaped, and we think he's there."

CHAPTER FOURTEEN

There have only been a few moments in my life when I have experienced true, soul-chilling terror. Our final visit to the hospital to say goodbye to our mam, when Calum was struck down by a dark wizard, when hobgoblins shot Liam, and when the Unseelie Prince Keldane was slaughtering Dart and Dillan, and I thought we'd die there and fail to save Sloan.

There have been other harrowing times when I've been afraid, but true terror only grips me when the people of my heart are at risk.

Like now...

In the brief moments between figuring out we delivered our greatest enemies right to our doorstep, and when we materialize on the back lawn a few seconds later, that icy terror takes root...

Sloan, Gran and Granda, Aiden, Kinu, the monkeys, Shannon, Nikon, Ciara, Tad...even the yeti queen and her people.

Oh, Sweet Mother, please let them be all right.

The moment we take form, I release Bruin and race up the grass toward the house. Aiden and Kinu are there...Jackson and Meg...

"Sloan! Gran! Granda! Where are you?" I push my legs to cut

the distance between my family and me as quickly as they can carry me.

Aiden turns, and I can see by the sorrow in his big, blue eyes that all is not well.

"Mingin and Melanippe…"

"Where are they now?"

"Gone. They portaled out."

"And Sloan?"

Da, Calum, Emmet, and Dillan are right behind me.

"Where's Ciara?" Emmet shouts.

"I'm here, Em." Ciara vaults off the deck of the treehouse and lands gracefully on the cushioned grass. Emmet breaks away and runs to pull her into his arms.

"Shannon? Mam? Da?" my dad shouts.

"Shannon's in the house with the twins while we calm Meg and Jackson," Aiden says. "She's fine."

"The babies are fine?"

"They are."

"What of our young?" Kimne shouts.

Ciara points up at the deck of the treehouse. "They're safe and up there. We were havin' a snack when Mingin and Melanippe blew through here."

"Where are my parents?" Da repeats.

Aiden shakes his head. "Gran and Granda were out here puttering around, and I couldn't get to them fast enough. When Sloan and the others first appeared, we thought they had the yeti kids. Then the illusion dropped, and there was a scuffle. Gran and Granda rushed to intercede. Then they were all gone."

"Gone?" I ask, my voice pitchy. "All of them?"

"Gran and Granda as well as Tad and Sloan."

"What about Nikon?"

"Once they had Sloan, Tad, Gran, and Granda, their quota seemed to be filled." Aiden tilts his head toward the kids. "Mingin puffed up like a toxic storm cloud and released some kind of mortal harm at us. Nikon got in front of the attack and absorbed the brunt while Ciara and I got shielding up."

Mortal harm? I scan the grounds. If Mingin intended the attack to kill and Nikon took the brunt of it…

Aiden nods, understanding that I'm piecing together what happened without him saying it in front of the kids.

"I assume he's at the vineyard in Greece visiting with his Papu after a hard battle," Aiden says, forcing a cheery tone.

I pull out my phone and call up the contact info for Nikon Tsambikos Senior. "I'm sure you're right. I'll send a quick text to double-check."

Thank the goddess for Nikon's immortality.

If Mingin killed him, he'll resurrect at his place of origin—the family vineyard on the Isle of Rhodes. He'll be out of the game for a few days, but hopefully, there won't be any lasting effects, and he'll be fine.

Sloan and the others don't have the same option. We need to figure out—

"Where is our queen?" Kimne says, interrupting my mind-spin. "You mention only your people. Where is our leader? Our queen was the third person portaled here. She is majestic and wears a bronze laurel and neck sash."

Aiden nods. "The third person portaled here sort of fit that description."

"Sort of? What do you mean? Where is she?"

"I don't know. The moment the illusion dropped, she disappeared, and only Mingin and Melanippe remained."

"That's because it wasn't your queen," Eva says, appearing in a burst of golden mist. "I escorted the yeti queen Thorra of the Alps to the Great Peaks."

Kimne straightens. "But how? We saw her taken."

"I don't know what you saw, my friend, but I assure you, your queen has passed." Eva lowers her chin. "My condolences to your people. She was a lovely female."

"Another misdirect?" Da suggests.

Caith and the others recoil. "How can we be sure?"

"Evangeline is a reaper," Dillan says. "She sensed a death and was called to duty not long after we arrived outside. If she says your queen has passed, that's what happened."

"But why?" Caith says. "We were complying with their wishes."

Eva takes her hand. "Mingin intended to use your people as part of his army. He planned to have Melanippe possess her body to lead your people into the coming war. Your queen refused to become a puppet. She chose to stop that from happening."

"That sounds like Thorra," Kimne says.

Evangeline smiles. "I only spent a few hours with her, but I liked her very much."

"Where was her body?" Caith says, still sounding unconvinced. "We were all in the audience hall. There was no body."

Eva nods. "Correct. If someone discovered a body, their deception would be moot, and their leverage over you wasted. They destroyed her body, but I promise you, I safely escorted her afterlife entity to its end."

I'm trying to stay with the conversation. I need to figure out what Mingin is up to, but my brain is misfiring.

"Sloan, my grandparents, and Tad have been taken. I still don't understand why."

"Kidnapping is about an exchange of power," Da says. "It can be about leverage to force us into an action or to stop an action or to attain something we have or they think we can get."

"Money?" I say. "Sloan and Tad both control family money and are multi-millionaires."

Da shakes his head. "I don't think that's it, luv. Certainly, money helps when building an evil army, but they have magic on their side and can simply take what they need."

"Are they trying to back us down?" Calum asks. "We're the

strongest force readying for the Culling. Maybe they're trying to cripple us before the fight begins."

"Possibly." Da's gaze falls on Shannon standing at the back door with one of the babes cradled in her arms. "Kinu, would ye mind takin' the monkeys into the house so Shannon can come to me? I need to hold her fer a moment while we work out the situation."

"Of course." She brushes Meg's hair back from her face. "We need to change some bums anyway, don't we, kids?"

"I wants to stay with Granda," Jackson says. "If the bad guys come back, I wants to help."

"Aye, yer a great help, Jackson," Da says. "Because of that, I need ye to go in with yer mam and keep her and the girls safe and happy. I don't expect the bad guys to come back, but if they do, ye'll need to be with them so ye can sound the alarm and keep them safe."

Jackson's face pinches as he considers that. "Okay, Granda. I can do that."

"I have no doubt, lad. Yer a Cumhaill, after all."

Jackson gives a sharp nod and takes Kinu's hand. "Come inside, Mommy. It's safe in there."

Kinu sends Aiden a look, and it's not a happy one.

I'm sorry, he mouths.

I feel bad for him. Of course, Kinu doesn't want these kinds of moments influencing her children's lives, but it's not Aiden's fault.

If anything, it's mine.

I'm the one who opened this whole druid can of worms, and I'm the one who's going to fix it.

"What's our move?" Dillan asks.

"You can take us home," Kimne says. "Our young are safe and, if what you say is true, our queen is gone. Nothing is holding us in the chaos of this world save the prospect of vengeance."

He's right. "Dionysus? Can you escort the yeti back to their compound? They've been affected enough by this madness. Eva? Maybe you could go too in case they have questions about the queen and what happened?"

She scans us, and I know where her mind is going.

"I promise we won't be rushing off and getting ourselves into battles just yet. You have time to go and be back to be our guardian."

"All right," she says. "But I'm holding you to your word on that, Fi."

"We'll stay put. Both of you hurry back. We'll figure out our next steps, and hopefully, be ready to roll by the time you return."

"Wonderful. I'll get the children ready to leave." She shifts her weight toward the treehouse and bursts into a white dove. A few flaps of her wings and she's back to being herself and stepping into our home away from home.

As she gets the yeti young ready to leave, Kimne turns to me. He extends his hand and squeezes mine with a surprising gentleness considering his size and strength. "I wish I could say it was a pleasure spending the day with you, Fiona."

"I wish you could too. I'm sorry the evil of our world spilled over onto yours."

"I am as well."

"If there's ever anything I can do for you or your people, don't hesitate to let us know."

"How would I do that?"

I run my fingers over my silver pendant and smile at Dionysus. "Tarzan? Might you have another one of these magical call buttons lying around that the yeti community could have for safekeeping?"

Dionysus arches a brow and smiles. "For you, I suppose I could scrounge up another."

"Thank you." I release Kimne's hand and step in to hug him. Damn, he's tall. I barely get my arms around his hips, but I squeeze him before stepping back. "Be safe, big guy. When we catch up with Mingin and Melanippe, we'll be sure to let you know how that goes."

"You do that. We might not want to involve ourselves in the wars of man, but that doesn't mean we don't wish to hear of justice served."

With that settled, Dionysus holds out his hand, and the yeti are gone.

***

While we sort through the aftermath of what's happened, Da takes a moment with Shannon, Emmet snuggles Ciara, and Dillan waits for Eva to return.

I would normally agree with simply deleting the part about Dillan and Eva getting close, but we're doing a full accounting of who's where and highlighting who *isn't* to ramp up the intensity.

I'm achingly aware that my plus-one is in the hands of a maniacal murderer and his traitorous bitch girlfriend.

"Da says kidnapping is an exchange of power," I say to Calum and Aiden. "If not Tad's and Sloan's money, we have to assume it's more personal."

"Mingin is in Riordan's body," Calum says. "It could be personal to him that his son isn't part of his crazy quest for evil."

"Maybe," Aiden says, "but from what Tad has always said, I get the feeling there's no real ties between the two."

"Maybe they're telling us to back off, or they'll take it out on our loved ones," Calum says. "Anyone who knows us knows that's an important factor in our lives."

"True, but I think it's something else," I say.

"Something like what?" Calum asks.

"We know Mingin and Melanippe hooked up with Yvain. What if this is about the grimoire?"

Aiden frowns. "You think they're going to ransom our loved ones for Morgan le Fey's dark grimoire?"

"It makes sense. In fact, it makes the *most* sense. Melanippe and I were sorta friends. She helped us rescue Granda and the other Elders of the Druid Order. She knows my tie to my grandparents, she knows I'm in love with Sloan, and if Yvain's in on this, she likely knows I have the grimoire."

"We talked about this as a pinch point last week with Merlin." Da joins us. "Ye removed the location from yer memory, didn't ye, *mo chroi*?"

"I'd like to say we did, but life got busy, and Sloan wanted time to set more wards on the location first."

"Did he do that?"

"He did, yes. He finished that right before we came here for the birthday party."

"Do you think they'll torture Sloan to find out where the grimoire is?" Emmet asks.

Calum and Dillan throw him a look.

The idea that Mingin and Melanippe have Sloan and might be handing him over to Yvain for torture and interrogation guts me. I was the one who brought that stupid grimoire into our lives. It shouldn't be him that pays the price.

"He'll be fine." Da cups my jaw and swipes my cheek with his thumb. "Sloan's as tough and smart as any man I've ever met, and he'll figure out a way to keep himself and everyone else safe."

I hear what he's saying and believe him, still… "What about Gran and Granda? I should never have dragged them into this."

Da scowls. "If ye remember, they were the ones who dragged *us* into this. I walked away from this life fer some very valid reasons—one of which was keepin' my family out of harm's way. They bypassed my wishes and pulled ye into the danger, not the other way around."

"You can't seriously blame them for this, can you?" Calum asks. "Granda was dying."

Da chuffs. "Och, no. I'm not talking about blame, son. I'm

talkin' about responsibility. I'll not let Fi take the lion's share of the guilt. There's plenty of it to go around."

Dionysus snaps back from the yeti compound with Eva and joins us. "If I get a vote, I say the blame falls squarely at the feet of the enemy. Whether or not Lugh and Lara brought Fi into druid life or she brought the grimoire here, none of this would be happening without the evil intent of others."

Dillan drapes a heavy arm across Eva's shoulder and kisses her cheek. "So, the question is, how do we get them back?"

"We track Sloan's Claddagh." I grin. "If he's spelled his to find mine, it stands to reason it might work the same way in reverse, doesn't it?"

Cue the blank looks of no one seems to know.

My phone buzzes and I check the incoming message. "Okay, Wallace says Ahren is stable, and Samuel and Quon Shen are asking about what happened. I'm going to get them, then talk to Wallace about tracking Sloan's ring. He's an Elder of the Order. He should know how to do that, shouldn't he?"

"It was Dora who helped Sloan with the locator spell in the first place," Calum says. "You should probably start there."

That sounds logical.

"Okay, Dionysus, if you don't mind—"

"I don't, Jane. Whatever you need."

I reach over and squeeze his hand. "I need a ride to Stonecrest Castle to catch up Samuel and the others on what's happened, then to speak to Wallace about his son's kidnapping. At the same time, if one of you could contact Merlin and see if he's available, maybe Dionysus can go get him and bring him here to help."

"On it." Dillan pulls out his phone.

"Consider it done," Dionysus says. "Who all is coming and who's staying?"

In the end, Calum, Dillan, and Eva decide to come with me, and Aiden, Emmet, and Ciara decide to stay with Da and the family.

"Ye'll not go off and do anythin' stupid without us." Da points at me.

"No. I promise. I'll only do stupid things when you're there."

That gets a hint of a smile out of him, but he forces it. He pulls me against his chest and kisses my forehead. "Fionn chose ye to represent because yer the one with the strongest natural druid talent. Yer instincts are strong, and yer gonna find a way through this that brings everyone home safe. I believe that to the marrow of my bones, *mo chroi.*"

"Then I'll believe it too because I happen to think you're always right."

He chuckles. "Now that's a lie and a big one at that. Ye absolutely do *not* think that."

I chuckle. "Maybe not always but when you're telling me how marvelous I am, for sure then." I give him one last squeeze and back away. "Okay. Let's get this done. We have people to bring home safe."

CHAPTER FIFTEEN

The clinic at Stonecrest Castle has become a regular stop in my druid journey. I wish I could say that's a good thing, but it's not. The only good thing about it is that Wallace Mackenzie is a marvel at what he does, and he's patched up me and mine more times than I can count.

Sloan gets his affinity for healing from him.

I try not to let thoughts of Sloan creep into my heart, but it's tough. Last year when the witches hexed him, I separated my emotions from what we needed to do.

I have to do that again.

I need to stay focused on what I can do and not get drawn into the what-ifs of worry.

"Fi." Samuel looks up from where he's sitting on the couch in the clinic's waiting area. His eyes are back to normal, and I'm pleased to see he's whole and healthy. "Melanippe and Mingin—"

I step over and sit in the armchair opposite him. "I know. You tried to tell us we portaled them away, but we didn't figure it out until it was too late."

"Are they gone?"

I nod. "They've made off with my grandparents, Sloan, and our friend Tad."

"Wasn't that the son of the man who gave himself over to Mingin?"

"That's him. We haven't figured out if taking him was part of the plan or a coincidence, but either way, he's one of the four."

"Do you think he might be working with them?"

I wave that off. Dillan and Calum back me up. "No. No way. He and his dad weren't close, but it's gutted him since it all happened."

"Dark Riordan tried to kill him when he first became Mingin's marionette," Calum adds, lowering himself to sit on the arm of the couch.

"Yeah, there's that," I add. "Dark Riordan hunted Tad through the forest like a wolf on a rabbit. Tad figured out Mingin had taken him over and tried to intervene, thinking his father was possessed."

"He wasn't?"

"No. Riordan chose it and tried to kill Tad like he did his wife."

Quon Shen whistles through his teeth as he joins us. He's just pulled on his shirt and is doing up the buttons. "Quite a keeper, that one."

"Yeah, and add that to the allure of a homicidal tainted soul, and you've got a real catch," Dillan says.

"I'd like to catch him," I say. "Any chance you guys have a line on how to track him?"

Samuel frowns. "We can track their evil energy signature if we're in proximity, but it's not a homing beacon. We have to have a starting point."

"I think that's where *I* come in." Merlin strides into the clinic with Dionysus. "I heard what happened. I'm so sorry, cookie."

"What's happened?" Wallace comes out with Ahren…who still looks awful even after Wallace's care.

"Dude. Tell me you don't feel as bad as you look," I say. "'Cause you look like shit."

Ahren grins. "And to think I missed you, Fi."

I hug him. "I'm glad you've stopped the shake-rattle-and-roll, but seriously, maybe you need to rest and sit this one out."

"And miss all the fun? No way."

"Then sit before you fall and I'll catch you up. Wallace, you too. There's news, and it's not good. You should sit too."

Once everyone is seated, I start from the top and bring everyone up to date. "So, I think if Sloan spelled our rings so he can track me, I should be able to reverse engineer it to locate him. Or, at least, I hope that's possible."

Merlin nods. "It's more than possible. I can do that. My only question is what then? We find them, Melanippe and Mingin, and possibly Yvain. They have four of ours captured and likely immobilized somehow...and then what? What's your plan of attack?"

I drop my head and run my fingers through my hair. "I'm barely stringing coherent thoughts together, here. Track the ring and find them. That's my idea."

Merlin nods. "Then we need to come up with a second part to the idea so we have a plan."

I lean back and close my eyes. "Not it. Somebody come up with something inspiring. I'm all used up."

Over the next hour, Merlin works with the Hunter-gods, my brothers, Eva, and Wallace. They elaborate on, mold, and reform the idea of tracking the others through the magic of Sloan's ring into a plan.

"Do you honestly think it'll work?" I ask. "Just say yes no matter what. I want to be lied to if necessary."

Merlin chuckles and pulls me against his chest. "It'll work, Fi.

You've led the charge enough for all of us that we can pick up the slack on this one and bring you a win when you need it."

"Awesome. Thanks."

I check the expressions of my brothers. As much as I don't want to hear bad news, I need to be ready for what's coming. Reading their take on things raises my hopes. They look serious but not overly anxious.

Even Dillan looks more calm delight than tortured night. That's a good sign.

"It's going to work out, Fi." Wallace steps in beside me and laces his fingers with mine. "I realized how strong Sloan had become when I started visiting him in Toronto. Maybe he'd always had it in him, but I believe yer love brought it to the fore. He's a smart, driven, resourceful young man and he will do whatever he needs to do to ensure yer grandparents are safe and they can all get back home where they belong."

"I believe that with everything in me and I need that to happen. I just found Gran, Granda, and Sloan. There's so much we haven't done yet."

"Ye'll get yer chance, I have no doubts about that."

I hope so.

Drawing a deep breath, I fortify myself and give myself a kick in the ass. "Time to get things done."

"Yeah, it is," Quon Shen says. He steps in close and leans even closer. "You never mentioned you know Merlin. What the hell, woman? That's not something you keep secret from your best friends."

I chuckle. "Sorry. He hadn't gone public yet, so his presence wasn't my story to share."

"But he is Merlin, right? *The* Merlin?"

I nod. "Yep. The same. The living legend of spells, stilettos, and stage."

I lose him a bit on that one, but that's fine.

It's good to keep people guessing.

Gaining some distance from the water dragon of our spectral plane group, I join the conversation between Merlin, Eva, and my brothers. "Are we almost ready?"

Merlin nods and hands me back my Claddagh band. "Everything's set. One quick stop at Lugh's and Lara's to gather the others and we'll be on the attack."

"Excellent. The sooner we leave, the sooner we bring everyone home."

"From your lips to this god's ears." Dionysus taps the side of his head. "If everyone would gather around and put a hand in, we'll get this party started."

I smile and do as he asks. Technically, Dionysus doesn't need physical contact to portal a group like Sloan and Nikon do, but that's the way we roll. I think he craves physical contact, even if it's platonic affection.

Considering how many centuries he longed for genuine affection and got denied, I'll never disappoint him.

If he wants a hug, I'll give him one.

If he calls for hands in, that's what we'll do.

My hand covers his, followed by Calum, Quon Shen, Dillan, Eva, Ahren, Merlin, and Samuel. When Dionysus tops those with his other hand, the circuit is complete, and we snap back to the treehouse living room.

Ciara and Emmet are on the couch chatting and startle a bit as our group materializes.

"*Annnd* you're back," Emmet says. "Hey guys, glad to see you're doing better."

I scan the room and ensure everyone knows and remembers everyone else. "Where's Da?"

"In their wee love shack," Ciara says.

Emmet nods. "Yeah, I think knowing Shannon was in danger was too much for the old guy. He's not bouncing back well from Brendan's loss."

Dillan scowls. "And what? We are? Don't be dumb."

Emmet rolls his eyes. "Don't be a dick. You know what I mean."

"We do." I cut them off. "Da is understandably sensitive. Shannon was here when Mingin and Melanippe swept through. He lost Brendan, and he's not up to losing anyone else."

"Yer right about that, *mo chroi*. So, if ye don't mind, I'd rather get started on the rescuin' part of the plan and not dwell on what we'll lose if we don't get them back." There's an edge to Da's tone that I don't think I deserve.

It was the boys who were stirring up the trouble.

I was calming the waters.

Still, there's no use arguing about it.

I stride over to the cookie jar and snag a few home-baked delights. I need a sugar hit to take the edge off my day. "We have a solid plan on where to start. Merlin's confident he can take us to Sloan by tracking the magic infused in our Claddagh bands. Then it's a matter of getting them away from the opposition and home."

"The three of us are on Mingin with Fi." Merlin points at Emmet and Samuel. "Dillan, Eva, and Quon Shen are on Melanippe. If Yvain is there, Calum, Aiden, Ciara, and Ahren are on him."

"What about me?" Manx says.

"You and Bruin are wild cards." I make things up as I go. "Whatever needs doing to ensure we get them out of there is your task. You're in charge of all the things we can't plan for."

"And Dionysus?" Da asks.

"He's the only one we can be sure can still portal," I say. "He'll disrupt any illusions or glamors and go straight to evacuation."

Da seems to agree with that. "It seems ye've thought things through."

That's good to hear. Da is a great strategic planner. All his years of organizing beat cops and detectives on the job have made him uniquely suited to run an empowered task force of fighters.

"Wallace is waiting, ready for us to arrive at the clinic." I envision the outcome I want. "I promised him he would see his son very soon and I won't let these people make me a liar."

Da extends his hand and smiles. "Then let's go make yer promise into a reality, shall we?"

I lace my fingers with his and squeeze. "Yeah, let's do that."

Our rescue force might be an eclectic group, but I've never been so thankful for my friends and family in my life. I wish Nikon were here. Not only do he and I fight well together, but he also keeps me smiling...and often chuckling when things get difficult.

During the planning session back at the clinic, I called Papu and made sure Nikon arrived after being killed by Mingin's and Melanippe's attack.

He had.

Papu promised me he's safe and on the mend.

Thank the goddess for that.

Da gives my hand another squeeze and meets my gaze. I release our connection, ready to get this over with. If it's the last thing I ever do, I'll make sure our enemies regret taking my family hostage.

With Dionysus supplying the power of travel and Merlin steering the ship, we arrive *en masse* at our destination. I'm not sure what I was expecting, a warehouse, another compound in the forest, or maybe an ancient castle with ramparts and a moat.

This is none of those.

We're standing on the polished deck of a luxury yacht with nothing but the flat, blue plane of ocean stretching out on all sides and a gentle roll and sway under our feet.

"We're on a boat?" Emmet asks.

"I think when you're this big, they call you a ship." Dillan waggles his brows.

"Whether it's a boat or a ship, let's hope it's where we need to be," I say.

"It is." Merlin glances across our group. "The spell to follow the signature of your ring is elegant and inventive. I think the man who enchanted them in the first place was a bit of a genius."

I chuckle, knowing that the man who enchanted them for Sloan in the first place was him.

Da scans past the group to where the ship rises three stories above. "There's an awful lot of ground to cover. Melanippe and Mingin could be hiding anywhere."

"I believe that's where we come in," Samuel says. "The three of us are quite adept at tracking the dark energy of the two of them. We'll do that, and with any luck, they won't be anywhere near your family and friends. If we can engage with them, you'll be able to liberate the hostages without a fight."

"Yvain might be here as well," I add. "We can't forget he's in the mix."

Samuel swallows, frowning as if he's got a bad taste in his mouth. "No. We can't. Be ready for anything because that bastard is a nightmare."

I imagine he is.

He was a powerful wizard back in the ninth century when we first encountered him. I can only imagine twelve hundred years of hating Merlin and me and planning his revenge has soured his soul even more.

I release Bruin, and he materializes on the deck next to Manx. "You two are on point for the seek and rescue part of this mission. Between Manx's companion bond and both of your senses of smell, I hope you'll have an edge to draw you through this giant floating maze so you can find everyone and get outta here."

I scrub Bruin's boxy cheek and rub the long tufts of Manx's ears between my fingers. "Find them, boys. Find them, free them, and take them home."

Nothing more needs to be said about that.

By the cautious looks in the expressions around me, everyone is wondering and worried about the same thing. What have Yvain and Mingin done to them in the hours since they took them?

Samuel and Quon Shen lead the offensive group through the first door we come to and take the stairs up toward the next deck. Merlin, Emmet, Dillan, Eva, and I follow as planned.

Da, Calum, Aiden, Ciara, and Ahren go with Manx and Bruin as the defensive group. They head down the stairs and go below deck.

In a perfect world, Yvain won't be here, and they'll find our people and solely act as a rescue squad.

For once, let this be a perfect world.

I send that wish up to the heavens and hope that even if the goddess isn't listening at the moment that maybe the three Fates might be.

Honestly, I'll take any help I can get.

I've seen ships like these in movies and on shows like *Lifestyles of the Rich and Famous*, but it's a bit of a mind-boggle to take it all in. As gorgeous as it is, who needs this kind of luxury and this much space?

My entire family could live on this ship and still not see one another for days.

"I wonder who owns this ship," Quon Shen says.

"I wonder when their bodies will wash onto shore," Merlin says. "I have a bad feeling they received an unexpected sea burial."

Yet another reason we need to take down Mingin and Melanippe. They really are the Bonnie and Clyde of our time if that infamous couple were immortal and powered by the evil of our world.

"Maybe it's not as bad as all that." I hope there's a possibility

I'm right. "Maybe the owners and the crew are simply bound and tied somewhere below deck."

Emmett casts me a halfhearted smile and nods. "Yeah, maybe."

I don't look at Dillan because I know well enough his expression would destroy any illusion of hope I'm grasping for.

We reach the top of the second flight of stairs and head toward the front of the ship. Our route takes us past a business center, a spa, the gymnasium, and through a grand living space.

I'm intently focused on the warming of my tattoo against my back but am still mesmerized by the onyx and marble countertops, the area rugs over hardwood floors, and the plush blue velvety captain's chairs around an oval coffee table.

"Damn, is that a fireplace?" I follow Dillan's gesture to the marble hearth past the bar. "This place is stupid swank."

"It's a little over the top," I say.

Emmet snorts. "Who are we kidding? We're totally jonesing for another family Caribbean birthday bash on one of these, aren't we?"

"Yeah, sorta," I say.

Dillan nods. "Point to you, bro. I am now."

I'm about to mention that Dillan's birthday is coming up when my shield flares to life. My back bursts into the singe of molten fire and I spin, taking in the room.

"*Tough as Bark.*" I call my armor forward at the same time Birga appears in my palm. "Here we go, boys and girls. Let's do this."

CHAPTER SIXTEEN

"Well, if it isn't Little Red and the big bad wolf." Melanippe steps through the doorway to join us in the living area on the third deck. She's an extremely tall, brunette woman who is as fierce in battle as she is stunning. "And here my love thought you wouldn't be able to find us so quickly."

"You always did underestimate me."

She tosses her head back and laughs. "No, little girl. It was the four of you who underestimated *me*."

I can't argue that. "Yeah, you snowed us until the moment Mingin was free, and you flipped the switch and showed your traitorous colors."

She shrugs, unrepentant. "Don't make me out to be the bad guy. I did what I had to do for love. I'm sure we're not so different. What wouldn't you do to spare your Irishman a lifetime of torment?"

She steps deeper into the room, and two thugs follow, dragging Sloan in between them. Frick and Frack have their hold hooked around his arms and are dragging his legs along the floor.

My heart lurches.

I knew they wouldn't be kind to him but...

"Is he dead?" A firm grip tightens around each of my arms. I blink and turn to find Dillan holding me on one side and Emmet on my other.

"There's no way he's dead, Fi. There would be no bargaining if they killed him."

"Your brother's right. He's unconscious so he can't portal to safety. I need my little pawns in play, and for that to happen, they need to stay where I want them."

"Your pawn? He's been your punching bag."

"Cuts and bruises heal," she says. "There are many things that don't heal, so you should be thankful."

"Thankful..."

Dillan's grip on my arm is pinching me hard. "Lock it down and keep your eye on the end game."

Right. If Melanippe is here, we're halfway to our goal of engaging with her and Mingin while Da, Quon Shen, and their group get Gran, Granda, and Tad out of here. Sloan is alive, and he's mostly upright.

"See how the suffering of your love tears at your soul? I had to live with that for an eternity."

No matter how much Melanippe tries to impress upon me that we are one—we're not. I would never sacrifice the good of the world for a lying, murderous psychopath no matter how self-destructive I felt.

"What do you want?" I ask. "Is this revenge? Is it to get us to back off and stop hunting you down? Or is it just how the two of you get off on a Wednesday night?"

She grins. "So suspicious, Little Red. We don't have to end up on opposite sides. There was a time we worked well as a team. I'd even go so far as to say we were becoming friends. We could be that again and more."

I roll my eyes. "Spare me the rah-rah pep talk. You killed one of my for reals best friends. There's no coming back from that."

A cruel smile curls the sides of her mouth. "I never saw what you liked in Nikon of Rhodes."

"I suppose you wouldn't. Selflessness and loyalty aren't really your thing."

Dillan raises a hand and interrupts. "This girl-talk is entertaining and all, but can we move things along? Irish looks like he might need medical assistance and I for one feel bad for the guy. Pulped and pureed isn't a good look for him. He's more prep school primp."

"Here's the thing." Melanippe grins. "I'm not giving him back to you. This is me showing you what damage you've already caused to someone you love simply by being stubborn. What you need to do now is tell me where the *Eochair Prana* is, and we'll give you back your elders and be on our way."

"I'm sorry, what?" Not only is it hilarious how she brutalized the pronunciation of Morgan le Fey's ensorcelled tome, I'm also prodding the bear to see how anxious she is to gauge my reaction.

"I think you heard me."

"Oh, I heard you. I was laughing at you. You should call it Morrigan's spellbook and not butcher its authentic name. I would've thought with your ancient status you could've pronounced that better."

"You're not taking me seriously."

"No. I am. I can't help you."

"Huh, I thought you'd be more eager to comply. Well, he's not my only hostage. If you won't deal for him, I'll move on to one of the others." She glances over at Frick and nods.

A glint of silver catches the overhead light and a dagger swings in a lethal arc. A deafening roar erupts through the air and—

Bruin materializes in a wild rage.

With one fierce swipe, he brandishes his long, chestnut claws and rips five long trenches through Frick's chest and belly. Killer

Clawbearer stands several feet over even the freakishly tall Amazon, and she has the good sense to look shaken.

While she's distracted, I draw back and throw my spear with everything I have.

Birga is inspired as she sails through the air and catches Frack in the chest. The impact of her piercing his sternum sends a horrid *crack* of bone through the air.

I don't even wince.

The moment of her shock is short-lived, and I ready for the incoming force. Melanippe rushes forward and grabs Sloan herself.

Instead of engaging in the attack, she takes a few quick steps back, and the door to this section of the ship slides shut.

I race past Frack slumped and bleeding on the lovely ivory rug. As I pass, I grab Birga's staff and—

Get nowhere.

Dammit, she's lodged in there good.

Dillan and Samuel work on opening the door, and I knock Frack over and use my foot on his chest to brace his body. Birga doesn't want to come free.

As a necromancer weapon, she loves feeding off the blood of her victims. She loves it even more if they're also empowered, and she can drink in their energy.

That's not what's happening here.

That guy was run-of-the-mill muscle. Nothing special in the human enhancement department.

By the time I get Birga free, Bruin has bashed through the doorway and created a new, wider opening.

"Great job, Bear." Dillan kicks away the fallen framework and drywall to clear the path. "You should consider a career in home renos if the whole mythical battle bear gig ever dries up on you."

Bruin chuckles and smashes through a set of sliding glass doors. He's a bull in a china shop now.

"We *can* still open the ones that'll open," I say.

A cold gust of ocean air smacks me in the face, and I scowl as I scan the outdoor platform. I have no idea where this ship is sailing but judging by the chill in the air and the blackness of the water, it isn't the Caribbean.

"Up here," Manx says.

We follow the lynx without question.

Manx is in the front of the pack, racing on all fours. He knows Sloan's scent better than anyone. Despite the several directions we could take, it's Sloan's long-time animal companion for the win.

"That's far enough!" Melanippe snaps.

A purple bolt of power shoots past my head and explodes against an invisible field twenty feet in front of me. The heat and power of the magical energy tingle across my skin and raise the hair on my arms.

Melanippe smiles from behind her bubble of protection. "Now, now, Samuel. That wasn't nice."

Samuel catches up to me and has the next bolt of magic snapping in his palm. "You're right. You should come out from behind your screen, and I'll apologize properly."

I examine Sloan's limp form. He's still unconscious and now in the clutches of two more minions dressed and built the same as the last two.

I shall call them Mutt and Jeff.

"Where are you running off these clones? Did you tell them what happened to their clone brothers?"

Melanippe ignores me and glares. "The answer is simple here, Fiona. Tell me where the Morrigan's grimoire is, and I'll give you back your love. Deny me, and he'll plummet and drown."

I shout, racing forward until I hit the invisible barrier preventing me from getting to Sloan and killing her. Helpless to get to him, I watch as Mutt and Jeff lift Sloan and push his upper body out to hang over the rail. I stare at Mutt's fisted grip bunching the front of Sloan's shirt.

"Don't!" I shout, slamming my hand against the solid shield in front of me. "I swear to the goddess if you kill him there is no way you'll ever get your hands on the *Eochair Prana*."

"So, you admit you have it?"

I look around and shout up at the open air above. "Do you hear me, Yvain? If she harms Sloan, there is no way you'll ever get your mother's spellbook."

"But we're not finished playing our hand," Mingin says, his voice distorted. He steps out onto the outdoor platform one level up and on the other side of the ship.

A rush of queasy hits and I barf in my mouth. Hokie-doodle, he is *soooo* gross. The level of dark and dastardly he gives off is even worse than the last time I saw him…which I would totes mention if my focus didn't remain solidly locked on saving Sloan's life.

"You don't need to play your hand because it's not your hand to play. Despite what he might have told you, I don't have what Yvain wants. I'm surprised you'd let him highjack your quest for world domination to settle a score he's not man enough to handle himself."

Mingin grins, and it twists his face up in a macabre distortion of expression.

It's not a good look for him.

"I do nothing without reasons. Trust me. I'm not a pawn. I'm the one playing the board." He gestures behind him, and Granda floats forward.

Dillan and Emmet curse, shifting position to address an attack on two fronts. Bruin roars and ghosts out at the same time we're slammed with a magical pulse. I stagger, and Bruin's thrown back onto the deck in his solid form.

"Rule number one, Little Red. Your bear must remain in full view at all times, or our conversation ends, and all of you as well as our guests die."

I don't think even he has that kind of juice, but I can't risk it.

They've bound Granda's hands behind his back, and he's wriggling and fighting against the spell of restraint. Despite his struggles, he doesn't seem to be getting anywhere.

Without his hands, he can't defend himself. If they throw him into the water, his chance of survival is no better than an unconscious Sloan.

"Where is Yvain? This is all his doing, amirite? If he doesn't have the balls to face me and ask me himself, this conversation isn't happening."

Mingin smiles. "This isn't a negotiation. This is when you do as told or everyone you love dies."

"I realize that's a possibility, but like I told the Amazon, I don't have the Morrigan's spellbook, and I can't tell you where it is."

"Can't or won't?" Melanippe says. "Last chance, druid. Tell us what we want to know, or loverboy goes overboard."

"I can't do it. No matter how much you threaten Sloan, Tad, my grandparents, or anyone else I care about the answer will be the same. I can't help you."

"Then this discussion is pointless." Melanippe glances at Mutt and Jeff. "Drop him."

I dive to the side, trying to get around the invisible bubble but it's no use. Before I can get to him, Melanippe's goons release Sloan and drop him into the choppy ocean below.

When I was a kid, my parents took us to Canada's Wonderland to spend a day in the amusement park. I remember watching the cliff divers jump off the perch on the artificial mountain. I thought it was incredibly cool.

I take it back.

There's nothing cool about diving off the side of a luxury yacht and plummeting sixty feet toward the water below.

CHAPTER SEVENTEEN

F *lying.*

In that brief moment when I swan dive over the railing of a massive yacht without a thought, I hang suspended in the air. Then my brain catches up. Gravity takes hold, the sudden drop makes my stomach lurch, and the butterflies of common-sense flutter wildly in my belly.

Falling. That's where I am next.

Falling sixty or maybe seventy to a hundred feet straight down as my hair whips my face and my eyes stream with tears. It's the velocity of the wind blinding me, not actual tears. I don't have the luxury of emotion at the moment.

"Diminish Descent!" I cast the spell toward Sloan, hoping I'm close enough for it to take effect and that there's enough time before impact for it to matter.

"Resilient Sphere!" My attempt to wrap him in a protective bubble fails.

Dammit, my focus is shot.

I don't have time to slow my downward plummet because I need to catch up as much as possible. My armor is still active, so that should take care of the worst of it. Hitting the surface of the water is still going to hurt like hell.

My mind is spinning, searching for a way to save him. I can't prevent it. He's going to hit, and the surface will be like a block of concrete.

"I'm sorry, Birga." Gripping her staff, I propel her down with a power boost to give her some extra *oomph*.

Like the trooper she is, she slices through the air and breaks through the choppy surface. It does nothing to help. Right, it's choppy. No surface tension.

I call her back, my heart pounding.

Sloan is about to collide with the surface when a geyser bursts from the ocean and forms the shape of a hand. It flips upward, catches Sloan's crumpled form in its palm, and lowers him gently into the waves.

Thank the goddess.

I'm not close enough to hitch a ride and hit a few seconds later. The impact is incredible. Even with my armor up, my brains and bones rattle. A thundering rush invades my ears as icy water sucks me down.

My head swims. I fight to stay conscious.

Fucking Melanippe.

Getting pissed helps. I'm angry about the dead yeti queen, about them kidnapping my family, and about throwing Sloan overboard as if he's disposable.

Bubbles tickle my cheeks, and I snap out of it.

Sloan. I can't pass out...I need to find Sloan.

I'm dazed. The sensation isn't uncommon. I do some of my best work under the pressure of brain fog. Forcing my arms to work, I fight against the power of the ocean and figure out which way is up.

It takes a bit, but the confusion starts to clear. I break the surface. Frantically, I search my surroundings, bobbing against the waves as I choke for air.

"Sloan!" Opening my mouth probably isn't the smartest idea because now I'm choking and sputtering.

Where are you, hotness?

I can't see anything.

I dive and search the depths, and there's nothing...nothing but darkness.

Did he go under? No.

There's no way I'm losing him like this.

Something brushes against me, and I jolt to the side and try to see if it's Sloan. It's not. I stick my face into the icy water but see nothing there.

Another bump shifts my leg, and I screech.

It's a shark...I know it.

When a dorsal fin breaks the surface, my scream freezes in my throat. Worst. Fear. Ever.

I hate *Jaws*. The boys watched it when we were kids and told me it was too scary for me. Stubborn as I was, I watched it anyway.

I couldn't even take a bath until I was a teenager.

The throaty hack of someone coughing snaps me out of my panic. I tread water, swishing my hands to turn to find the source. There are a couple of fins circling Sloan.

I'll be damned if sharks get to eat my boyfriend.

Leaning forward, I start paddling. What's that safety fix? Punching them in the nose? That was sharks, right?

I'm a decent swimmer, but with the swell and bob of the ocean, it feels like I'm getting nowhere...until something grabs the back of my shirt and starts dragging me. What the hell?

Sharks don't corral their prey, do they?

I twist to see who is driving my water taxi and am relieved beyond words. "Flipper."

My dolphin companion lets out a long series of yips and clicks, and I take that as him introducing himself.

"Thanks," I say as he swings me into the same circle as Sloan and releases me. "I'll be sure to leave you a tip for your troubles."

Sloan has a hold on one of Flipper's dolphin friends and is treading water. "Are ye all right, *a ghra*? What happened? How'd we end up takin' a swim?"

"Long story. Yeah, I'm all right as long as you are—which is debatable because you look like shit—but assuming you're alive and well, you were tossed overboard as a powerplay by Melanippe. Naturally, I dove in after you without a moment's thought."

"Naturally," he says, reaching across the water to pull me closer. "Thank you for saving me yet again."

I shake my head, treading water right in front of him. "I can't take the credit. Do you know Hand from the *Addams Family*? Picture his magical cousin Water Hand. That's who saved you. I crashed beside you and nearly drowned."

He chuckles. "I'm sure that was Merlin. Now, where are Lugh and Lara?"

"I don't know. We need to get back up there and get back in the game. Two to beam up, please."

I reach over so he can take my hand. Only, when he makes the connection, we don't *poof* anywhere. "What's wrong? Are you broken?"

"I don't think so, but Mingin cast a spell on Tad and me to prevent us from portaling. It seems it hasn't dissipated yet."

"Well, that's disappointing. What now?"

"The ship isn't moving too quickly. Maybe we can catch it." Sloan glances around and points at the back of the yacht puttering off without us. "If ye wouldn't mind, friends. It seems we've missed our ride."

The dolphins encircling us sit up, lifting their heads and torsos out of the water. After a second or two, they flick their snouts and give us a happy laugh. Then, they let out a few clicks and circle us to dive.

"Put yer feet together, *a ghra*. They say they'll push us back to the ship."

"You speak dolphin?"

"I'm a druid. If ye focus, I'm sure ye'd be able to communicate with them too."

I love the way he says things so matter-of-factly. Of course, I speak dolphin. Doesn't everyone? I'm laughing to myself as something pushes against my feet, and I pay closer attention to locking my knees to make this easier for them.

As we skip across the surface of the water, several things dawn on me at once. One: people pay a lot of money to have an interactive dolphin experience like this. Two: now that the excitement of saving Sloan is over, I'm cold and shivering. Three: my family and friends are still on that floating hotel, and I have no idea how the battle is going.

Sloan and I make our way to the ship and get dropped off when we each grab hold of one of the two ladders running up the flat slope at the back of the yacht.

Water is churning in a steady froth of white foam from the engines, but the dolphin brigade comes in from the side, and we're able to get our hands on the bottom rungs to pull ourselves aboard.

Dolphin power for the win!

I love to portal, but that was fun. If we were in Caribbean waters and lives weren't at stake, it would've been even better.

But we're not. And they are.

Sloan and I climb the slope and flop onto the wooden deck when we get to the top. It takes us a moment to catch our breath. Then I roll onto my hands and knees to get back in motion.

My clothes are soaked and heavy, and there's no graceful way to sneak up on someone when your sneakers are sloshing, and your clothes make *plop* and *smack* sounds with every step.

"Where were you being held?" I wring out the length of my hair into a puddle on the deck.

"Below deck near the bow."

"And the bow is…"

"At the front."

"Right, because it would be much too convenient to get there undetected if it was at the back of the boat and we were close by."

Sloan flashes me a patient smile, and I realize how much this ordeal has taken out of him. "Are you truly all right, hotness? You got pretty badly beaten up, and I know you'd take the hits for Gran and Granda if you could."

He leans forward and kisses my nose. "Nothin' that a quiet weekend and a bit of soup and TLC can't fix. What I don't understand is what this is all about."

"You can't make sense of cray."

"That's just it. I don't think any of this was crazy."

"What do you mean?"

"I mean, Melanippe and Mingin were askin' about the dark grimoire."

I pull my shirt from my body and wring it out as we walk. "Yeah, I figure they want it for Yvain and also to make the dark side much more powerful if they get it."

Sloan nods. "That makes perfect sense. So, they kidnap us to make either me or ye talk. I didn't, and I'm guessin' ye didn't."

"Nope."

"So why then would they throw their best leverage point into the ocean so the only other person who knows where the book is hidden follows? Then, if we assume they didn't mean for ye to jump, why would they leave the two of us in the water and sail away? It seems counterintuitive to them gettin' what they want."

It always amazes me how Sloan's mind works. He boils down logic like it's nothing. I would eventually get there, but right now my mind is busy worrying about my grandparents and cranky about being cold.

It would've taken me ages before I thought to start asking the questions about the motives of our foes.

"Did you see Yvain here at all?" I ask.

He shakes his head. "No. Apart from yer Hunter-god friends sayin' they saw him with Melanippe and Mingin, I haven't seen nor heard any more about him."

"So, if I follow your questions with mine... Why wouldn't Yvain want to interrogate us himself? Even if he doesn't know for sure if we have Morgana's grimoire, he knows we were the last people who did have it. You'd think he would want to beat it out of us or something equally violent."

Sloan's head tilts to the side, and his gaze goes soft.

I fall silent. I know this look. He's gone from his logical expression of insight and wisdom and has now transitioned into the heavy lifting look of figuring out the mysteries of the ancient world.

A gust of wind hits us, and I stiffen and clasp his wrist. *"Internal Warmth."* As heat blooms beneath my skin, I start to thaw and unclench.

Much better.

I bask in the influx of heat and take a moment to be thankful for my druid powers.

Sloan curses, and it breaks my moment.

"What? What did you figure out?"

"It's another feckin' misdirect." He grabs my hand and tugs me back into motion. "Melanippe and Mingin weren't questionin' us. They were distractin' us. They kidnapped yer friends knowin' it'd draw ye into the fight. Then they took yer lover and yer grandparents and knew ye'd be so focused on gettin' them back ye'd miss the real play."

"Which is what?"

"I'd bet my balls the reason Yvain isn't here is that he's in

Toronto. If I'm right, he's searchin' close to home knowin' that between Merlin and the two of us, we would want to keep an eye on the wicked tome."

Nonononono.

"Did any of your alarms go off to tell us he's there?"

He shrugs. "Mingin shorted out my powers. I'm officially offline."

"Crap. And Yvain can sense his mother's magical signature. Do you think he'll be able to find it?"

"I don't know." We slosh up a set of stairs and jog along the outside rail toward the front of the ship. "It's sealed in Merlin's box to avoid magical leakage, and it's five hundred feet beneath the ground."

Exactly. It's not the most secure hiding spot, but it's also not sitting on a shelf somewhere in our house.

Even so, I have a very bad feeling Sloan is right. "We need to get back."

"I still can't portal, and I'm guessing neither can Tad. We'll have to find Nikon or Dionysus."

"They killed Nikon back at Gran's. He hasn't come back from regenerating in Rhodes yet."

Sloan's scowl deepens. "Then Dionysus. Tell me he's still here with us somewhere."

"As far as I know, he is… Except, we can't leave everyone here with Melanippe and Mingin and take the only person who can portal away from the fight."

"No, we can't. Whatever is happenin' in Toronto will have to wait until we end what's happenin' here. One disaster at a time."

Except the disaster in Toronto could mean a huge power shift toward Team Evil. We're already fighting an uphill battle.

It'll be fine…

I'm sure it will.

Except my instincts say differently. My instincts say Sloan's right again, and we've spent the past two days being led around on a wild goose chase to keep us busy so Yvain can find his mother's dark legacy to evil.

Fuckety-fuck.

My shield flares hot, and I pull back on Sloan's hand, tugging him to an abrupt halt. A split second later, the cabin wall to our left explodes across the deck in front of us.

Lumber and debris fly around as a raging fire spews out over the water. A massive rectangle of flames shoots forty feet off the ship's side and crashes into the water below.

"Was that a couch?"

Inching forward, I peek around the jagged opening and into the ship's interior. Two bolts of blue energy shoot past my head. I call Birga forward and check on Sloan's state of readiness. "Samuel's fighting someone. I should see if I can help. Are you up for it, or do you want to pass and recuperate a bit more?"

Sloan gestures toward the gaping hole in the side of the ship. "Off ye go, Cumhaill. I may not be top-shelf quality today, but I'm sure I can still get the job done in a pinch."

CHAPTER EIGHTEEN

Holy hell. If this was a luxury rental, these people are *soooo* not getting back their damage deposit. Well, if they were alive, that is. Which, knowing Melanippe and Mingin, they aren't. I duck behind the stocked bar and take in the scene. Instead of royal luxury, this yacht now screams ode to post-apocalyptic ruins.

It's quite the transformation.

The renovation work hasn't ended. From what I can tell, there's an all-out, last-man-standing battle going on in the living room between Merlin, Da, Bruin, Samuel, and Dionysus against Mingin.

Then, through what used to be the glass doors leading out to the pool deck, there's another war raging between Ahren, Dillan, Eva, and Calum against Melanippe.

My father casts a quick look over at us as we join the room and relief washes over his expression. "Fi, help Dionysus with the evacuation. We're holdin' our own."

"No doubt." I come out from behind the bar. "Because they're not trying to win. This is a misdirect. Yvain's after the grimoire. He's off searching for it while they're sidetracking us."

Mingin tips his head back and laughs. "Figured that out, did you?"

Damn it. I didn't doubt Sloan's logic, but it sucks that he's right. Throwing my powers into the mix, I jog over to talk to Merlin. "We need to end this and get home."

Merlin blinks at me. "Oh, sorry. Here we are screwing around for the hell of it."

"Your sarcasm is coming along beautifully."

"Your family is rubbing off on me."

"You're welcome." I twist to find the Hunter-gods. "Samuel, what's our best chance to obliterate this asshole on the quick?"

Samuel glances at me and shrugs. "Your guess is as good as mine. He's a toxic fog bound with a corporeal host. My guess... kill the host."

I guess that's an option now.

Several months ago, we decided we couldn't kill the host because we needed to save Riordan. That's no longer a concern. Riordan chose this. He wants to be the Whoopie Goldberg to Mingin's evil Swayze.

Sucks to be him.

Da, Merlin, Samuel, and the others continue to bombard Mingin from all sides, and I search for a way to take him out of the equation quickly.

I admit, between worrying about Sloan and my grandparents, I'm not firing on all pistons. My creative idea cartridge is running on empty.

When in doubt, throwing energy balls is always good. I set my focus and call the power of electricity in the air. Glancing down at my palm, I enhance the pull as my first energy ball forms.

Samuel is throwing magical bolts of energy.

Merlin is zapping Mingin with electrical streams he's calling from the ship's lighting and circuitry.

I call for the dispatched power to come to me, and it responds eagerly. The first law of thermodynamics is the law of conservation of energy. It states energy is neither created nor destroyed—only converted from one form to another.

That's where I come in.

Even as a new druid, I seem to have a natural affinity for energy.

Da and Dillan go at Mingin with a physical attack of staff and daggers but are having trouble getting inside his defenses. I bet they'd have better luck if Riordan weren't a druid.

There must be some kind of magical canceling factor considering our magic and knowledge come from the same source of prana.

Still, this is where we are.

The energy building inside me has the hair on my arms prickling and standing on end. It's gratifying, but I ease up on my call a little. I have what I need, pull my arm back, and make my first pitch.

Mingin grins unaffected and watches me like he's in on some dirty little secret only he knows about.

Such a creeper.

Energy snaps in my cells and I hold out my palm to form another, bigger ball of energy this time. If I were building an energy snowman, the last one would've been his head, but this one is easily his torso.

Thunder rolls overhead and the light from outside clouds over. Great...a thunderstorm is all we need.

Merlin glances over at me. "Release that before you fry us all."

I raise the orb of snapping orange energy and thrust it at Mingin like a basketball chest pass. Again, the energy hits an invisible field and dissipates ineffectively.

My fingers have barely stopped tingling when I have my hands up, dealing with another massive buildup of energy. "Guys? I don't think this is me doing this. Either that or I took too many Flintstone vitamins this morning."

Merlin looks over at me and frowns. "What do you mean, it's not you?"

"I don't know. There's more and more power drawing to me, and I can't seem to shut it off."

"Yer tired, luv." Sloan's worry is thick in his voice. "Maybe yer focus is off."

I throw the next energy ball and barely pay attention where I'm chucking it. "I *am* tired, but I don't think that's what's happening. It feels like my energy valve is stuck open and I need to shut it somehow."

Dillan shifts closer as Da and Sloan turn to me.

"Describe what it feels like, *mo chroi*. Maybe we can help if we know what's happenin'."

I yelp as my fingers burn. The game has now switched from Mingin energy balling to druid hot potato. "It feels like I'm a conduit and not the one in control. I started by calling energy to join the fight, but now it's coming too much too fast, and I can't slow it down."

My fingers burn, and I curse, dropping the energy ball right in front of me.

Sloan leaps back to escape my widening radius of damage. "I think yer right, luv. I've never known a druid who gets burned by their spell."

"No, that shouldn't happen," Merlin says. "Maybe use your shaman powers to close that door. If you're a conduit, try to break the circuit."

Another long rumble overhead brings my focus back to the darkening skies outside.

"I have a bad feeling I'm about to be made into a spinning rooster on the top of a weathervane."

In fact, it's more than a feeling. I know it with everything in me that the environmental energy building up is coming for me.

"Niall and Sloan, cover me." Merlin breaks free from where he hunkered down to battle against our soulless foe. He rushes toward me, but even he can't get much closer than ten feet. *"Dissipate Energy."*

I feel the power of Merlin's spell wash over me, but aside from a momentary reprieve from my skin burning with pins and needles, it does nothing else.

"Dispel Magic." Merlin casts his spell but again, other than sensing the soothing signature of his power for a brief moment, nothing changes.

"Crap on a cracker, that hurts!" I'm no longer calling energy to build in my palms. Now my palms are shooting a steady stream of fireworks five feet into the air. "Me no likey. Make it stop."

"I'm trying, Fi, but you're right. You're not driving this train. This is Mingin testing your control and toying with you."

I glare at his stupid, spider-webbed face. Man, I hate that jerk. I also hate being the passenger of my magic train. I'm a freakin' engineer.

Fine. If he wants to supercharge me on elemental power, I'll use it to my advantage.

If we can't attack Mingin from the side or front, an attack from above might work.

I grit my teeth as my muscles quake with the influx of energy. At the very least, a bolt from the heavens should land with enough force to finally use distraction against him for a change.

The power of lightning builds fast, and I close my eyes, drawing as much power as I can harness. If I manage a solid strike, maybe it'll be enough to do some real damage...maybe even fry Mingin free from Riordan.

Potential energy rumbles and rolls in the sky above, pushing down on me, fighting to break free. Its power snaps in the air, and it's incredible.

Mingin is testing me. If I'm reading him right, he thinks he's got me, and this will be too much for me to come back from.

I don't know if he's misogynistic, if he's underestimating me, or if he's overestimating himself, but I'm not out of this yet.

The power continues to build, and I fight for control. Is he trying to make me the target of the strike? Does he think it's going to overload me and blast me into bits?

Wrong. Or, at least, I hope he's wrong.

"*A ghra*, what can I do?"

"Nothing, babe," I say from between clenched teeth. "I've got this. S'all good. Everyone, stand back. I'm about to get all up in my Zeus impression."

The others clue into my intention.

"Fi?" Da says. "I don't think ye—"

Merlin's head cranks around and his eyes bug wide. "Fi, wait!"

When I can't hold the energy back any longer, I free the strike and pull to tether it to the target.

"*Command Lightning.*" A deafening *crack* splits the air as a hole blows open in the ship's roof. The room explodes into a whirlwind of debris, and I twist and close my eyes. Tightening my grip on the energy, I focus the power of the lightning bolt with everything I have.

Mingin may be a powerful, tainted soul but I'm the chosen one of Fionn mac Cumhaill and hold dominion over nature. Power vibrates in my cells and rattles in my bones. It's violent and powerful, and when it's over, the air is full of the smell of burning ozone and a creepy black smog.

I smile at the giant hole where Riordan McNiff stood only moments ago.

Take that, asshole.

As chunks of superyacht rain down around us, I search the room for remnants of Tad's father.

Nada. Nothing.

The only sign of what he used to be is the toxic cloud seeping out the yacht's new moonroof.

I'm about to celebrate when the floor beneath us heaves and

buckles. A series of grinding *crunches* sound and water fountains up the hole I made in the floor.

"Oh, crap."

"Understatement." Dillan grabs the end of the bar to keep from getting sucked down toward the glugging water. "I think this is why Merlin and Da were telling you to hold on before you blew a hole in the middle of the ship we're on."

"I may have jumped the punchline on that one."

"Never mind that now." Da points at the hole in the wall where the couch cannonballed into the ocean. "Dillan and I will assist the other group with the Amazon. Everyone else, get to the bow to find Dionysus and the hostages. We need to abandon this ship."

"Aye, aye, Captain."

"There's a shuttle boat in the lower hull," Sloan says. "I saw it when they led us to our cell. I'll see if I can get it launched before we take on too much water and things go off-kilter."

I've got a hold on the metal rail of the outer deck and am pulling myself uphill to keep from falling into the vortex of bubbles as the boat fills with water. "I think things are already off-kilter, hotness. Remember when we watched *Titanic*? It's time to climb over the rail and look for floating doors."

"What did you expect would happen when you call a lightning strike to a boat in the middle of the open water?" Samuel asks.

I yelp and lift my legs out of the way as a sun lounger slides at me and nearly takes me out. "Everyone's a critic. I got rid of Mingin, didn't I?"

"Aye, luv." Sloan pulls himself along behind me. "Ye did at that. Fer now anyway."

"I wish we could hang around and see Melanippe's face when she realizes we've struck down Mingin."

"I'm with you there, Red." Samuel reaches for the door to the lower level at the front of the boat. "I might be petty, but I hope I'm in the front row when her world collapses."

"That's not petty." I grimace as the ship *creaks*. "Speaking of the world collapsing…"

Sloan wraps an arm behind my waist and heave-hos me into the next section of the ship. "We need to find the others and get gone."

"Marco!" I shout down the stairwell to the level below us. Thankfully, the water hasn't gotten into this section of the ship yet, so there's nothing to worry about other than the extreme angle of the floor and walls.

At least that's what I'm telling myself.

"The boat launch was over here." Sloan fights to stay on his feet as the ship groans and makes another adjustment to where the floor should be. "It'll only take a moment to check…"

"Oh, poop." I tilt my head like a confused cocker spaniel. "I don't suppose that boat will float any better than this one."

Samuel frowns. "Not with a giant metal gear shaft rammed through the hull, no."

"It kinda looks like a metal toothpick through what used to be a very pretty sausage."

"Regardless of what it looks like, it's not going to float." Sloan backtracks the short corridor to where we were. "Back to search and rescue."

I'm all for that. The impending danger of a rapid influx of icy water is alarming but not finding my grandparents before it happens is worse.

"Gran! Granda! Dionysus!"

Sloan reaches up to grab the handle of the sliding door closing off the hall to the next section. "Watch this doesn't hit ye, luv. It's heavy, and gravity hasn't always been yer friend."

"True story." I climb out of the way, and Sloan unlatches the door. It slides so fast and with such weight behind it that it snaps free of its track on the bottom end and tumbles down the slope of the hallway. "You broke that, not me."

Sloan chuckles. "If ye want to compare the damage done to

this ship, I think ye've proven yerself a much more destructive force. However, in the grand scheme, I don't think it'll matter."

"No, probably not. Where to now, hotness?"

"To the end of the hall. The room they had us in is at the end there on the right."

I follow Sloan's instructions, but my wet feet are sliding, and my aching muscles are starting to fail me. Between the battle and swimming and lassoing lightning, I'm pooped.

"Granda!" I shout down the hall.

There's still no response up ahead.

"Sloan, can you *poof* yet? Please say yes."

"No."

"Very not helpful."

The ship shifts and the three of us tumble and slide back down the hallway. We crash in a mess of arms and legs and jolt to a groaning stop on top of the door Sloan just broke.

"Ow. I think I broke my ovaries."

Samuel pulls his arm out from under me and starts to wriggle free. "At least your tender parts are inside. Someone's foot is crushing mine."

"Och, this is maddening." Sloan fights to untangle himself.

It is. With no idea where Tad, Gran, and Granda are or if we're going to get out of this, I squeeze my Dionysus pendant and hope he's able to respond.

"Jane? What are you three doing down there?"

I push up from the pile of crushed corridor tumbleweeds and extend my hand. "Searching for you and the hostages. Where are Tad and my grandparents?"

"At Wallace's clinic. Your grandmother wanted me to drop them there because Tad hasn't woken yet. Do you want to go too?"

"Yes, but we have to make sure we get everyone. Da and the boys were still fighting Melanippe on the outdoor platform of the third deck."

"Don't worry. I'll find them."

Before I can answer, Dionysus flicks his wrist, and the three of us are lying on the cold, stone floor of Stonecrest Castle.

Manx is the first to respond, and he bounds over and rubs his furry cheeks against Sloan. "Yer a sight. I'm glad yer not dead."

Sloan chuckles and lifts a brow, pegging me with a look. "Yer spendin' too much time with my companion."

"Your companion is my companion. We now have joint custody, don't we, Manxy?" I reach over and scrub his ears. "Good to see you safe, sweet boy."

"Right back at ye." Manx lets out a long purr. I wish we had more time and were lounging on King Henry and were warm and cozy. Manx is a champion snuggler. "Where are Gran and Granda?"

"Wallace put them into recovery room one to assess them. Tad's in room two."

I kiss the top of his head and push up to my feet. "Gran? Granda?" I rush through the receiving room and hurry to the private corridor that leads to the recovery rooms. "Gran?"

"Fi, come here to me, luv." Gran waves for me to hurry over. As I cross the room, I take a visual inventory. Everything seems to be working and in the right place.

As I expected, Sloan took the brunt of the violence.

Gran stands and reaches out to hug me, but I hold her at arm's length. "I'm soaked. You don't want to be cold and wet on top of everything else."

"I don't care about a little water, luv. How'd ye get so wet, anyway?"

"It's Sloan's fault." I ease back from hugging her and move to Granda. "He's so irresponsible. There we were, all focused on rescuing you guys, and he decided to take a swim. As it happens, I went in after him."

Sloan *harrumphs*. "When she says 'decided to take a swim,' she means I was tossed overboard while unconscious."

"Oh, my wee lad." Gran moves in to hug him. "The two of ye do take more than yer share of hits."

"Kids, there ye are." Wallace catches sight of us from the hall and rushes in. "Ye look awful, my boy."

I chuckle. "That's what I told him too. The moment we know everyone is safe, we're taking a hot bath and locking the doors on the world for a month."

"No." Sloan accepts his father's hug. "The moment everyone's safe, we need to get back to Toronto to see if Yvain invaded our lives and stole the Morrigan's grimoire."

I groan. "Right, and after we find out we've single-handedly let down the world of good and light, then can we have a hot bath and lick our wounds?"

"Och, luv." Gran pegs me with a warm gaze. "I doubt ye did any such thing. Bad people do bad things. What happens next isn't yer responsibility because ye couldn't stop them."

Da, Merlin, and Bruin appear out of nowhere and look around.

"I take it Dionysus found you?"

Da nods. "He did. Who are we still missin'?"

Dillan, Eva, Ahren, and Calum appear in the next wave of arrivals.

"Go, Dionysus," I say, a rush of big love going out to my favorite Greek god. "That just leaves Emmet, Quon Shen, and Dionysus himself."

The words have barely left my lips when the last of our party appear, coughing up seawater and pooling large puddles on the clinic's floor.

I jog over to hug Dionysus and give him a smackeroo right on the lips. "I lurve you, Tarzan. Big. Warm. Gooey. Luuurve."

He straightens, grinning. "Well, if I knew all I had to do was save everyone you love from drowning to get a kiss, I would've done it sooner."

I laugh and hug him again, patting his chest. Of course, he's not wet like the others. Being a drowned rat wouldn't be a good look for someone so image-conscious as he.

"As much as I wish we could rest, I need an emergency return to our back yard. Sloan and I believe this entire Mingin and Melanippe debacle has been a misdirection while Yvain seeks out his mother's dark tome."

Merlin frowns and steps forward. "I'm coming."

"Us too," Dillan says, tugging Eva along at his side. "Everyone here is safe. If there's guardian angel work to be done, we're in."

I nod. "That's fine. Bruin, are you with me?"

He materializes and joins me. *Nowhere else I would rather be, Red.*

"The rest of you rest and take care of Tad. We'll get back to you as soon as we can. Love you all."

"Love you right back, sista," Emmet says. "Safe home."

I take Sloan's hand and extend my free hand toward Dionysus. "Home, James."

"James? Who is this James you speak of?"

With that, we snap out to face whatever awaits us back in Toronto.

CHAPTER NINETEEN

The moment we materialize in the backyard of our Toronto home, Sloan and I head toward the back gate, accompanied by Dionysus, Merlin, Dillan, and Evangeline. The two of us have been very careful over the past months to guard the location of the *Eochair Prana*, but I have a feeling that's become moot at this point.

My childhood home next door is the last house on the street and running along the side of the yard is a long dirt laneway that borders the edge of the Don River conservation lands.

The Don is a wild and wonderful neighbor.

We cross the side lane and duck into the trees.

The old St. James Cemetery is part of the wildlands that border our houses, and when Sloan and I were considering where we could hide Morgana's spellbook, we chose to bury it here to keep an eye on it without drawing attention.

"In the cemetery? Seriously?" Dillan asks.

I make a face at my brother. "There are always people exploring the gravesites and making etchings of the mausoleum inscriptions. We thought us walking around to check on things would seem as natural as two lovers out for a nature walk."

Dillan snorts. "A romantic walk among the dead?"

"Not among them so much as adjacent to them."

"You're nuts. You thought hiding the evilest grimoire known in the realm in a dead-adjacent hiding spot was a good idea? Have you never seen a horror movie? The cemetery is where all bad guys hang out."

"Books aren't evil." I get my ire up. "The people who covet the spells in books and use them to do evil things are evil."

"Says the woman almost possessed by taking the totally not evil book into her system to transport it through time," Merlin says.

I make a face at him. "You *are* cranky today."

"Yes. The prospect of evil forces taking over the world in two months doesn't make me happy. I want to be in the dragon lair in Iceland, spending time with my family."

I love that Cazzie and the dragons are his family.

We come out of the trees at the back of the cemetery and Sloan gestures to the right, toward the spot where we buried the Morrigan's grimoire.

The soles of my shoes *squish* and slosh as we walk. Sloan and I are still drenched, so I call *Internal Warmth* to keep us from getting pneumonia.

"It's quite secluded back here." I draw attention to the fact that there's no one around and therefore, it was a decent hiding place.

"I wouldn't say secluded," Eva counters. "There's quite a lively post-life presence here."

I frown at her. "Post-life? Are you saying you see dead people?"

"Of course, silly." She giggles. "Did you forget about the part where I've spent my entire existence being a reaper for Death?"

"No. Right. I suppose that makes total sense. It's just a little..."

"Uncommon." Sloan helps me out.

"Yeah, uncommon. Good one, hotness." Seriously, that was a

save because I was spinning on words like gross, horrifying, ghastly, or distressing.

Yep, that's me, queen of winning people over.

"At least tell me the ghosts stem from the *Casper* variety and not the *Poltergeist* kind. Hell, I'll even take a Slimer if I have to."

Eva glances blankly over at me, and Dillan grumbles something under his breath about me being a moron.

"Look, D. I've had a crap day, and the idea of ghosts is unsettling. Sorry if I'm not saying or doing everything right with your girlfriend, but you're going to have to give me some friggin' wiggle room here. Things are going to shit, and if I'm about to have my face eaten off by the undead, I'd rather know now."

Eva offers me a sympathetic smile. "They're ghosts, not zombies, but I understand your point. To answer your question, no, there will be no faces for dinner. For the most part, ghosts are harmless."

I take the comment as the reassurance it's meant to be and ignore the 'for the most part' bit.

When we arrive at the spot at the very back of the cemetery near the tree line, the earth is upturned. The lead box Merlin fashioned to seal in the grimoire's evil mojo has been pried open, and it's empty.

Awesomesauce.

The cherry on my screw you sundae is the exhumed skeletal remains of some poor soul propped up on the hill of fresh earth with his middle finger raised to greet us.

"Classy," Dillan says. "Your Yvain guy has a sick sense of humor."

"Like mother, like son, I suppose."

Sloan steps off and stares into the trees. While Merlin gathers the lead box and Eva communes with the ghosts to find out where the skeleton belongs, I go over and check on my guy.

"Hotness?" I place a gentle hand on his shoulder and step around him so I can see his face. "Are you okay?"

"Not really," he says, his voice deep and quiet. "I failed ye. Ye trusted in my ability to safeguard the book and where did that get us? Yvain's got his mother's evil spells and will wield them against us in the days to come."

"First of all, you've never failed me—not ever. Even when you couldn't stand me and wanted nothing to do with me, you came through for me every time. Yes, Yvain got the book but like Gran said, evil people do evil things. We're not going to win every battle."

"No, but this was an important one."

"Maybe too important."

He scrunches up his face. "What do ye mean?"

"I mean, maybe it was too big and too important to the enemy that they never would've stopped, and we never would've truly been able to keep them from winning. If everything happens as it's supposed to, maybe this is a one step back and two steps forward moment."

He's so cute when he arches one eyebrow and stares at me like he thinks I'm ridiculous. "So, what do ye suggest we do from here?"

I draw a deep breath, and the air is cold in my lungs. "I don't know about you, but I need to go home, get warm, and call Garnet and Myra. Maybe Yvain got the book and left, or maybe he's lingering, I don't know. Either way, there's nothing to be done tonight. Let's take a moment to regroup and look at things in the morning."

He shakes his head. "Do ye think it's wise to put things off until tomorrow?"

"Do you have something we need to do tonight?"

He considers that for a moment and shakes his head. "Nothin' comes to mind."

"Same. The important thing is a bad situation just got worse. We have to see how that plays out."

"Is this you cheerin' me up?"

I chuckle. "Is it working?"

"Not a bit."

"Then let's go home, and I'll come at things a different way. Would you rather a hot bath or time in the grove in the hot springs?"

He rolls his eyes. "Not every situation improves by gettin' naked."

"Wrong." Dionysus lopes over to join us. "Sorry, I wasn't eavesdropping, but I'm a god and I happened to hear that last part. You couldn't be more wrong. Every situation improves by getting naked. Trust me. I'm the resident expert on the subject."

I turn Sloan to return home and link my arms with two of my favorite guys. "He's got you there, hotness. He does know the most about being naked."

Sloan chuckles. "Fine. I'll give ye that, but we still can't just go home and pretend like nothin' happened."

"No? Why not?"

"Because Tad is at the clinic. We need to check on him and give him our condolences about his father. He might not have liked the man, but that doesn't change the fact that we killed him tonight."

I sober and sigh. "No. Of course, it doesn't. Do you think he'll hate me for lightning bolting him?"

"I don't think so, *a ghra*, but death is tricky."

It is.

"He won't hate you, Jane. Take it from the son of a horrific asshole father. He'll know you did what you needed to do. You'll see."

I take his hand and check in with the others. "Who's coming to the clinic to break the news to Tad?"

Everyone steps up, and I breathe a little easier.

Once everyone puts in a hand, Dionysus powers us up, and we snap to Stonecrest Castle. As we step apart, I meet Sloan's gaze. "This is going to suck."

He nods. "We're right here with ye, luv."

The brass bell over the door chimes as I step into Myra's Mystical Emporium the next morning. I take a moment to center myself. This otherworld bookstore is one of my happiest of happy places, and it feels like ages since I've been here.

Striking off toward the back, I think about how long it has been. A week?

Maybe a couple of days more than a week?

It's crazy how days blur when chaos rears its head.

"Fi, my favorite employee, you're here!" Myra rounds the old wooden display table we use as a check-out desk and hugs me. "Tell me, tell me. Your text this morning was so cryptic."

"My reality is cryptic right now."

Myra eases back, and I smile at the silver streak through her electric blue hair. "Me likey. Sexy *and* sassy."

"You think?" She checks herself in the old, leaded mirror. It's a great antique, but the actual mirror doesn't do anybody any favors. It makes everyone look blurry and a little warbly.

"Absolutely. You look young and super hip. In fact, when people see you with Garnet, I bet they're thinking he robbed the cradle."

She snorts. "You're too much. We both know *I* robbed the cradle, but thanks, that was fun for me."

"I'm serious. I do love it."

She holds out the strip of silver hair in question and grins. "Yeah, me too."

The two of us each make a cup of tea—mine chai and hers a special blend nymphs enjoy—and put them onto a tray with some macaroon cookies to take into the back so we can catch up.

The bookstore is a two-part experience. The storefront is

where the business happens, and there's the back, which is more like a glorious library.

It's a three-story space with bookshelves rising all around and a beautiful stained-glass ceiling to light things up. The spines of thousands of books line the walls while iron ladders on rails slide along tracks so customers can reach them.

It's magical.

Not only because many of the books are magical and sentient. There's simply something inspiring about sitting in the reading area on the ground level and staring up at the selection.

Myra leads the way to the grouping of leather sofas beneath the old ash tree she's bound to, Leniya, and sets the tea tray down on the coffee table.

I take a moment to pat Leniya's trunk and send him some loving druid energy. "Hey, Mr. Tree, you're looking extra full and healthy today. You've been taking good care of our girl, I see. Great job. Keep that up."

Myra chuckles and pours a splash of peppermint into each mug. "Our bond is symbiotic, duck. I take care of him too, you know?"

"Oh, I know. Still, I like to think that even when I'm not here, you're not alone."

The leather of the couch *creaks* as I take my seat. After heeling off my shoes, I tuck my toes under my butt and sip from my mug.

Myra settles on the couch perpendicular to mine, and the two of us lean on the wide arms so we can chat. "I ran this shop with Leniya for decades on my own, then for decades more during the dark years, and will run it for decades to come. Between my tree and my books, I've never been alone a day in my life."

The dark years are what Myra calls the years she and Garnet were apart after the death of their son, Grant. As bonded shifter mates, even though they weren't together because of their grief, neither could ever truly move on and be happy.

Thankfully, that's over now.

"It's your connection with books I want to talk to you about."

She blows across the top of her tea and smiles up at me. "What about it?"

"I'm worried about your Fae Historian status and what that might mean in the coming months. Did Garnet tell you we had some trouble in Ireland?"

"Nothing specific. He doesn't let the harsh realities of the world into the compound. Our life with Imari is sacred and off-limits from the bad stuff. He did mention there was trouble but said you were home and everyone is safe in the aftermath."

I savor the minty taste as my chai succulence flows down my throat. "True, but something significant happened last night once we got home. Since it might involve you, I'm hoping you'll stay at the compound for a while until we determine the danger."

"Danger to me? What happened that could be a danger to me?"

"It's a long story. I should probably start at the beginning." Over the course of five cookies and a second cup of tea, I recap the magical hexing at the fair, the dragon birthday party, the yeti fiasco, and the yacht hostage recovery. Then, I move on to tell her how Sloan figured out all the Mingin and Melanippe bologna was a ploy to distract us so Yvain could do his thing.

"Now, because we messed up, Yvain has his mother's grimoire, and we're in a whole heap of trouble."

Myra sets her empty mug down on the tray and turns to face me. "There's no sense beating yourself up over it. You got outmaneuvered on this one, but you can't win them all. What matters is how you handle things now."

"I agree, and that's where my concern stems for you and your safety."

"Because of the *Eochair Prana*," she says.

"Exactly. The last time the cockroaches of the dark and dirty world crawled out of Hell's ass crack, you were attacked and almost kidnapped. I don't want you self-inducing another coma. That was awful."

"True, but I did that to keep bad people from finding out how to get their hands on the book. Yvain already has it. He's likely the most ideally suited to read it and decipher his mother's spells. He shouldn't need me."

Which is a good news-bad news thing.

It's good he's self-sufficient and might not need a Fae Historian to unlock the book's mysteries, but it's bad because nothing is slowing him down or stopping him from unlocking the book's secrets.

"I can't imagine what Melanippe and Mingin will do once they have access to Morgana's dark knowledge."

Myra sits back and shrugs. "Maybe that won't come into play. Men like Yvain don't necessarily play well with others. If they allied to find it, that doesn't mean Yvain will honor it if he considers the book and its contents his birthright. I doubt he's inclined to share."

"That works for me. I'd rather have two powerful pain in the ass foes and one evil-inspired dark power than all three of them brimming with the kind of dark energy I know that book contains."

Myra reaches over and pats my hand on the armrest. "How do you feel about the book resurfacing? Have you noticed anything alarming yet?"

"Alarming how?"

"Like maybe a residual connection with the book calling to you now that it's out in the world?"

Normally, I'd blow that off, but the question is too serious for a dismissive response. Myra's Historian status gives her an understanding of magical books few others in either realm possess. If she's concerned enough to ask, I'm concerned enough to consider it.

Closing my eyes, I focus on my energy flow and take inventory of the factors influencing me.

My connection to nature is strong here at the store—it always is. Between Leniya and the books and the ambient fae power in the air, my cells are active and alive.

There's no darkness.

During those days and weeks while I was fighting the evil possession battle after internalizing the book, I felt the darkness slithering inside me like a snake in the shadows. It was cold and hungry.

I don't feel that now.

"No. There's nothing. The only negative mojo I have is the guilt and regret I'm carrying from failing on the monumentally important task of securing the book."

"Which you need to let go of."

I open my eyes and draw a cleansing breath. "I'll try, but regret is tricky."

Her smile dims. "It is. It can hollow you out and steal years from your life. It's also useless. It's done. The question now is where to go from here."

"Well...I suppose we have two choices. We can either try to track down Yvain or not?"

"Do you have a way to track him down?"

I consider that for a bit and shake my head. "Not that I know of. He's either still in Toronto or he's not. He's either seeking Melanippe and Mingin to regroup or he's not."

"And you're not part of the in-crowd."

"Nope."

"So, I guess you wait and see what happens."

I snort. "Not sure if you're aware of this, but patience isn't my best event."

A deep male chuckle breaks into our conversation. "You don't say..."

CHAPTER TWENTY

Myra and I turn our attention from our quiet conversation on the couches to Garnet flashing in over by the display of Tarot cards by the entrance. He strides over to join us, his gait strong and filled with the swagger of him being the alpha in charge. "Sorry, ladies, I didn't mean to interrupt your chat."

I wave that away. "No biggie, boss. We were discussing the possible doom of the free world and the part I played in helping the opposing team."

Myra clucks her tongue and pats the leather seat next to her. "No, we weren't. Maybe you can convince her that no matter how prepared we think we are or try to be, sometimes bad things happen."

Garnet unbuttons his suit jacket and sits next to his beloved mate. Tailored and refined, Garnet projects an air of aristocratic power and sharp edges. Myra, on the other hand, is all softness and flow. She's eclectic and Bohemian from her blue hair cut at a crazy angle to her flowy, new-age blouses and culottes.

I adore them both.

"The one thing I've learned over a lifetime, Lady Druid, is

Myra is always right. We might as well take anything she says as the undisputed truth and not argue."

I chuckle. "That's very enlightened of you. I'm not arguing. I'm simply concerned about how losing the grimoire will impact the Culling and the balance of light and dark."

He stretches his arm along the back of the couch and rests his fingers on Myra's shoulder to play with her hair. "I understand you take the whole 'chosen one' appointment very seriously, but Fionn chose you to represent the Druid Order, not to stand as the salvation of the entire empowered society. Don't take on the weight of the world or it will crush you."

"I hear what you're saying—I do—but it's upsetting because this matters."

He nods. "It certainly does, but as a snarky, know-it-all redhead once told me, all we can do is what we can do, so stop growling."

I let him get away with the know-it-all comment.

My mind is too full to add anything else right now. Dropping my head back, I stare up at all the books filled with magical knowledge and wonderment. "How many sects and empowered societies do you think there are?"

Garnet chuffs. "I have no idea. Any idea, babe?"

Myra shrugs. "Hundreds for sure…maybe more. There are the ones who live here and many more that live behind the faery glass because they can't pass as humans and can't hide their existence. I couldn't even guess how many that would be."

"Do you think the societies there will be affected by the Culling? I mean, if evil gets a solid foothold on the dominion of power, do you think that will reach into the fae realm and the Greek pantheon and the Norse gods and everywhere?"

"I don't know, duck." Myra offers me a sympathetic smile. "Those are big questions."

I sigh and meet their gazes. "Don't we need to ask those questions? Rocking chair lady said there is strength in numbers. She couldn't mean only druid strength. She had to be saying everyone needs to fight for the balance of the future, don't you think?"

Garnet nods. "We're working toward that. Because of you and your family, the awareness has begun, and the forces are rallying."

"And not only in Toronto," Myra says, smiling at her mate. "Garnet has been contacting the Moon Called alphas in all the major cities, and Xavier has spoken with many of the more progressive vampire leaders."

Good. That's good.

"Granda said the Order has been contacting druids worldwide as well, and I know Dionysus spoke with the Fates and Pan and some of his Greek friends. He also visited with Hel. She's aware of what we're facing and will let us know where the Norse gods stand on things."

Garnet leans forward, resting his elbows on his knees. "There's still time to figure this out, Fi."

"Not much."

"No, but if it weren't for you figuring out about the Culling, we'd be much worse off. Let's focus on what we know and what we can do. It's not time to panic yet."

I suppose that's fair.

"So, since we're at a bit of a standstill on the Yvain front and Melanippe is probably off somewhere searching for a new body for her smoggy boyfriend, what are we working on here on the home front?"

Garnet smiles. "While you were off in Ireland, Anyx and I worked on tracking down the source of trouble related to the hex bags at the fair."

I still can't quite wrap my head around that.

"Don't you think it's weird someone picked a country fair outside the city to instigate an exposure leak? Why not a trade show or a concert at Scotiabank Arena or something with thousands more people?"

Garnet smiles. "We had the same question."

"What answer did you come up with?"

"We think it was you."

I take in his smug smile and… "You're serious. Me? What about me?"

"We traced the signature back to wizard magic, but when we confronted Markdale and asked him about the possible involvement of the Toronto wizards, he said he didn't know anything about it."

"You believe him? He's had it out for me since I killed his cousin and stopped their power play of releasing Asmodeus."

"That's true, but he can't lie to a Moon Called."

No. I suppose not. Shifters can smell a lie no matter how skilled the fibber is.

"Also, Markdale lost a member of his coven at the fair, remember?"

An image of a severed head spraying blood over a panicked crowd comes to mind. I make a face. "Yeah, Eva got a little scythe happy in the excitement. Sorry about that."

He arches an ebony brow. "If she could refrain from lopping heads in the future, I would appreciate it."

"I'll mention it. She's new to the whole guardian angel thing and her actions gaining notice on the human plane. She's always been more behind the scenes."

Garnet nods. "There's always a period of adjustment, but less decapitation would be great. Especially when involving the other empowered sects we're trying to govern and control."

"I suppose Markdale hates me even more now?"

"No doubt he does. The important point of this conversation is that he denied any involvement in placing the hex bags."

"Would you expect otherwise?"

"No, but I allowed him to examine the hex bags to see how he'd react."

"And?"

"He seemed genuinely curious and agreed that the magic behind the spell was wizardry."

"So, if not someone within the West Village Wizards, who are we looking for?"

"Markdale said to force a blanketed loss of control like the empowered members of the crowd experienced would require a very high level of magic. When he held the hex bags, he swore the source of that magic leans heavily into the realm of ancient sorcery."

"Ancient sorcery?"

"Uh-huh. Bring anyone to mind?"

I groan. "You think that was Yvain too?"

"We didn't have a name to pin on the perpetrator until you called me last night, but yes, Yvain is now the front-runner for our top suspect."

"Amazeballs." I let that tumble over in my brain for a bit and straighten. "What exactly do you think he was testing for when he forced the empowered to lose control? What did he learn about us?"

"I suppose if he knows you belong to the Guild and the policing agency, he might've been testing your response to a public event?"

"Or how we handle exposure?" Myra adds.

Garnet nods. "If he was paying attention, maybe he watched how your family responded, maybe learned a bit more about Bruin, possibly how the other sects interact, and maybe about the djinn and how we covered everything up."

I replay those panicked moments in my mind and wonder if Yvain was there and what he saw. "What advantage would that information offer him?"

"I'm not sure," Garnet says. "The problem with supposition is there's no way to know if you're on the right track. There's no way to know what's in someone else's head unless you're that person."

I grab the last cookie from the tray and bite off the edge. "I don't imagine any of us want to be in Yvain's head. Honestly, I think he has serious mommy issues."

Garnet frowns. "Like anger issues toward her or more abandonment?"

"Neither. When we hit head-on back in the ninth century, he was all about finding the way to set mommy dearest free. He seemed loyal and devoted. He blamed Merlin and me for keeping him from his mother."

Garnet sits up, scowling. "How so? Is she entombed in the grimoire somehow?"

"Not that I know of, but the book is imbibed with her blood and flesh, so it carries a strong tie to her essence. When I first came across it, a sorcerer named Bathalt of Anglia was using it in a ritual of lightning and dark magic to free her from her banishment."

"How close did he get? Do you think it could've worked if you hadn't interfered?"

"I'm not sure...maybe. It all happened really fast, and I was only a few weeks into my training."

"Try to remember," Garnet says. "This could be important, Fi. Tell me about how that sorcerer used the book to try to release the Morrigan."

I sit heavily on the couch and close my eyes. Part of my shaman ability is to enter a plane of meditation. Not that I practice enough, but in the past, I have been able to calm my mind and recreate moments in my memory.

I do that now.

I focus on what I need to do to relax. It's Sloan's voice I hear. No surprise, he's the one who's taught me the most about meditation and getting in touch with my natural abilities.

Don't force yer breath to be anything but what it is. Ye don't need big or long breaths. Let it come naturally. Nice and natural. In and out.

Feel the weight of yer legs and the connection of yer seat to the floor. Let the tension drain from yer arms.

I pull a deep breath into my lungs and release it.

Let the last of yer anxieties go. There is nothing but this moment and yer intention.

I breathe in and out, my cells pinging to life with little tingles. The energy around me builds to a slow surge and my equilibrium shifts a little off-balance.

"Fionn, and I were at the Castle of Carlisle," I say, envisioning it in my mind. "I finally convinced Merlin that Bathalt was up to no good and he needed to help us intervene."

I picture the sorcerer standing at the end of the upper balcony, arms raised, with Morgana's amulet glowing against the night sky.

"The book was on a podium of stone, and it was pulsing with a creepy light. Merlin mentioned he dreamed about a sleek, black raven riding the wave of a violent storm. He said the black bird covered a great distance, calling darkness to feed the storm. When she finally landed, she perched on the balcony of the castle and transformed into Morgana."

"But that didn't happen?" Garnet asks.

"Almost. We had the freak lightning storm, and the sky darkened into shadows, and a massive raven formed in the sky but we eliminated Bathalt in time to stop it. Then I took the book and returned here."

"But it seemed like Morgana would've gained her freedom if you hadn't intervened?"

I consider that. "Yeah. I'm pretty sure we were about to meet her face-to-face when we managed to shut things down."

I finish with the end of the memory and open my eyes. "That's it. Then I came back, and the fight to get free of the book began. Merlin—Dora then—had worked on how to remove it from the time I left Carlisle Castle and was ready to help."

Myra looks from Garnet to me and frowns. "Do you think

that's what this is about? Do you think Yvain will attempt to free his mother?"

Garnet tilts his head to the side. "Either the man wants his mother's legacy to live on with him, or he wants his mother herself. There's no way to know."

"Both alternatives suck," I say.

Garnet nods. "Agreed."

I finish my cookie, but it's dry in my mouth. "If he's gone off somewhere remote in the world, there's no way we'll find him in time to stop him."

"I doubt we will."

"So, there's a real chance Team Evil might be calling up a ringer for the Culling."

Garnet nods. "Seems like a real possibility."

I groan, flop to the side, and bury my face in the leather cushion. "Tell life to carry on without me. I'll stay here with my head in the sand until it's over."

Myra chuckles. "Your head isn't buried in the sand, duck. It's buried in my sofa."

"Yeah, well, there's that."

***

By the time I summon the energy to return home, I've convinced myself we should pull a Noah, gather everyone and everything, and set sail. Forty days and forty nights sound about right for starting up a yurt community somewhere remote enough no one will ever find us.

When I tell Sloan my plan, he's totally non-supportive. "Hotness...you can't dismiss the idea without considering it. I've given this real thought."

Sloan rolls his eyes, stares blankly at the ceiling for a few seconds, and shakes his head. "The answer is still no."

I scrunch my face at him and climb onto a stool at the breakfast bar. "Why not? Garnet started the conversation by saying we can't take on the responsibility for the fate of the world."

Sloan chuckles, sprinkling cilantro on the top of our cashew chicken and lime zest rice. "There's a difference between not taking on responsibility for the world and ignoring the needs of the world to hide."

When he pushes a full plate toward me, I tug it into place and get myself set up. I never used to eat so much but being a druid takes more fuel than I used to burn. Well, that and the three-hour workouts we've begun doing each day to ready ourselves for what's coming.

"Wine?"

"No thanks. Water is good."

Sloan fills two glasses with water from the fridge and sits on the barstool beside me. "Yer worn down at the moment, luv. It's perfectly understandable. Ye'll feel better about things in a day or so."

I take my first bite and die a little inside. How a rich boy with a live-in chef knows how to make such yumminess is a mystery to me. "I don't think so."

"Trust me."

"I do, but I doubt there's any way to feel better about the probability of Morgana joining the opposing team."

"That's only conjecture at this point."

"It's logical conjecture, and it sucks."

"No argument, but so far there have been no freak lightning storms or evil darkness culminating into an evil sky raven."

"That we know of."

He nods. "That we know of."

We eat in companionable silence for a moment, but I can't shake the panic that everything is about to blow up in our faces. "I hate this."

"I know ye do, luv. Deep breaths. Ye have no control over the intentions of others. It's out of yer hands."

"I hate that too."

"I know ye do." He finishes chewing and sets down his fork. "How about, for tonight only, we ignore the fate of the world and count our blessings. What are ye most thankful for at this moment?"

I shovel another bite into my mouth. "At this moment, I'm most thankful for your cashew chicken. It's delish."

He nods. "After dinner, we'll go next door and hold the wee babes, and ye can tell them funny stories. Ye'll feel better."

Yeah. Even the thought of that makes me feel better.

Damn, he knows me so well.

My phone vibrates in my pocket, and I reluctantly set down my fork and check the message. "Oh, yes!"

My thumbs can't move fast enough. After hitting send, I hop off my stool and turn to welcome the fallen hero home from the war. The moment Nikon snaps into the living room, I check to ensure he's all right, and I launch against him and hug him big.

"I'm thankful for you, Nikon Tsambikos. I'm thankful you're alive, that you took the poisonous hit to save my family, and that you are my dear friend."

Nikon chuckles, hugging me back. "Wow, that's quite a welcome. I'm thankful for you too...and this hug...and you're welcome, by the way."

Sloan moves in next, and the two of them meet chest-to-chest. "I told Fi we need to count our blessings and focus on what we're most thankful fer. I think ye just ranked higher than cashew chicken. Congrats."

Nikon laughs. "I'm honored, but honestly, it smells amazing. I would understand if I only ranked a close second to the cashew chicken."

I wave that away and tug him to the breakfast bar to join us. "Nope. You definitely take first place. In fact..."

I pull the foldable stepstool out from beside the fridge and climb up to open the upper cabinet. Grabbing a handful of yellow wrappers, I step down and place a stack of chocolate bars in front of him.

"Nikon Tsambikos, I award you with a six Oh Henry! bar salute. Congratulations, you earned it."

Nikon grins. "Six? That's too generous."

"You saved my family from whatever poisonous death Mingin had planned for them. Six doesn't begin to cover it."

Sloan offers him a plate and some cutlery and Nikon dishes himself a meal and leans against the countertop. "This smells amazing."

"And tastes even better," I say.

He takes his first bite and nods. "Irish, your gifts never seem to end."

"True story. It's a meal fit to feed the Clan Cumhaill hero of the hour."

He finishes chewing and swallows. "Thanks, Red. Just so you know, I'd die for you and your family for real if it came to that. Chocolate bars or no chocolate bars."

And just like that, I'm ready to take on the world and get back into the fight.

How can I not be with guys like this in my life?

CHAPTER TWENTY-ONE

The next couple of days pass unusually smoothly. I check in with Samuel about the hunt for Mingin and Melanippe, I cover at the soup kitchen while Merlin goes back to Iceland to spend the weekend and gather Dart to bring him home, and Sloan and I manage to get further on our plan to help Calum and Kevin expand their lives to foster.

I sense when my dragon boy is close, and Sloan and I go out into the backyard to welcome him home.

When he drops within the protective ward surrounding our house and the house next door, he releases the glamor to hide his presence. I straighten and smile, surprised to find Saxa here too.

Dart has been crushing on the yellow dragon since their first meeting back in the ninth century a few months ago. I worried at first that it was one-sided, but Merlin assures me Saxa adores him.

Apparently, she's holding him at wing's length to give him the chance to grow and find himself.

"Hello, Saxa. Welcome. This is a lovely surprise."

Saxa lowers her chin and stretches out her wing in a very graceful bow. "I am relieved you think so."

"Saxa thought she might stay with us for a time," Dart says. "With the coming of the Culling, I want to increase my training, and we thought having a second dragon on the property might be wise. The evil forces are building, and our homes and family are where we're most vulnerable."

He's not wrong.

"You're welcome to stay as long as you like. My only concern is whether the backyard and grove can hold two dragons. Dart can, at least for now, downsize when not in battle mode. You're full-sized."

Saxa chuckles, and it's an oddly charming sound. "Ancient dragons possess a great deal more magical power than a hatchling, Fiona. Creating a spatial pocket for a lair will be the work of a moment and considering it'll be within a sacred grove powered by magical energy, even less than that."

I blink at Sloan, looking forward to seeing this. "Then, by all means, make yourself at home. Our backyard welcomes you."

I feel a giant surge of relief coming from Dart, and I turn to my boy. Did he not think we'd welcome Saxa? Does she mean that much to him that he was twisted up at the prospect of us not being on board?

"What do the two of you have planned for training?" I ask. "Merlin is setting up late-night sessions with a couple of empowered friends of his. We're to start meeting them at the druid stones at midnight."

"That sounds wonderful." Dart glances over to gauge Saxa's reaction. "Are Bruin and Manx going?"

"As far as I know."

Sloan nods. "Aye, Manx enjoyed bein' in the thick of things last week. I think ye'll find he's more involved in the battles to come."

I'm quite excited about that myself. Manx is a smart animal with keen senses, and he loves Sloan. When I can't keep an eye on my druid boyfriend, it'll be nice to know he's there as the next line of support.

"Dartamont? Will you show me where your nest is and where you think you'd like our lair to be?"

Dart turns in a rush and trots off toward the grove and into the trees.

"*Our* lair," I whisper to Sloan and waggle my eyebrows. "Well, well, it seems my blue boy might be shacking up with his dragon crush."

Sloan chuckles. "Yer ridiculous. Don't make this weird for them."

"Me? Do I make things weird?"

"More often than not." Calum jogs across from the back gate in his police blues. "Was that Saxa I saw going into the grove?"

"Yeah, she's going to stay with us and help us ready for the Culling."

"*Noice.* I bet Dart's busting his buttons."

"He seemed pretty jazzed, yeah."

"Thus, my comment fer yer sister not to make things weird fer the two of them," Sloan says.

"Ah, yep, I'm with you now. He's right, Fi, don't make it weird for them."

Rude. "Et tu, Brute?"

Calum laughs at me and tilts his head toward the house. "Is Kev home? He had a meeting with Garnet's people about Bizzy and how the investigation is going into her mom's death. Garnet had a driver dropping them off afterward."

"They aren't back yet, but I talked to Kinu earlier, and she said Garnet is forming a Guild sub-committee regarding orphans, adoptions, and fostering."

Calum frowns. "I don't love the idea of a sub-committee. In my experience that only gives more people a say in whether or not to do the right thing."

"I hear you, but I think after Garnet's experience finding and bonding with Imari, he's taken a personal interest in the idea. He'll make sure things keep moving."

"How are things goin' with little Bizzy?" Sloan asks. "With the Ireland fiasco and the fallout after, we haven't been much help with yer wee charge, I'm afraid."

Calum shakes his head. "Don't worry about that. The fostering thing is our commitment, not yours. You guys have been great with us taking over the house and having a toddler as crazy as Bizzy-B invading your home."

"About that…" I check in with Sloan. When he nods, I continue. "We have a surprise on that front. Get changed, and we'll meet you in the kitchen. There's something we want to talk to you about."

Calum locks his sidearm in the gun safe in the hall to the kitchen and heads upstairs to change out of his blues. While he's upstairs, a large, black SUV pulls up in front of the house, and Kevin gets out carrying a little brown river otter curled up in his arms.

"Fatherhood looks super sweet on him," I say absently.

Sloan hugs me from behind and looks out the front window with me. "It does. It suits them both."

We watch as he strides up the walk, then I step back, hurrying to get the door so Kevin doesn't have to jostle the sleeping babe for his keys.

"Hey, welcome home," I whisper, leaning in to see how cute she is when she's sleeping. "How'd things go?"

Kev steps inside and lets the strap of the baby bag slide off his shoulder. After setting it on the floor inside the door, he adjusts Bizzy's blanket and smiles down at her. "Fine, I guess. They wanted to check that a fae child could thrive with two human parents. I guess we cleared the hurdle because they said we're good to continue doing what we're doing."

"What about them findin' other members of her family?" Sloan asks.

"Apparently her mother was estranged from her family because they're purists. Bizzy's father wasn't otterkie, so it looks like they have no interest in pursuing a relationship with Bizz."

"That's horrible," I say.

"Horrible of them, yes. Not horrible for us. If they're not interested in giving this little monkey everything she needs, we sure are."

"Damned straight." Calum jogs down the last steps to greet his husband and foster daughter. "It couldn't work out better for us. Their loss."

Kevin kisses Calum. "Yep. S'all good."

I grin. "In that vein, Sloan and I have an announcement. If the two of you would follow us outside, we'd like to show you something."

I'm grinning ear-to-ear as I step out on the porch and wave for them to follow. "You don't need shoes, Calum. We aren't going far."

Kev still has his coat and shoes on, so he's good to go. Calum grabs his hoodie off the hall rack and follows. "What's this about, Fi?" he asks.

"My three most favorite things."

"Sex, chocolate, and working the bar with Liam?"

"No."

"King Henry, Hawaiian pizza, and naked hot springs time in the grove?" Kevin asks.

I give them the stink eye. "You two suck. No. My three most favorite things are family, love, and people finding a place to be accepted and belong."

Kevin chuckles. "Oh, yeah. Those would've been my next guess."

I roll my eyes. "Do you want your surprise or not? I'm beginning to think you don't deserve it."

Calum laughs. "I'm standing on the front walk in my socks in October. I deserve it."

I take pity on him and cut across the lawn, up the street to the house next door. Our childhood home is the other way. This house is the one that gets rented out by a local real estate company.

As we climb the front steps, I take out the keys and jingle them in front of my brother and his hubs. "Are you excited yet?"

"I'm terrified, actually." Calum studies first me, then Sloan. "What did you two do? Irish? You didn't buy another house, did you?"

"Not yet. No. The owner lives in China and has been rather difficult to nail down. I did, however, have my barrister broker a long-term lease with the real estate company that manages the property. I also added a clause in their contract that they'll notify me if the option to purchase comes up."

"You rented us a house?" Kevin says. "If you want us to move out, you don't have to finance it."

I'd smack him in the shoulder, but Bizzy is still sleeping, so I smack Calum instead.

Calum makes a face at me. "Rude. He comments, but I take the beating?"

"You both know if I had my choice, I'd live in a ginormous house and have all of us together but segmented with private spaces. Living separate lives but together."

Calum chuckles. "Kind of like your millionaire boyfriend buying up all the houses on the block?"

I make a face at him. "No. Not like that."

Kevin shakes his head. "We get what you mean, Fi, but seriously, you need to explain. My mind is spinning. I don't want you two paying our rent, and I'm damned sure we can't afford a four-bedroom in downtown on the salaries of a cop and an artist."

I hand Sloan the keys and smile. "Totally true. That's why we went another route."

Sloan opens the door and swings it forward so Kevin and Calum are the first to enter. In the front entrance of the house, there are a couple of reception chairs, a quaint antique desk with a banker's lamp, and a computer set up ready for people to arrive.

"Guild Guardians?" Calum asks, reading the sign on the wall behind the desk. "What does that mean?"

"It means Garnet and I worked out some of the details regarding the placement of empowered kids who need a home. We're making this place the primary drop-off center where little ones will be brought and cared for until we figure out about placement."

Sloan hands them the keys and grins. "Kinu is on board for intake and counseling, and Emmet and I will be yer triage team if any of yer new arrivals need medical attention. Ye'll need to take some certification courses to seal the deal, but otherwise, yer all set."

I nod. "The Lakeshore Guild of Empowered Ones is covering a considerable chunk of your rent. As well, the house has a monthly stipend allotted to ensure you have everything you need to keep the place running."

Kevin and Calum blink at me.

"This is a good stunned, right?" I get a little nervous. "I didn't misread your aspirations, did I?"

Calum turns to me and rolls his eyes. "No, Fi. You nailed it. I just...I can't..."

"What he's so eloquently trying to say is thank you, Fi. It's an amazing surprise, and it's so far beyond perfection we can't even begin to thank you enough."

Calum nods. "Yeah, that's what I was saying."

I exhale a long breath. "Okay, thank goodness. I was scared there for a sec."

"Does this mean we can take another fence down and expand the grove again?" Calum asks.

I laugh. "We better wait until the owner gets back to us and agrees to sell. He might not appreciate us remodeling the place when we're technically only renting."

"While *they* are technically only renting," Sloan corrects. He gestures for them to step farther inside. "Go ahead and look around. Everything is in yer name and yer set to take possession."

Calum grabs me up in a bone-crushing hug. "You're the best, baby girl. How did we get so lucky?"

"Well, I'd say Mam and Da kept having kids until they finally got it right."

He barks a laugh and eases back. "I'm not even going to argue. You earned that one."

"Yeah, you did," Kev says. "Big love coming your way, Fi. Big. Huge."

I gesture for him to give me Bizzy. "Right back atcha, boys. Now go on. Take a tour and start making your plans. Welcome to your new home."

"All good?" Sloan asks as I come in from the back yard later that night. I take off my jacket and hand it to him as I unzip my boots and drop them on the mat beside the door. "Is everyone settled fer the night?"

"Saxa has successfully made her and Dart a lair—it's mind-boggling and incredible. I moved the earth to create a hole under our fence so Daisy, Doc, and Manx can come and go without difficulty. Nilm says Pip is feeling huge but happy. He expects their young to arrive within the week."

"That's exciting. Have they got everything they need fer the birth and their nest?"

"I'm assured they do." I close the back door, lock us up for the night, and activate our wards. "Now, your turn. How did things go with *poofing* Kev's and Calum's stuff next door? Did they get Bizzy settled? All good?"

"All good. I told them there was no need to rush, but they were so excited to spread their wings and explore the potential of their new lives, they insisted. They don't have groceries, so they'll be back in the morning for breakfast, but other than that, I think they're set."

I link my fingers with his and walk toward the back of the house. Dozens of tea light candles glow across the fireplace mantle, on the coffee table, and all along the window ledges.

"What's this?" I let him tug me along behind him.

"This is us enjoying an empty house and a quiet night. Yer brothers have found their own homes. Manx and Bruin invited Doc and Aurora from across the road and are havin' a sleepover with Daisy next door. They want to ensure she doesn't feel like she's leaving them by moving out."

"That's sweet. They love her so much."

"It's a big brother, little sister thing."

I grin. "I might be familiar with that."

He pours two glasses of red wine and hands me one. "I thought we could unwind a little before life closes in on us once again."

I laugh. "Are you predicting it, or do you know something I don't?"

"The second one."

"Oh? And what's that?"

"Merlin called a moment ago and said he might have a way to track Yvain. He wants us to come to the club first thing in the morning."

"That's all he said?"

"That's it."

"Okay then, I'm with you." I tip my glass toward his. "Let's enjoy our night alone before all hell breaks loose once again."

CHAPTER TWENTY-TWO

Queens on Queen is a local treasure. I'd heard all about it from girlfriends who'd been to bachelorette parties and special events long before I met Pan Dora or became friends with Merlin. Dora's Merry Queens and Scots event is a yearly sellout as well as many of the summer weekend shows. And not long ago, the *Rocky Horror* night was a huge smash.

So fun.

Since Empress Cazzienth was released from Merlin and restored to her amazing dragon-y self, Dora hasn't had quite the same passion for fashion. More often than not, it's Merlin we meet up with now.

That's both a great thing—because he and Cazzie reunited—and a sad thing—because Dora was and still is one of my favorite people.

When we don't find anyone down in the club, Sloan *poofs* us up the narrow stairwell to the door to the apartment upstairs. I raise my hand to knock, but the entrance swings open before my knuckles rap.

"Thanks for coming, Fi," Merlin says. "I appreciate the house call, but I needed to show you something."

"Not a problem. Sloan said you think you have a way to track Yvain. I'm all for that. Whatever you need from us, we're in."

He steps back to allow us to enter and frowns. "You might not be quite so eager when you hear my idea."

Sloan pegs me with a serious gaze, and I shrug.

The first time I came to the apartment, I described it as an eclectic mash-up of Old World ancient meets bedazzling bathhouse meets brash and sassy drag queen delight. That much hasn't changed.

Sloan and I follow the zebra-print runner into the living space, and the Pan Dora-ness of it all warms me. I honestly wasn't sure if Merlin would redecorate with swords and medieval manliness now that his empress influence is gone.

"Have a seat."

I sit at the table and stare at the Tarot spread lying out on the wide, round table. I don't know much about Tarot beyond the fact that reading the cards is an art form that takes time and study.

Also, Merlin is very good at it.

"This is a big spread." I count the cards. "Twelve cards."

Once we're both seated, he joins us, sitting in the chair addressing the cards. "It's a complicated situation. It deserves a large spread."

"Is this how you came up with your idea about how to track Yvain down?"

"Yes and no." He drapes a finger over the Nine of Wands, sending me a poignant look. "Reading the cards gives me clarity of mind, and it was during that when the idea struck me."

I stare at the warrior woman with wine-red hair. We already determined a few months ago that when this card came up, it signified me. Between the hair, the battle-ready disposition, and the heraldic dragon embroidered on the center of her tunic, it was a bit too on the nose to ignore…

And there she is.

She's standing with a quarterstaff ready to defend her turf. Dora suggested it's the universe's way to show that I'm on guard to ward off trouble.

"Okay, I'm ready. What's your idea?"

He sits back. "Well, you know how I said you can never be truly free of a darkness like the kind Prana's Key left within your cells?"

"Right. It merged with my body, so somewhere in my cells, there will always be a residual trace of it. Though we extracted most of it and bound and buried the rest, it's still there. You said I'd likely never have to worry about it again, but I'd never truly get rid of it."

"Exactly…that's true. So, what if we unbound it and dug it up again?"

I sit up. "Wait. What? You want to dredge up the residual darkness of that book possessing me?"

He holds up his palms. "I want to discuss it, yes."

Sloan goes eerily stiff. Judging by his full marble statue impression, he hates this conversation. He won't weigh in without being asked because he believes in me making up my mind.

He's a keeper, that one.

I take a moment to calm my nerves and swallow. "Okay, give me your pitch, and I promise I'll listen before I freak out."

Merlin points at the Nine of Wands. "I believe you came up in this position because, like it or not, you have a connection with that book."

"I don't like it. Go on."

"Since energy is neither created nor destroyed, the memory of its magic and pull is evermore in your cellular memory. I think we can enhance that darkness and maybe get a lock on it."

I blink at him. "You want not only to wake up the sleeping darkness but feed it and try to harness it?"

"That's one way to look at it."

I frown. "I think that's a fairly accurate way to look at it." I point at the Death card next to me. "I know that the Death card doesn't necessarily mean dead, but it also doesn't look good."

"Death isn't a literal translation, no. It's more about the essence of an ending."

"Does my ending have anything to do with that?" I point at the card above the Nine of Wands. It's card fifteen of the Major Arcana, The Shadow Side.

A dark-haired man is holding a book, the power he's giving off threatens a woman, and a cloaked figure in the darkness behind promises something ominous to come.

"I hate how they paint such an eerie foretelling."

"The cards don't lie, Fi."

"I know." I might not understand how the power of Tarot works, but the times when Dora or Merlin have worked with me, the messages have been much too accurate to be lucky guessing or them trying to convince me of a given outcome.

"Maybe this was bad luck. If we shuffle things up and ask the universe a different question, maybe things might look better."

"Fi. This isn't the first spread I laid out. I did over twenty, searching for an outcome where we find Yvain in time to affect the future positively. This is the only one where there's some hope of us pulling a win out of our asses."

I groan. "Fine, Doctor Strange. So, you're saying we need to allow Thanos to snap his fingers and I'm the one turning to ash and whisking away on the wind."

Merlin looks at Sloan. "Has the needle skipped the record? I don't know what we're talking about anymore, but I don't think that's what I was saying."

"It happens sometimes when she's stressed," Sloan says. "In her mind, her mental hamster is running in its wheel, making connections. She'll bring it back around to the topic at hand. You just have to give her a little line to run with it and tire herself out first."

I frown at them both. "I'll have you know I have a beautiful mind, and there's nothing wrong with my mental hamster."

Sloan chuffs. "Ye realize that the point of the beautiful mind was that the man was insane, right?"

I stick my tongue out at Sloan and return my attention to Merlin. "Ignore him. He's cranky because I'm being tossed into the fire again."

"Tossing you into the fire is the last thing I want to do, Fi," Merlin says apologetically.

I sigh and point at card twenty-one. It's a pretty depiction and has people and animals skirting the Green Man's face. "What does The World represent…well, other than the obvious?"

"It's exactly the obvious. It's in the final position of the spread representing the possible outcome of the future. For the world to thrive, I believe this section back here with you and the dark shadows must come to pass."

I scan over the other cards, trying to make sense of it. Some of them I recognize. Some I don't know the full meanings of. The Lovers I get…The Magician…

"What's this Knight of Swords here for?"

"Swords are representative of thoughts, actions, and, in this case, the assertion of power. To have the Knight of Swords to the right of the Nine of Wands and next to Strength is representational of the building strength of our forces in the battle to come."

Okay, I see how that works.

"Is there anything in here that states how quickly I need to decide? Because honestly, I hate the idea of opening up to the sensation of being possessed by darkness. Been there, done that, really not a fan."

Merlin squeezes my hand. "I know. I wouldn't even suggest it if I thought there was another way to get a positive outcome. I figure, even with Yvain's level of experience and understanding, he won't try something as monumental as trying to free his mother until he's thoroughly comfortable with the spell. He'd need a few days to verify wording and meanings, and he'll want to find a location that suits his needs."

"Tell me that gives us another week or more."

Merlin shakes his head. "I'm thinking we're seriously running out of time. I figure if we're not already too late, it'll be today or tomorrow at the latest."

Well crap. I let out a long sigh.

"Fi, if we're going to do this, it needs to be now."

Not what I wanted to hear, but it's time to pull up my big girl panties. "Give Sloan and me the morning to noodle it over. He's super smart. Maybe if we put our heads together, we can come up with an offshoot plan that saves me from being the darkness homing beacon."

Merlin nods. "Good luck. I seriously hope you do."

"Well, that was a downer start to our day." I lace my fingers with Sloan's as we leave Queens on Queen, and we strike off in a stroll down the sidewalk. Trying to thaw him out enough to have a conversation won't be easy. He's currently in the silent stewing state of his cerebral process and has tuned out the world.

We walk along for a few more minutes, and I point at a new storefront with a "Just Opened" sign in the window. "What do you say to mid-morning crêpes with tons of whipped cream and berries?"

"Whatever ye like, luv."

I steer us to the door and head inside.

La Belle Crêperie mimics an authentic Parisian café with small iron tables, decadent pastries, and a menu board that entices and delights.

"*Bonjour*, welcome to La Belle Crêperie." The proprietor says in a thick Parisian accent.

I step forward so Sloan can close the door and draw a long breath deep into my lungs. "Wow. It smells incredible in here. If I worked here, I'd eat myself out of my salary every shift."

She chuckles. "Luckily, I'm not one for sweets anymore."

"Luckily, I work in a bookstore."

"The Emporium," the woman says. She catches her slip and stiffens. "Do you love crêpes or are you intrigued to try them out?"

Despite her quick recovery, the hairs on the nape of my neck stand on end, and I take a much more discerning look at the server.

She's pretty, brunette, with eyes that could look a little too large for her face but because they're such a rich hazel green, they don't.

I search my instincts but come up blank. My shield's not weighing in, so that's good. "Do I know you?"

Only empowered community members are aware of Myra's Mystical Emporium, so that means this woman isn't as human as she appears.

I reclaim Sloan's hand and tap the bone ring that chose him from Fionn's treasure trove. He's way ahead of me. The magic of "seeing that which is not seen" has already been activated and the glamor of who and what the woman truly is falls away.

A vampire.

She's grown very still.

I glance around at the empty tables and realize we're the only people in here. All of a sudden, I'm not so sure crêpes are worth it, no matter how much soft serve and berries are on top.

I'm about to make our excuses and leave when she holds up her palms. "*J'excuse*, I didn't mean to make you ill at ease. I'm sure you think I shouldn't know where you work."

"It crossed my mind."

"I am Clara Bellefleur, a new member of Xavier's family."

"Uh-huh. And what? He's giving everyone coming to town a

dossier on me? Why would you need to know who I am and where I work?"

She sighs and presses her hands against the frill of her apron. "*Non*, it had nothing to do with Xavier. I'm usually better at keeping my thoughts to myself."

"That doesn't explain how you know things about me. If Xavier didn't tell you, then who?"

"Well...you."

"Me? But you said we haven't met."

"*Non*, we haven't."

"You are a confusing woman, Clara Bellefleur."

She holds up a finger and starts again. "Before I transitioned, I was very empathetic to those around me. When I started my second life, that gift intensified."

"So, you're psychic?"

"Not exactly. I don't predict things. I simply hear and see thoughts and emotions...especially if the person has a strong mind, which you do."

I'm not sure I like that, but hey, people don't always get to pick their gifts. "So, you read minds?"

"*Non*. What comes to me is only the surface thoughts and images. You mentioned working in the bookstore and images of the Emporium came through so clearly, I could tell you what sections of books are where."

I draw a deep breath and exhale. "Oh, that's cool."

"Not when I slip up. Then, as you did, people assess me as a threat."

"That's not personal. There are a lot of people who consider me a threat. I've learned the hard way I have to stay on my toes."

"Somehow, you saw me not only as a threat but also as a vampire. How?"

I won't out Sloan and his ring, so I go the aloof route. "You're not the only one who can see things."

"*Non*, I suppose not. Your mind ran through the faces of a

great many vampires. Considering how private Xavier is, I'm surprised you've met so many."

I shrug. "Xavier and I have a complicated history, but I consider him to be an ally and a friend."

"Which is why you chose to leave instead of engaging. You weren't sure if I was of his family or not and you didn't want to insert yourself into conflict."

"Correct."

"You have a very interesting mind."

I feel the brush of Sloan's mental energies in my mind as he throws up a block on my thoughts and battens down my hatches.

I smile at him. He's sweet. He worries.

"As fate would have it, you caught me in a very tumultuous life and death, good versus evil moment. I'm sure you got a mind full."

She lowers her chin. "*Oui*, that's likely what caused me to lose focus and say too much."

Sloan grunts. "As fate would have it, that's your normal state of being. When are ye not faced with tumultuous topics of life and death?"

"Point to you, Mackenzie." With the mystery of the mindreading solved, I fall back to my original reason for coming in. "On that note, I'd like to indulge in a sugar overload and drown my worries in crêpes and sinful toppings. When faced with the fate of the world, I find it best to eat my emotions."

"*Bien sur*, what can I get for you?"

Sloan and I make our selections and choose a two-seater table in the farthest corner. It's not that I doubt Sloan's mind-shielding capabilities or Clara's intentions. We have personal stuff to discuss, and I don't need a third party involved. Before the conversation gets off on the wrong foot, I hold up a finger and start things off.

"You don't need to say it. You hate everything about the idea of unlocking the resident evil, and I do too. I suffered, and you hate it when I suffer. You're worried about the long-term effects of awakening that kind of darkness, and so am I."

Sloan frowns at me, a bite of bananas fosters on his fork. "I'm not sure if yer aware, but a conversation involves the give and take of ideas by both parties. If ye don't let me speak, it's a monologue."

"Right. Sorry. I just want you to understand that I recognize your reservations and I share them." I fork in another bite of sweet, strawberry goodness, and OMG they're good.

Still, I try to control myself and not groan so loud and enthusiastically this bite.

There is another couple in the café now, and they must have thought I was performing the diner scene from *When Harry Met Sally* because the looks they threw me were very odd.

Can't a girl just really love her crêpes?

"Go ahead, hotness. Tell me what you think."

He finishes chewing, wipes his mouth with his napkin, and straightens in his seat. "We know time is of the essence. Odds are, wherever Yvain is, he's at least considering how to free his mother from her imprisonment."

"Agreed."

"We also know he can do that anywhere in the world. He's not bound to Toronto now that he has the book and likely isn't here."

"Agreed again."

He frowns. "As the man who loves ye, I think it's a terrible idea, and I want to vote it off the table and punch Merlin in the face fer even suggestin' it."

"Thank you for not doing that."

"It was touch and go there a few times. It truly incenses me when others take the liberty to place ye in danger."

"You are forever my black and beautiful white knight, and I love you for that."

He nods. "As a fellow warrior in this battle we're in, I can't think of any other way to track Yvain or find him quickly enough to have a chance to stop him. If we sit idly waitin' fer inspiration to strike, we'll miss our chance."

"So, you think I should do it?"

He reaches across the table and takes my hand. "I won't tell ye what ye should do, *a ghra*. I'm much too selfish and protective to be objective. I will say I understand the risks and will support ye through it if ye decide it's what you must do."

"And if I don't want to?" I push a couple of berries around in a melted soft-serve and berry juice puddle on my plate. "Because I really don't want to."

"Och, I know that well enough, luv. Even if ye agree, I healed ye through some of the worst moments of that possession. Who would ever want to revisit that?"

"It sounds like there's a but coming."

"I also know how stubborn and brave and dedicated ye are to the cause and to the prospect of takin' down the evil of our world. I know ye don't want to, but I also know ye will because ye feel ye must."

My eyes sting as I stare at the berry puddle. "I feel selfish because I really don't want to."

Sloan pushes out from the table and opens his arms to me. "Come here to me, *a ghra*."

"What? Here?"

"Yes, here. Don't mind them. The biggest worry they've got on their minds is whether or not this morning after the night before awkwardness will end with an invitation fer another date."

I glance over at the other couple and yeah, he could be right. There is all kinds of sexual tension and fluster going on over there.

"Come here, luv."

I do as he asks and sit on his lap with my back to the restaurant. When he wraps his arms around me, I feel his healing energy tingle in my cells. "I've said before the world asks too much from ye and it's true. Yet, it keeps askin'. There are simply things yer uniquely suited fer that no one else is."

"Lucky me."

He chuckles, running his hand down my back. "Aye, lucky you."

I rest there, absorbing the warmth and the healing energy. After a few minutes, I feel much better. Sloan has that effect on me.

When I sit up, I grip both sides of his face and kiss him. "The world sees me doing all the things, but the only reason I have the strength and confidence I do is because you love me."

"Then it's our little secret."

"You must get so tired of propping me up."

He pegs me with a serious gaze. "Fi, it's my greatest honor. Before ye agreed to date me, I stood in yer room and told ye we were goin' to happen. I didn't care how long ye needed to realize it. We would be together."

"It was very romantic—cocky, but very romantic."

He chuckles. "I was cocky because I feel it down to the marrow of my bones. We're meant fer great and important things. Ye have a destiny that's bigger than the both of us, so it's goin' to take a village. Not all of it will be pleasant. Sometimes things will go wrong, but we'll never stop tryin' to set things right."

I chuckle. "You're now in charge of the Cumhaill pep talks. You're really good."

He smiles and gives me one last squeeze. "I'll remind ye of that the next time I piss ye off."

I laugh. "You never piss me off."

"Then, at the risk of makin' this the first time, I think we need to get ye back to Merlin's apartment. There's work to be done and time is of the essence."

I draw a deep breath and exhale. "Okeedokee, but it's going to suck huge."

"No question, luv. It is at that."

CHAPTER TWENTY-THREE

"Are you ready to do this, cookie?" Merlin is standing over me, with Sloan, Emmet, Dillan, Eva, Nikon, and Dionysus nearby. It's funny hearing him use the term of endearment. It seemed so natural coming from Dora but with him...it just seems funny.

"Not really, but this is where we are, amirite?"

"Sadly, you are right."

"We're here for you, baby girl." Dillan winks at me while looking on.

I'm lying out on the stage of Queens on Queen with a ritual circle drawn out beneath me. It has a pentacle, candles, sigils calling to Morgana's darkness, and me as the sacrifice offered up as its host.

"I heart you, Jane." Dionysus stands next to Nikon, looking rattled.

"I heart you right back, Tarzan. It's fine. Everything's going to be fine."

"I know it is." He doesn't sound at all like his normal, confident self. "You're sure the balance of humanity is worth waking up the darkness? You said it really hurt last time."

"It did, but there's the whole balance of humanity thing to consider."

"We're with you no matter how many flowerbeds you fertilize, Red."

I smile at Nikon. "You still owe me a replacement dinner at BlueBloods, Greek."

"Name the time and place, babe. I'll be there."

Merlin steps into the pentacle with me and kneels at my side. "Okay, everyone. I'll need you all to be quiet while we get this done. The next part is a bit tricky."

The prospect of something being tricky for Merlin silences the nervous chatter. I don't blame them. It's hard for me to imagine that too.

When he places his hand on the bare skin of my thigh where the book once lived, a rush of hot tears spills down my cheeks. I don't mean to get emotional in front of everyone, but that doesn't mean I can stop it.

"Okay, Fi, here we go…and for what it's worth, I'm sorry it's come to this."

I draw a steadying breath and nod. "Not your fault. Do your thing and let's getter done."

"I really wish ye'd let me be yer strength, Red," Bruin grumbles beside me.

"No, buddy. We're reactivating evil in my cells. I don't want you affected. You're an outtie for the time being." He doesn't like it, but I won't budge on this one.

If evil is taking me down, it won't take him too.

"Ready?" Merlin asks.

I nod. "Ready."

Merlin begins working over me, and I close my eyes. I'm scared enough as it is without seeing the panic and upset in the gazes of the people who love me.

Relaxing into the inevitability of things, I sink back into myself. I haven't gone into my meditative retreat to speak to

Brendan in a while—too long. I don't go now because too much is happening, but I make a mental note to check in with him once this is over.

Merlin's voice is deep, and when he casts, he has a natural cadence I find incredibly relaxing. I'm sure it also helps that he's speaking in tongues.

I'm glad I don't know what he's saying.

If I heard him saying, "awake darkness and possess this vessel" or "I free you evil to grow and consume your host," I wouldn't find it as relaxing, I'm sure.

Instead, I listen to the change in pitch and tone, searching for a word I recognize while not wanting to understand him at all.

"Augh!" I gasp as he unlocks something significant. When we put this behind us last fall, he said we'd never be able to banish it completely, so we'd wrap it up, bury it deep, and spell the area to hold it prisoner so I would be free of it.

Yeah, well, we took the same approach with the actual book, and look where that got us.

I open my eyes, and a haze clouds my vision. It's like the darkness of Morgana's power taints not only my cells but the air around me.

Merlin winces, his lips moving in a steady flow despite the discomfort we both feel because of his enchantment.

Nausea is building in the pit of my stomach, and there's no question I'm going to puke in front of my friends. I try to hold still, sensing Merlin coming to the end of his spell.

Or maybe it's wishful thinking.

The moment he eases back, I sit up and press my hand over my mouth. "Barf bucket."

Dionysus is there a moment later with the *Pirates of the Caribbean* garbage can from his powder room. "Here you go, Jane."

I accept the offering with a brief smile and double over the receptacle, revisiting my big idea to go for a sugar overload right before this.

Hindsight, amirite?

Yeah, that should be my middle name. Fiona Hindsight mac Cumhaill.

Sloan is there, his hand on my back as I retch while everyone watches. Yay, me…dinner and a show.

Thankfully, the turmoil doesn't last long. By the second round of out-you-go, my stomach is empty, and now my throat is on fire.

Dammit. I remember this part.

"I'm sorry about Capt'n Jack," I say, not sure what to do with the bucket.

Dionysus is on his knees beside me. He touches the garbage can, and it's refreshed and good to go. "Better?"

"Much. Thanks, dude."

I think about how this whole possession nightmare started the last time…

One minute I was sucked back into medieval times and watching jugglers practice in the courtyard of an ancient castle, and the next I was internalizing an evil grimoire and poisoning myself for the sake of humanity.

Who would've guessed that would come back to bite me in the ass? Twice.

"How do you feel, cookie?"

I meet the dark storms in Merlin's gaze and appreciate his concern. "I've been better."

"I bet. So, now that I've unbound it, I'm going to let it out into your system."

"Fuckety-fuck. You mean it's not even free yet?"

"Not yet, so grit your teeth because that's next."

I do as Merlin suggests and lock myself down. I lay flat on the stage again, close my eyes, and raise my hand for someone to please grab hold.

It doesn't matter at this moment who it is.

I simply need someone to anchor me to what's happening instead of me getting swept away by the poison about to be set free inside me.

"I'm here, luv," Sloan says quietly next to me. "We're all here."

"You've got this, baby girl," Calum says.

"Sac up, Cumhaill," Dillan says, "and get ready for the impending suckage."

Funny enough, Dillan's militant approach helps the most. I tighten up and get ready for the next wave of darkness. When it hits, it doesn't hurt or make me sick as the first wave did. It's more like adding water to a puddle. It builds and expands.

That should make me more nervous than it does.

For the moment, I'll take the reprieve. I close my eyes and focus on what's happening within my body. In my mind's eye, I imagined the darkness would be pleased to gain its freedom.

It's not. It's nothing. It just...*is*.

Over the past year, I built up the darkness as a sentient foe in my mind. I envisioned it entombed and trapped like a prisoner with a life sentence.

It's not like that at all.

It's dark and cloying, and it's powerful.

And it's growing.

"Fi, are you ready for me to turn things up?"

I swallow and give Merlin a nod. "Can't wait."

The pressure of Merlin's hand on my thigh increases and a rush of dark power floods my system. It's cold and eager to pool with the like energy in my cells. It hungers to build and grow.

When the weight and heat of Merlin's touch disappear, I open my eyes. "Am I done?"

"For now. How do you feel?"

I sit up and hold my hands out in front of my face. I turn them over, taking inventory of myself. "Everything seems to be working. My core temperature might have dropped a couple of degrees, and my throat is burning, but other than the internal game of hot-and-cold going on inside me, so far so good."

Merlin takes my one hand, and Sloan takes the other. They pull me up onto my feet, and Sloan steadies me against his hip until I'm sure my footing is sound.

"Are ye all right, luv?"

I pull my jeans up and meet his worried gaze. "Yeah. I'm okay. It was no fun doing the unlocking, but now that things are settling, it's better."

"I wouldn't say better," Dillan says.

"No. Not in the sense that I've just invited the evil possession of Morgana's grimoire to set up shop in my cells, more in the 'not about to puke on my friends' kinda way."

"Your friends won't hold it against you." Nikon comes over to squeeze my wrist. "Who are we kidding? Having you bleed, puke, or nearly die on us isn't that unusual."

I laugh, swallowing against a bad taste in my mouth. "Thanks, Greek. You sure know how to make a girl feel special."

As the group's tension eases a little, everyone strikes up a conversation and the spotlight on me dims.

Thank you, baby Groot.

Now that I'm up and about, I think I might have been premature with the "no biggie" celebration. I stretch my neck from side to side, and the vertebrae pop.

Emmet and Sloan are watching me closely, and I give them a thumbs-up. "S'all good, guys."

Sloan arches a brow, and I regret the fib.

"Okay, so not one hundy percent good but not as bad as I feared."

They seem to accept that.

Merlin comes over to check on me, and his gaze narrows. "Anything to report? You have to be straight with me, Fi. I can't get ahead of things if I don't know what's happening inside you."

A shiver races the length of my spine, and I wrap my arms

across my body and try to hold myself together. "I'm good. Certainly not as bad as the last time. Why the worried look?"

He sighs. "I think it'll be stronger this time around. If I'm right, the darkness will gain strength and hunger now that the *Eochair Prana* is free and likely being read and utilized."

"Do you think the darkness in me can sense when the book is used?"

"Of course, it can. The darkness in you stems from the book's power. It's not inert residue left behind. It's a dislodged piece of the whole. Having the book activated anywhere in the world should activate it within you."

I take a moment to inventory what's going on with me and shrug. "Nothing ebbing horror or clawing at me to murder the world yet."

"Yet?" Sloan scowls. "Perhaps joking about such things is in bad taste."

I smile. "Oh, hotness. Bad taste commentary is my happy place. When the shit hits, it's my salvation."

He rolls his eyes. "Yer such an oddity."

"Thanks for noticing…but back to the point of our story, me becoming overcome by dark and ebbing power is the reason we unlocked it in the first place. If nothing happens, we can't track the source book, and this whole resurrecting ghosts of possession past was for nothing."

"I suppose that's one way to look at it."

A long, eerie howl of a wolf's call interrupts our conversation, and I jog over to where I dropped my purse and jacket for the ritual. Digging out my phone, I answer the call. "Hey, Samuel. What's up?"

"Fi. I need you and Dionysus to meet us at Newgrange as soon as you can get here. I think we've figured out a way to reinstate Mingin's banishment back into the Neitherlands."

"No way. Seriously?"

"Yeah, but we'll need five, so we're calling in you and Dionysus."

I grab my purse and jacket. Hustling across the stage, I point at Dionysus and hold my hand out for him to join me. "We're on our way. See you in a few."

CHAPTER TWENTY-FOUR

"Are ye sure yer up for a plan that involves takin' on Mingin, luv? Ye just finished with Merlin's plan to unlock Morgana's evil. It's been a big day already."

Our group has barely materialized in Ireland, and my beloved champion is already up in arms.

I squeeze Sloan's hand and tug him toward the farmer's field below the Newgrange tomb.

Samuel whistles from up by the mounded tomb and waves us up. "Up here, guys. There's no one here."

Even better.

As we change direction and tromp through the brittle grass toward the ancient tomb, I address Sloan's concerns. "The darkness hasn't taken hold yet. Until it does, there's nothing I can do about stopping Yvain except worry and get antsy about sitting around."

"And rest," Sloan says as if that should have been obvious. "These things take a lot out of ye. It couldn't hurt ye to excuse yerself to rest."

"No rest for the wicked, hotness. If we're lucky, Mingin is still in fog form and vulnerable. If Samuel has a plan, there's no way I'll pass so I can don a onesie and watch a rom-com."

"Although that does sound awesome." Dionysus grins. "Maybe with a trip to the junk food store and some of those fruity vodka coolers too."

"Exactly. We'll have to do it again soon."

Sloan grunts. "I can't decide if yer forgettin' or glossin' over the hits ye took the last time ye were here."

"Neither. I revisit that night in my nightmares often and am acutely aware of the beating we took. Several key factors led to our defeat."

I lift my fingers to count them off. "One, Melanippe tricked us and caught us off-guard. Two, there were four fog fugitives to battle at the same time. Three, Quon Shen was down, and Samuel wasn't there. We were two men down and with Melanippe and Barghest forces moving in we were hugely outnumbered."

Dionysus laughs. "Samuel picked a bad time to go joyriding with Scarlet through the dragon tunnels. I'll never forget the look on his face as she snatched him up and dragged him off. Hilarious."

I try not to laugh. Funny-not funny.

"The point is, if we can get one mega-evil player off the field it's worth a bit of a scramble. I promise, as soon as the darkness starts taking hold, I'll let you know, and we'll search for Yvain."

"That's not my concern, and ye know it. It's not about wastin' time. It's about wastin' yer strength."

"She's right, Irish," Merlin says, chiming in. "If Samuel has a plan for Mingin, let's strike one of the bad guys off the roster. Fi's strong, and she's smart. She'll let us know if things get to be too much. Won't you?"

Merlin sends me a warning glare, and I hold up my palms. "How did I become the bad guy here?"

"Yer not," Sloan says, "but Merlin's not wrong. Ye tend to

ignore dangers to yerself when the world is closin' in. We're not wrong to worry."

Poor Sloan. Stewing over what could go wrong is kinda his thing.

"Fi! You made great time." Samuel jogs over to join us, followed by Quon Shen and Ahren. "Dionysus. Thank you for being our fifth."

Dionysus waves that away and chuckles. "Fifth, sixth, tenth, twelfth, what does it matter as long as everyone gets a happy ending and leaves satisfied."

I burst out laughing. "Dude, this is a banishment ritual, not an orgy. You know that, right?"

Dionysus grins. "Same concept."

"I wouldn't know."

Dionysus looks like he's about to make another suggestion toward educating me on the joys of hedonism, but I raise a finger and cut him off. "What have you boys come up with?"

Samuel tilts his head and gestures for us to go inside. "Come in, and I'll explain."

The entire group mills around in the main chamber while Samuel goes over his plan. "I was watching a movie last night in the hotel, and I had an epiphany. The two characters were bound in a struggle for power and survival. The magic between them created a locked loop and began recalling the most recent battles fought with their wands."

I chuckle. "Were you watching *Harry Potter and the Goblet of Fire?*"

Samuel's cheeks flush pink. "The movie doesn't matter. The point is, the magic passing between the two characters linked and locked."

"Yes, both their wands held a feather from the phoenix, Fawkes, at their core. Poor Cedric."

He frowns at me. "This isn't about the movie. It's about the idea it sparked when I watched it."

I pat his shoulder. "That's all good, but you guys need lives outside the quest to take down Mingin and Melanippe. The three of you sitting in a hotel room watching *Harry Potter* is a sad commentary on your lives. But, you're right, that's a problem for another night. Go on."

Samuel rolls his eyes but doesn't engage. "So, I was thinking about what's coming on the horizon and about the Winter Solstice. When the light hits the right angle and shines down the corridor to light this tunnel, it's game on, right?"

"So the stories go, yeah."

He moves to stand where the seam to the Neitherlands is weakest. The spot isn't visible on this plane, but when a Hunter-god walks the astral plane, the rift lights up like a golden zipper between two realms.

We were supposed to reinforce the zipper when it was at its weakest, but Melanippe grabbed the pull-tab and yanked that sucker open to let out her maniacal lover and his friends.

"So, this epiphany of yours…care to share?"

Samuel nods. "We need Mingin back in this tomb if we're ever going to send him back. How do we do that?"

I don't know, or I'd have done it by now. "Forcing a cat back in the bag is much harder than letting it out."

"Preach," Dillan says. "Especially a psycho cat with poison claws that goes straight for your nuts."

I chuckle. "True story. We'd either have to put the Min-genie in the bottle in gaseous form or tackle him in whatever physical human form he assumes next and snap him here before he can break free."

Dillan frowns. "Did you miss the part about the cat having poisonous claws and targeting our nuts? You don't want Sloan or Nikon that close to him, do you?"

"Of course not, but the question was about how we could do it."

"Both of those options will be one helluva fight," Emmet says.

"You're absolutely right." Samuel points at Emmet like he won the prize. "What if we could eliminate the fight?"

I give him a look. "How do you expect to do that, Wolfman?"

"Dustbuster." Emmet snaps his fingers, nodding. "We spell a powerful, hand-held vacuum and suck him up, then flash here and reverse the flow and blow him through the cracks."

Dionysus makes a face. "Suck him and blow him? Are we still talking about how to take down an enemy? This sounds more like a Friday night at my place."

That breaks all semblance of order.

Sloan shakes his head. "Sorry, Samuel. Only this group would veer off into the distasteful while discussing how to save the world."

"Distasteful?" Calum says, looking offended. "Don't judge, Irish. There's nothing wrong with a good suck and blow job."

"There are no blowjobs." Samuel scowls at us. "Dammit, you guys. It's like trying to get frat boys to focus during a wet t-shirt contest with you."

Yep. Now they're all smiling and imagining that.

I wave in front of Samuel to get his attention. "Ignore them. I take it your epiphany has something to do with not tackling Mingin or thinking we can trick him into this chamber."

"Right you are." He turns to focus on Sloan, Merlin, and me. "Instead of going after him, we spell the chamber. For sure, sometime in the next two months, he'll come to check the strength of the seam."

Merlin frowns. "You think he'll take another run at releasing his friends?"

"I do. He wanted his friends released from the Neitherlands for a reason. He knows the Winter Solstice is coming and that will give him another chance."

I nod. "Because the seam is weaker during the solstices and holidays on the wheel of the year."

"Exactly. I'm betting they'll take another run at opening the seam to free more exiled exhaust."

"I like the logic, but I still don't see what we're going to do."

He smiles. "Leave that to me. What I need is for the five of us to open the pentacle circle and go astral. Dionysus, I know you can't god this to work, but if you could maybe give me an extra bit of *oomph*, I'd appreciate it."

"Of course. What's our objective?" Dionysus asks.

"The five of us will set an invisible trap. Since Mingin was the last entity to escape from the Neitherlands, I'll set the chamber to recognize his energy signature and seal him in here the next time he returns."

"Oh, I get it…like how Harry's wand recalled the lives it took until it wound back to his parents."

"*Priori Incantatem*," Emmet says.

Samuel looks at him and me. "Your family is so strange."

I grin. "You're welcome."

Dionysus steps beside me and lays his arm over my shoulder. "I'm an honorary Cumhaill now too. Not sure if you got the memo."

Samuel blinks and shakes his head. "No, but it makes perfect sense. Now, if we've covered all the shenanigans, how about the five of us who have work to do, get to it, and no offense but everyone else go away."

I chuckle. "No offense taken. Everyone outside. If setting this trap gets us closer to snaring Mingin, we need to focus. Dionysus…" I gesture at the sandy ground. "A pentacle circle if you will, sir."

Dionysus bows deeply at the waist and sweeps his hand across. A moment later a glowing orange pentacle circle appears. At each of the five points, a pillar candle sits lit and waiting.

"All right, let's take our places."

Rounding the circle, I wait at the top point while the others get set. Quon Shen is to my left, then Dionysus, then Samuel to my far right, and finally, Ahren.

When Samuel lowers himself to kneel in the sand, we follow suit. He lays down and places his head at the point of the star, and we mirror the action.

"Set your minds free and focus on our intention. We are keepers of the balance, and it's our duty to return the escaped evil back into its prison. Expand your presence beyond the physical plane and reach out to the universe that surrounds us."

I draw a deep breath and make a concerted effort to relax… which isn't as easy as it sounds. This is the first moment I've been truly still since Merlin unlocked the darkness of Morgana's book.

I feel it now.

Within me there is dark, and there is light, each side struggling to gain the upper hand. I sink heavily against the sandy ground reaching into myself, pushing the darkness back to focus on our task.

First, I'll help Samuel set this trap. Then I'll worry about the darkness growing within.

"Everyone, enter the astral plane," Samuel says.

I settle in. "May the Force be with you."

By the time we finish with Samuel in the Newgrange tomb, my awareness of the darkness within has passed discomfort and gone straight into a definite possession level of dark mojo.

As masochistic as it seems, my suffering is good.

The stronger the pull toward Morgana's dark power, the better the chance Merlin will be able to track the pull, and Dionysus can take us where we need to find Yvain.

It's long after dark as we leave the chamber and I smile at my family rocking a bonfire in the parking lot.

"That's a little ballsy, isn't it? What if one of the tour guides forgot something and swings back or security comes by to make sure no trespassers are having a bonfire on sacred grounds?"

Sloan rises from his seat and meets me with a kiss and a worried gaze. "This site doesn't open fer a few more weeks, luv. The tourist season at Newgrange is from November through March."

"Oh, that's good."

"So, how did it go? Is it done? How are ye feelin'?"

"It went well. Yes, it's done. I'm fine, though I admit my frog started to boil a little while I wasn't paying attention."

Sloan frowns. "Can I get some clarification on the frog metaphor?"

Emmet chuckles. "You don't know the boiling frog analogy?"

"No. Enlighten me."

"Well, the story goes that if you drop a frog into boiling water, it will immediately hop out and save itself. If you drop a frog in room temperature water and bring it up to a boil, the process of heat rising over time isn't enough of a shock to trigger its survival instinct. It'll remain in the water and boil alive."

Sloan looks at me, and the horror in his gaze is regrettable. "That's the analogy ye chose to describe how ye feel?"

I hug his arm and tug him toward the fire. "My bad. It's not that horrible. My point was simply that I didn't notice the darkness gaining momentum while I was busy astral projecting. When we finished up, it struck me how much the dark influence built up."

"How built up are we talking, Fi?" Merlin asks.

"On a scale of one to ten based on last time, I'd say it was a one when we got here and a four now."

Sloan frowns. "Four times worse now than it was an hour ago?"

"If you look at it that way, yeah. That sums it up."

Sloan scowls at Merlin, but I shake my head. "It's not his fault.

This was my decision, and we knew this would happen. In fact, we *need* this to happen."

"I don't have to like it."

"No, you don't."

"Do you think it's strong enough to call you to the source?" Merlin asks. "We need it to really pull at you."

"What are we talking about?" Samuel asks.

I tell Samuel, Quon Shen, and Ahren about the whole grimoire fiasco and the horrors it could lead to.

"You intentionally infected yourself to connect with the tome?" Quon Shen asks.

"She did," Sloan snaps.

"We're running out of time," Merlin says. "We know Yvain will either use the book for its dark contents or to free his mother from banishment."

Quon Shen frowns. "We can amp up the draw quickly enough. If that's what you want."

I turn my attention to him. "How do we do that?"

"The same way we brought it from a one to a four. By spending time on the astral plane."

Samuel nods. "Magic exists on the astral plane more readily than on the physical one. That's how we're able to banish magical beings beyond their lives here to contain them behind a veil. With the personal grimoire imbued with flesh and blood of a sorceress like the Morrigan, its presence on the astral plane will be monumentally powerful."

"How so?" Calum asks.

"Because the sorceress herself is imprisoned on the astral plane. The darkness of the book will be seeking itself. If Fi is there, it will sense her and seek her too."

Dillan sighs. "So, you're saying the longer Fi spends on the astral plane, the faster the darkness will take hold because it's seeking itself."

Samuel nods. "That's what I'm saying."

I look at Merlin, and he nods. "The logic follows. The problem is...like your boiling frog analogy. If it's growing while you're in the astral plane, will you know when to leave or might the darkness boil you alive?"

I groan. "I regret the choice of that analogy now."

Sloan scowls at me. "You and me both."

CHAPTER TWENTY-FIVE

Quon Shen, Samuel, Ahren, and Dionysus all join me in the astral plane, and I'm thankful to have them with me. I knew Ahren had a weird thing with energy because being near him in the physical plane made me nauseous until I learned to turn it off. I didn't realize it related to him having a higher energy sensitivity.

Which is quite handy in this instance.

Despite Merlin's concern that I might stay in the astral plane too long and overdo baking my evil soufflé, Ahren keeps a close watch on things and lets us know when he thinks I've been in long enough.

I'm certainly not going to argue.

When I open my eyes and sit up, Sloan and my brothers are right there looking as queasy as I feel.

"And?" Calum gives me a close once over. "Are you still in control of things?"

I take a quick poll of all my Fi-ness and nod. "I feel like me... maybe a bit edgy...definitely more hostile...but me. There's a strange churning inside me like an evil eel swimming around looking for an orifice to pull an *Aliens* maneuver and make me the next Ellen Ripley."

Emmet and Dillan recoil, looking horrified.

When I bust up laughing, Sloan rolls his eyes. "Was that necessary?"

I press my lips together and sober. "Sorry. You guys teed me up so beautifully. I had to take the swing."

Emmet smacks his chest, chuckling. "Dayam, sista. I was totally expecting you to spew an eel."

"Wouldn't that be gross?"

"Yep. Totally would."

"Fi?" Merlin says. "Close your eyes and give us a number. Where are you on the possession scale? Do you feel the pull of the book?"

I settle down and do as he asks. "My number would be an eight and a half. I think the presence is as strong as before, but it doesn't hurt this time. I'm not sure why, but I seem to be a more suitable host for the evil this time."

Dillan flashes me a look. "What the fuck does that mean?"

"No idea. I'm only reporting here."

"Can you feel the pull of the book?" Merlin asks again.

"Oh, yeah. It's like I'm homesick. I'm craving to reunite with the book or Morgana or whatever it is that's pulling at me."

"Excellent, then let's reunite you with your precious." Dillan rubs his hands together. "Are you boys joining the fun or have you got big plans tonight with *The Order of the Phoenix*?"

Samuel gives Dillan the finger, and I have to laugh.

That was funny.

"Okay, boys." I rub my hands over the tops of my arms. "I'm getting prickly here. Let's get this done."

Merlin nods and extends one hand to me and the other to Dionysus. "Let her drive the train. You're simply the power behind getting her where she yearns to be."

Dionysus leans in. "Is it just me or does that sound dirty?"

"You think everything sounds dirty, but you're not wrong. I can absolutely drive my train."

Dionysus barks a laugh and wraps an arm around my shoulders. "Hell yes, you can."

The group gathers in tight, and we get ready to snap out. I take Dionysus's hand and close my eyes, focusing on the pull to reunite with the grimoire. "Ready or not, here we come."

We materialize at the base of a stone tower on top of a bluff in the middle of barren countryside. The crash of waves rises from somewhere close by, and the air feels sticky with a salty mist. The dark yearning of the *Eochair Prana* intensifies ten-fold the moment we take form.

"Well, we're in the right place." I use Sloan to steady myself.

"Can you feel it, Fi?" Emmet asks. "Is it bad?"

"I feel it, yeah, but I also hear it and see it." I point up at the night sky and cringe.

The night span above is darker than dark, and when lightning shoots sideways through the clouds, it highlights the image from one of my worst nightmares.

"Check it," Emmet says. "Cloud-spotting. Doesn't that cloud look like a big crow?"

"Raven," Merlin and I say at the same time.

"That's Morgana," I add. "We saw this once before, and it was the same. That's Morgana edging to the seam of the veil. She's testing the boundaries of her imprisonment and if we don't stop Yvain—like, right now—she's going to be free."

There's a collective curse, and everyone reaches to hold hands again.

"Get us up there, boys."

Except…nothing happens.

Sloan, Nikon, and Dionysus all shake their heads.

"Time to go old-school, boys and girls." Emmet strides over to grab the iron handle on the door. "Follow me—*Augh! Fuckety-fuck!*"

Magic snaps in the air and Emmet snatches his hand back and doubles over, cursing. The air sizzles with the stench of burned flesh as an iridescent barrier ripples around the outside of the stone tower.

"Dirty pool, asshole," Emmet snaps.

Sloan uncurls Em's fingers and forces open his blackened palm. "Hold on, Em. I'll have ye fixed up in a flash."

"You do you, Irish."

The sight of the charred digits and the putrid stench makes me gag. As concerned as I am about my brother and his injury, I don't have time for the distraction. "How do we get up there?"

"If at first you don't succeed…" Dillan sweeps a hand toward the door. "Who's up next? What do you say…Calum extra crispy?"

I ignore my brother and join Merlin and Samuel to help examine how the magic locks us out. "How strong is the warding?"

Merlin frowns. "Too strong to unravel in the time we have left. By the time we get in, Morgana will have breached the veil and be alive and well on the physical plane."

"Well, crap. What do we do?"

Another crack of lightning strikes off.

My gaze turns skyward, and I groan. "Dammit! She's so close I can practically feel her here with us."

"That's it!" Samuel says. "Fi…the barrier will be spelled to keep us out, but that might not include you. Yvain has obviously allowed his mother's energy to pass through the warding, so maybe you have enough of her in you that you might be able to get in too."

"Then can I open the door and let us all in?"

Merlin shakes his head. "More likely you'll be able to pass through, but we'll still be here trying to unravel the wards."

"Then I'm coming," Bruin says, his voice more growl than words. "I understand yer reluctance, Red, but this isn't up fer discussion. I'm the mythical battle beast here, and I'm comin'. The. End."

"I hate the idea you'll suffer from this, buddy."

"Understood and overruled. Now, let me in."

I won't argue. Opening my arms, I pat my sternum and give him my blessing to come aboard.

"Good luck, Fi," Dillan says. "Between Sloan, Merlin, and Samuel, we'll be right behind you."

"I'll try to join you from the skies," Eva says. "I'd be surprised if Yvain's warding extends to restrict an Angel of the Choir from entry, but you never know. It'll take some doing either way, but I'll get there as soon as I can. I don't suppose you want to give me a head start?"

"No time, girlfriend. Get there as soon as you can. That will be great."

The prospect of having Bruin and Eva with me makes me feel loads better. Normally, I don't mind going in on my own, but the darkness is doing a happy dance inside me, and that's alarming.

Part of me is afraid I won't get there in time to stop Morgana, and part of me is afraid I'll get there, and I won't *want* to stop her.

"Okay, girlfriend. Let's give this our best effort."

Eva shucks off her jacket and hands it to Dillan. "Don't get dead, Fi. I don't want to fail and lose my chance to change my stars."

"I'll try my best." I move quickly toward the door, kiss Sloan—who is still working on Emmet's hand—and face off with the door handle. "Little pig, little pig, let me come in."

As I contact the long, iron handle, I focus on Morgana and our connection and my desire to be one with the book again. The iron warms to my touch, but it doesn't burn. I lift the finger latch, undo the door, and swing it open.

Dillan nods and steps in behind me, just to make sure. He moves tentatively, but the moment the fingers of his outstretched hand touch the barrier, he hisses and pulls back his hand. "Sorry, baby girl. It's all you for the moment. Go get him."

I let out a deep breath and turn for the stairs. It was a long shot anyway. Pushing that out of my mind, I start the climb.

The stairs of this tower spiral up the inside of the cylindrical structure. As I climb, I glance up and gauge the distance from me to the clusterfuck I'm bolting into.

Two hundred feet…

One hundred feet…

The muscles of my thighs are eating up the distance, and I keep pumping upward. Normally, I'd feel the burn and start getting tired climbing this many stairs this fast.

Tonight, each step higher takes me one step closer to my precious.

As much as I hate that I'm totally Golluming here, it's my reality.

Fifty feet…twenty…ten…

The door leading to the tower's roof is open, and the cyclone of wind hits me before I reach the top stairs. I feel Morgana's presence before I see her. Even though she was banished centuries before I was born and we've never met, I know her.

Part of me *is* her.

I step out onto the roof and take in the scene. Yvain has the book on an altar and is speaking in tongues. He's gotten farther than Bathalt did.

The raven has landed.

I stop in my tracks, my mental hamster assplanting as I try to make sense of the night sky funneling down into the winged form of a twenty-foot raven.

Absently, I grab the hair out of my mouth, lost in the draw pulling me toward the undulation of shadows. The raven is here, but not. Her form has taken shape but hasn't solidified.

Still…I feel her presence.

Morgana is majestic, powerful, and breathtaking. I am awed and honored to witness her return and yet afraid. Why am I afraid?

Red? Why are we waitin' here? Release me. We still might be able to stop her.

Stop her? Why would I want to stop her?

Because she's the batshit source of evil we've fought to keep contained? C'mon, Fi, ye know this. I don't care how affected ye are by her poison. This woman threatens everyone ye love.

I draw a deep breath, Bruin's words resonating inside me more than I like. *But…*

There's no but, Fi. Release me.

But you want to hurt her.

He growls, and his frustration confuses me. *What if I promise not to? What if I only take care of Yvain? Ye don't have any fondness fer him, do ye?*

It's difficult, but I pull my gaze from the raven taking form and look at Yvain. The spell of wonder breaks. *Crap, Bruin, what are we waiting for?*

My question exactly. Fi, stay focused on Yvain. Whatever happens, you worry about him.

I hear the plea in his voice, and I'm not sure what it's about, but I know it's got something to do with the haze of darkness wrapping me in its cocoon.

Yvain. Got it. Good luck, buddy.

I release my bear and turn toward the altar. Yvain has his arms up with an amber amulet in one hand and the book glowing in front of him.

How did he get the amulet?

Was that another big win of his thieving days in Toronto while Merlin was with us in Ireland? Is that the amulet Merlin's been safeguarding or did he find another trinket in mommy's jewelry box to use to release her?

I know it's irrelevant, but I hate this guy.

As I think about that, darkness flares inside me. Hate feeds the power and makes me stronger. I clench my hands, reveling in that strength.

Lightning flashes in the sky and I lift my face and soak in the fierceness of nature.

Morgana is coming and wants the book.

I want the book.

Yvain orchestrates the storm and is too caught up in his spell-casting to notice my arrival.

The moment I see the grimoire glowing on the altar, my course is set. The axis of my world shifts and my desire takes control. I call Birga to my hand and launch at the man who trespassed into my life and wants to keep me from what is mine.

"My book. You stole my book."

Yvain turns to defend, shock and confusion plain in his expression. "How did you—?"

I swing my spear and knock the amulet from his hand. It clatters across the stone and lodges in a tuft of vegetation rooted between blocks.

Yvain shifts position and recovers from my surprise attack. He throws his hand through the air, and a wall of flames divides us.

Nice try. Nothing will keep me from what is mine.

"Absorb Elements." I cast on the run, not stopping as I reach the fiery barrier. Crossing the fiery threshold bolsters my strength and gets me to within reaching distance of my book.

"Entangle." I call the sparse vegetation forward, giving it

strength and purpose. It grabs his ankles and wraps up his shins to his knees like snakes up a pole.

He curses, shouting something, and my vines are gone. Reaching over his head, he draws two swords out of thin air and vaults forward.

The sudden rush of his attack forces me back from the altar. *Rude.* The need to recover my book fuels the fire in me.

"Stealing is ungentlemanly, but what's unforgivable is using innocent yeti and my grandparents as pawns in your play for power."

"It's not about power," he grunts, swinging. "It's about family."

The edge of his blade *swishes* past my head and whistles in my ear. "If this were truly about family, you wouldn't have crossed that line."

That seems to spark a fire in him. "That was Melanippe and Mingin. We are not the same."

He lunges forward, his blades bursting into blue flame as he swings.

"Feline Finesse," I throw myself into a back aerial, landing ten feet away and inside the stone wall of the tower's outer edge. When my boots connect with the stone, I adjust my stance to keep the book in my sights.

Yvain might be an asshole, but he's a damned good fighter and keeps me on my back foot more than I like.

"Bestial Strength." I push forward to improve my position. Raising Birga with both hands, I brace as his next strike comes down with bone-shattering force.

I grunt and absorb the hit, anger and aggression feeding the darkness within. The book senses my fury and calls to me.

I lose focus for a brief moment...

My shield ignites with a fiery burn as the hilt of his second sword cracks into the side of my head.

The connection drops me to the stones as the world blinks in and out of focus. Without my armor up, that would've killed or crippled me.

I roll to avoid the downward thrust of his blade.

Clink…he hits the stone where my chest would've been a split second before.

Clink…I keep rolling as he follows me.

Clink…he's closing in, and I can only roll so far.

The roar of my bear brings Bruin into the fight, and a meaty *thwack* sends Yvain flying across the tower.

I push up onto one knee and take a moment to let the funhouse ride come to a stop and allow my equilibrium to catch up.

Wow…that rattled my cage.

"Are ye all right, Red?"

"Yeah, buddy. Thanks." I get to my feet and send Birga back to my forearm. Jogging over to the altar, I smile at the *Eochair Prana*. "Hello, my precious."

Touching her again is like nothing I can describe. I'm full of the rightness of it, the need to keep her safe, and the need to have her for myself.

In the back of my mind, something niggles at me that my connection with the book, the burning of my back, and the darkness snaking its way through my system isn't a good thing…

How can it not be?

At this moment, there is only me and my book.

A bolt of power hits my shoulder and knocks me spinning. It tears the book from my hand, and I claw through the air trying to retain possession.

"Gust of Air." My call to the elements brings a surge of wind to my aid and the book changes direction to return to me.

It tumbles through open space, flipping and fluttering. I grab pages and the back cover. Yvain grabs other pages and the front cover.

There's a moment of a standoff. Then several things happen

all at once: Bruin rears and swings...Eva appears and swings...
Yvain raises his palm as his head flies off his shoulders.

Eva strikes again.

Shit.

Without him to cast it, the magic Yvain called forward
unleashes in a violent detonation. I scream, twisting away, my
white-knuckled grip on my book tightening more than ever.

Even in death, the asshole won't let go.

There's a moment of resistance, and something gives. Dark
magic erupts, and it thrusts me off my feet behind the force of a
second explosion.

I soar over the side of the tower and plummet.

My only consolation is to clutch the half of the book I was
able to save.

CHAPTER TWENTY-SIX

"Here she comes," Merlin says. If I had to guess, I'd say he was fifty feet away, but when I open my eyes, he's hovering over me next to Sloan, my brothers, and everyone else. He tips a glass vial with a brilliant red liquid into my mouth and doesn't stop until he's upended it. "You know the drill. Every drop."

With no choice in the matter, I swallow in gulps. The gloopy liquid burns down my esophagus and something inside me rears, needing to stop this.

I'd say so if I had the energy to speak.

What's happening? What is he doing to me?

The snake of dark power wriggling inside me reacts to Merlin's potion, not liking it any more than I do. "Where's my book?"

"It's all right, Fi." Merlin offers me a placating smile. "Forget about everything except getting better. We've got you."

I arch my back as the clawing darkness within me yearns for my lost connection with my book. "I need my book. Who took it? Where is it?"

"It's gone, *a ghra*." Sloan shifts to block my vision. "The battle badly damaged it, and it's gone. Focus on—"

"Liar!" I shout, scanning the faces of the people who profess to love me. "You want it for yourself. Who took it? Where are you hiding it?"

Merlin is casting a spell over me, and I don't want it. Whatever he's doing is making me feel sick. I struggle to get out from under his ministrations, but the others hold me down. "Stop. Let me go."

"Try to relax, baby girl," Calum says. "Everything's going to be fine."

"Everything will be fine if you guys let go of me."

I cry out as I struggle and get jostled back, their hands holding down my ankles, hips, and shoulders. An icy chill creeps under my heated flesh, and I start to shiver.

"Don't hurt her," Emmet says. "She's cold. Couldn't we get her off the ground?"

"She's not cold, Em," Merlin says. "She's boiling up. It's the darkness trying to consume her."

"Em, help me." I plead to his sympathies. "They're hurting me. I just want to be left alone."

Emmet curses and Sloan pushes into my view. "Yer provin' Merlin's point. Our Fi would never manipulate her brothers."

"Maybe you don't know me as well as you think you do," I snap.

"Aye, I do, so ye can save yer breath."

"How's it going?" Dillan rushes into the mix.

"Where were you, D? Did you take my book? Where did you put it?"

Dillan frowns. "Why am I getting a strong *Exorcist* vibe here?"

Sloan grunts as I twist my wrist free and manage to elbow him in the face. As he reels back, I push up to take advantage and am slammed back down hard by Dillan. "Settle the fuck down, Fi.

Consider yourself under arrest until Merlin and Sloan have weeded the taint out of your system."

"How dare you," I hiss, fighting against Dillan's hold. "You can't keep me here."

Dillan laughs. "You and I both know different. Remember the summer when you sheared my hair while I was sleeping? How long did I hold you pinned to the carpet until you admitted it was you?"

That memory breaks through the fog and fight, and I chuckle. "Two episodes of *Fresh Prince* and a *Buffy*."

He nods. "I could've held you longer."

"I don't doubt that, but I was eight. Besides, you deserved it. You shaved my guinea pig."

"Walks With No Legs didn't mind. It was summer. He was hot."

A rush of healing energy tingles up my arm and the gnawing pain in my stomach ebbs into the background. It's not gone so much as held at bay.

"Better, *a ghra?*"

I hear the worry in Sloan's tone and meet his mint-green gaze. The moment our gazes lock, I'm home. "Hey there, Mackenzie."

"Hey there, Cumhaill. Glad to have ye back."

"Fi, if you will?" Merlin hands Sloan a second vial, and he uncorks it and holds it to my mouth.

I drink it down, the fog finally clearing. "You improved the taste. The last batch tasted like licorice vomit, but these are fruit punch."

Merlin chuckles. "I thought you'd appreciate that."

"Trust me, I do."

"How's our boiling frog scenario, cookie?"

I think about that. "The darkness is relenting, but the pain of withdrawal has replaced the taint. It's excruciating. I want my book back."

I bite my bottom lip to keep from begging for it.

Another wave of shivers racks me.

"Emmet, I *am* cold. Can you give me some warmth while they work? I promise I'm me again."

My brother shifts his hold on my wrist from pinning it in place to rubbing it between his palms. "I've got ye, sista. Anytime, anywhere."

Merlin does something, and I gasp and suck in a breath. My murderous desire to level everyone and reclaim my book subsides even more.

I still feel out of control, though.

"Is there a spell to battle book addiction?"

Sloan smiles, the worry in his eyes held at bay. "I think that's a one day at a time thing, isn't it?"

"I've never been great at pacing myself."

"I might have noticed."

Another pulse of his healing energy chases away the fire in my veins, and the shakes downgrade from shivers to feeling slightly achy. "Help me up?"

"Take another minute, luv. The world can wait until you're ready."

I do take another few minutes, but I wriggle over to rest my head on Emmet's knees. "So, what did I miss? The last thing I remember is Eva lopping heads again and me getting blown off the roof of the tower."

Eva nods. "Yvain is dead."

"Score one in the win column. And Morgana?"

"No idea. That shadow raven thing blew apart when you and Yvain ripped the book in half."

"Is that what the second explosion was?"

She nods. "There was a massive disruption on both the physical and astral planes."

"So, we don't know if Morgana is free or if she got blown back into the astral plane of her prison?"

"Not definitively."

Dillan chuffs. "If she is free, I'm sure we'll know soon enough."

"What about the book?"

"I told ye the truth, *a ghra*. It was badly damaged. There was the half ye had in yer arms when ye landed but no sign of the other half when the Greeks searched the aftermath of the scene."

"We ripped it in half?"

Eva nods. "It was a real King Solomon moment."

"Only we didn't save the child. We ripped it in two."

"Then it exploded," Calum says.

"I take it that no one is going to tell me where my half of the book is now."

Cue a group of shaking heads.

"That's likely for the best. I truly thought I was strong enough not to be lost in the lure of coveting darkness. I was very wrong."

Sloan grumbles. "Och, don't get down on yerself, luv. Ye did have evil implanted directly into yer system and amplified as much as we could as quickly as we could. I don't think we can hold ye to blame."

Merlin sits back on his heels and sighs. "Agreed. But I think, going forward, we need to avoid activating those cells in Fi. That was too close to a full maniacal meltdown for my liking."

The thought of that kills me. "I'm so sorry, guys."

Sloan shakes his head. "Don't be. Ye may not have been yerself, but ye weren't totally gone either. Even when we had ye pinned and were takin' yer precious darkness, ye never cast a spell to defeat us. Ye may have wriggled and spouted off a bit, but somewhere deep down, ye wanted us to win."

"Well, I'm glad you did." I sit up. "Thank you all for all you do. Now, can we go home?"

Instead of home, we end up at Stonecrest Castle. Sloan wants me checked out by his father, and if I'm honest, I feel better about that myself. Losing control of who I am and what I believe in undermined my confidence and I want to be sure I'm me again.

"Yer energy is in quite a state of flux, but after what ye went through, I'm not surprised. Other than that, and ye needin' some rest, I give ye a clean bill of health."

Sloan arches a brow. "There now. Yer doctor has said ye need rest. Maybe ye'll listen to him."

I chuckle and hop off the exam table. "I always listen to you, Mackenzie. I just don't always *listen*."

He rolls his eyes and looks at his father. "Do ye see what I'm up against, Da?"

Wallace's smile is sweet and a little sad. "I see, son, and I couldn't be happier ye found her. Ye share something rare, kids. Don't forget that."

I pull my jacket on and hug Wallace tight. "We won't. I'll annoy your son for as long as he'll have me."

Sloan chuckles and steps in to hug his father as I step back. "Then it's good yer dragon bond gives ye longevity because yer not goin' anywhere without me."

I chuckle. "Is that because you love me or because you don't think you can trust me on my own?"

"Both."

The three of us are still chuckling about that when the brunette from the hot tub comes into the clinic carrying a box of supplies. Wallace goes over to help her with it, and I make eyes at Sloan.

The scathing glare he gives me is too funny. "Well, we'll be off, Da." He grabs my wrist and squeezes. "Take care."

Wallace rushes back. "Yer welcome to stay a few days if ye like. I'd welcome the company."

"We'd love to," I say, "but our dance cards are full until after the Winter Solstice. So much to do. So little time. But if we survive that, how about we plan a week after and really get our Yule on?"

Wallace nods. "I look forward to it."

"We'll see ye before then, I'm sure," Sloan says. "If ye need anything in the meantime, let us know. We'll be here in a flash."

"Och, I'll be fine. Don't worry about me. Now, off ye go. I'm sure Lugh and Lara are lookin' forward to sendin' ye off."

I nod. "Da and Shannon too. They're going to be a permanent fixture around here now."

Wallace smiles. "It'll be nice to have him back. With Riordan's betrayal, the Druid Order is a bit *out* of order and can use his experience."

I chuckle at his joke and nod. "I'm sure he'll need a project to work on. He's not the kind of man to be idle."

"On that note, I should get back to work myself. Safe home, kids. All my love."

Sloan *poofs* us to Gran's and Granda's back lawn and the gang's all here. Before I can even say hello, I'm swept up in a hug and twirled around. "What did Sloan's father say, Jane? Are you fixed? You're not evil anymore, are you?"

I go with the hug and lean back to reassure him. "All fixed. Although Wallace wants me to lounge around as much as possible for a few days. Do you want to join me for a onesie marathon?"

"Was Medusa the Beyonce of the Gorgons?"

I have no idea, but I leap. "Hells, yeah."

"Right you are."

I chuckle and take the win. "Great, then when we get home, we'll veg out."

"Be still like vegetables. Lay like broccoli."

I laugh at the quote from *Pretty Woman*. "Well played, Tarzan. Point to you."

Dionysus sets me back onto my feet, and in no time flat, I get spun to face a much scowlier puss. "Fiona Kacee Cumhaill, tell me yer brothers got things wrong. They said ye invited the darkness of Morgana's book into yer life again and keyed it up to catch yer man."

I scowl at Dillan, Calum, and Emmet. The three of them are glancing around at the birds and the scenery but avoiding my gaze won't save them. "Seriously? You ratted me out? What happened to honor among siblings?"

Da leans in closer, and yep. He's really pissed. "It's honor among thieves and yer avoidin' the question."

I sack up and jut my chin. "I did activate the evil, but it worked. We got Yvain, and I'm fine—"

"Are ye off yer feckin' gob?" He runs rough fingers through his russet hair and makes it stick up all cockeyed and crazy. When it goes like that, we always say he looks like an angry rooster. "Ye could've been lost to it this time."

"But I wasn't. Wallace says—"

He lifts a finger and stops my argument. "Ye promised if I moved on to a quieter life with Shannon, ye'd take care of yerself and wouldn't be reckless. Ye swore to me. Here we are, only days and weeks later, and yer makin' deals with the devil and nearly gettin' yerself killed. How am I supposed to live here and retire if I can't trust ye'll take care of yerself?"

My brothers are so dead.

"I do take care, Da, and as much as I appreciate you loving me and worrying, the truth is, dangerous things are coming for us. The next two months will be hairy, and I'm sure we'll take our hits, but I come from tough stock. I've got stone fists, a fighting spirit, and my instincts are sharp. Fionn chose me, and I won't let him down. I won't let any of you down, I promise."

"What about lettin' *yerself* down, *mo chroi*? Ye've proven yer smart and resilient, but there's always someone tougher and more prepared to fight."

I nod. "That's why I have all of you. When this all began you told me you had faith in me, but you worried because I didn't know how to ask for help. You said I always tried to take on the world myself and I was going to get myself killed."

"I remember."

"I learned, Da. I have a team, and they are amazing. Maybe I take risks, but if I do, I have faith in the people around me that they'll catch me if I fall."

"Off the side of a stone tower," Dillan interjects, waggling his brows. "You owe Nikon thanks for that one, by the way. He plucked you right out of the air."

Nikon shrugs. "It's a new skill I picked up at the dragon birthday bash. Glad it came in handy."

I wink at Nikon and smile at my dad. "You deserve a quieter life, Da. No one faults you for wanting to take a breather. You've always been there for everything with us, but it's different now. You'll be there for important things, but you'll miss other stuff. You have to have faith we'll take care of each other because we will."

"We'll catch her when she falls, Da," Emmet says.

"And watch her six," Calum adds.

"And pin her down to exorcise her if she gets possessed by evil," Dillan says.

By his pinched expression, Da could've lived without that image, but hey, that's where we are. It's hard for him—I get that. He always kept us safe until Brendan's death, and now he's suffering.

I take his hand and smile up at him. "Our entire lives you taught us how to survive and thrive. We are Clan Cumhaill because of you. We have our guiding principles, we live and love, and we do what needs doing to keep others from harm."

"Yeah, baby," Dillan says.

Calum nods. "That's who we are, and it's all your doing, Da."

Emmet holds out his arms. "Good or bad, this is us."

"It's good." Gran smiles at us. "Ye taught them well, Niall."

"You did." I squeeze his hand. "Whatever comes at us, we'll tackle it. We've got this. I promise. You rest up and get refreshed because when the shit hits, we're going to drag you right back into the heat of things."

"Ye better." He eyes me up.

"We will." I hug my father and ease back. "Now, before we leave, I want a tour of the new love nest. Dionysus told me he got you all set up for the next chapter of your life. He even mentioned a hot tub. Everyone loves a hot tub, right hotness?"

Sloan frowns at me. "Don't ye dare."

I snort and link my arm with Da. "Oh, I dare. Now, how about that tour?"

THANK YOU!

Thank you for reading *A United Front*. While the story is fresh in your mind, and as a favor to Michael and me, please click HERE and tell other readers what you thought.

A quick star rating and/or even one sentence can mean so much to readers deciding whether or not to try a book, series, or a new-to-them author.

Thank you.

If you loved it, continue with the Chronicles of an Urban Druid and claim your copy of book fourteen: A Culling Tide.

The story continues with *A Culling Tide*, available now at Amazon and Kindle Unlimited.

Claim your copy today!

AUTHOR NOTES - AUBURN TEMPEST

DECEMBER 13, 2021

Thanks for being here, for loving this series, and for spending time with Fi and the Cumhaill fam jam.

Here we are in the aftermath of another holiday season looking at the beginning of 2022. Happiest of Happy New Years to you.

I wish you and yours health, happiness, and endless laughter with friends and family. If you can't be with the ones you love, maybe spending time with Clan Cumhaill will offer you some levity and lift your spirits.

I hope it does.

Now… On the good news front, Michael and I had a face-to-face back in November and came up with some exciting plans for Fi and friends and the Urban Druid world. You said you love them…we love them too.

We won't let you down by breaking up the band.

Exciting druid-y things happening in 2022.

Stay tuned for more info on that.

For now, I wish you an amazeballs 2022. Eat great food, laugh inappropriately, and if the mood strikes, tip back a glass and celebrate health and happiness.

Slainte Mhath,
Auburn Tempest

AUTHOR NOTES - MICHAEL ANDERLE

JANUARY 17, 2022

Thank you for not only reading this book but these author notes as well!

No notes from Auburn

So, I don't have any author notes from my collaborator to read and riff off, so you are stuck with just me.

I hope your health and mental insurance are paid up.

I am presently in Sharjah, UAE (United Arab Emirates), after twenty-eight hours of flying and airports. I am now trying to acclimate to a day that is twelve hours ahead of the schedule I'm used to in Las Vegas.

I called a seven-hour dive into sleep a nap yesterday to try to convince myself that nothing is amiss. It is working...I think.

For those who missed the memo, LMBPN Publishing announced we are opening a new business front for LMBPN International FZC in the Publisher Free Zone of Sharjah. There are some business and tax advantages (to some degree, although not as many as one would think). More importantly, it is a goal of His Highness Sheikh Dr. Sultan bin Muhammad Al Qasimi that Sharjah becomes a nexus for the world in the publishing arena.

Just eight (8) weeks ago, the joint venture between Ingram

Content Group and Sharjah Book Authority opened its doors—November 24, 2021. LMBPN announced that we were opening an office (a company, actually) on January 12, but the papers to start the new company were actually in place in late December 2021.

I didn't want to issue the press release at the end of the year or the beginning of the new year, with everyone getting back to work.

As LMBPN grows, we wish to bring stories that readers love to read over and over. Further, I think we can help authors around the world as well as readers by taking our stories from English into other languages and also by translating stories from other languages to English.

As a reader first, I don't care WHAT language the story was written in. Now, I'll get the chance to find wonderful authors in other countries and introduce them to our readers.

You never know. One day, that story you are gushing about might help a family step out of poverty because that kid who couldn't get her mind out of the clouds is famous…in America!

And you helped by reading, enjoying, and perhaps telling your friends about a cool new story.

Personally? *I call that amazing.*

Have a wonderful year, and smile at someone just because. You never know if that is the one thing a person needs to make it through another day.

Ad Aeternitatem,

Michael Anderle

ABOUT AUBURN TEMPEST

Auburn Tempest is a multi-genre novelist giving life to Urban Fantasy, Paranormal, and Sci-Fi adventures. Under the pen name, JL Madore, she writes in the same genres but in full romance, sexy-steamy novels. Whether Romance or not, she loves to twist Alpha heroes and kick-ass heroines into chaotic, hilarious, fast-paced, magical situations and make them really work for their happy endings.

Auburn Tempest lives in the Greater Toronto Area, Canada with her dear, wonderful hubby of 30 years and a menagerie of family, friends, and animals.

BOOKS BY AUBURN TEMPEST

Chronicles of an Urban Druid

Book 1 – A Gilded Cage

Book 2 – A Sacred Grove

Book 3 – A Family Oath

Book 4 – A Witch's Revenge

Book 5 – A Broken Vow

Book 6 – A Druid Hexed

Book 7 – An Immortal's Pain

Book 8 – A Shaman's Power

Book 9 – A Fated Bond

Book 10 – A Dragon's Dare

Book 11 – A God's Mistake

Book 12 – A Destiny Unlocked

Book 13 – A United Front

Book 14 – A Culling Tide

Misty's Magick and Mayhem Series – Written by Carolina Mac/Contributed to by Auburn Tempest

Book 1 – School for Reluctant Witches

Book 2 – School for Saucy Sorceresses

Book 3 – School for Unwitting Wiccans

Book 4 – Nine St. Gillian Street

Book 5 – The Ghost of Pirate's Alley

Book 6 – Jinxing Jackson Square

Book 7 – Flame

Book 8 – <u>Frost</u>

Book 9 – Nocturne

Book 10 – <u>Luna</u>

Book 11 – <u>Swamp Magic</u>

Exemplar Hall – Co-written with Ruby Night

Prequel – Death of a Magi Knight

Book 1 – Drafted by the Magi

Book 2 – Jesse and the Magi Vault

Book 3 – <u>The Makings of a Magi</u>

If you enjoy my writing and read sexy/steamy romance, my pen name for the books I write in Paranormal and Fantasy Romance is JL Madore. You can find me on Amazon HERE.

CONNECT WITH THE AUTHORS

Connect with Auburn

Amazon, Facebook, Newsletter

Web page – www.jlmadore.com

Email – AuburnTempestWrites@gmail.com

Connect with Michael Anderle and sign up for his email list here:

Website: http://lmbpn.com

Email List: http://lmbpn.com/email/

https://www.facebook.com/LMBPNPublishing

https://twitter.com/MichaelAnderle

https://www.instagram.com/lmbpn_publishing/

https://www.bookbub.com/authors/michael-anderle

OTHER LMBPN PUBLISHING BOOKS